Donuts in an Empty Field

For the Love of Donuts Series

Book 1

RACHEL BARNARD

Copyright © 2016 Rachel Barnard

All rights reserved. No part of this book may be reproduced or transmitted in any form or by any electronic or mechanical means, including photocopying, recording or by any information storage and retrieval system, without the written permission of the Author, except where permitted by law.

This is a work of fiction. Names, characters, businesses, places, events and incidents are either the products of the author's imagination or used in a fictitious manner.

ISBN: 1944022023
ISBN-13: 978-1944022020

Life's a Book Publishing

DEDICATION

Dear Nichole,

You are and have always been larger than life. You brought me out of my shell and helped me become the person I am today. I wanted to immortalize us by telling our story because it's a story for everyone.

CONTENTS

Chapter one - Mementos 4

chapter two - Smoke Memories 14

chapter three - School 17

chapter four – Beach BBQ 24

chapter five – Tree Beach 42

chapter six – Fat Boy Run 48

chapter seven – Holding a Grudge 54

chapter eight - Grand Re-opening 60

chapter nine - The Movies 78

chapter ten - First Attempt 87

chapter eleven - Picture Hunt 93

chapter twelve - Tip, Don't Buy 109

chapter thirteen - Puppies 116

chapter fourteen - New Job 126

chapter fifteen - Now What 131

chapter sixteen - Ready for Anything 141

chapter seventeen - Vanessa Unleashed 151

chapter eighteen – Donuts in an Empty Field 166

chapter nineteen – Just Because 175

chapter twenty - Back to Ben 180

chapter twenty-one - Overcome Your Fears 195

chapter twenty-two - Hero's Challenge 201

Vanessa and Nichole's Bonus Bucket List

Read on for a sneak peek of Seize the Donut

Acknowledgements

About the Author

Other Books by the Author

"Just bring donuts."

- Bill Barnard

CHAPTER ONE - MEMENTOS

We haven't opened this room in five years.

"Are you sure you're up for this, Vanessa?" Mom asks.

I nod, but I'm not ready. How can I deal? Dad could be alive if he hadn't tried to be a hero.

I glance back at Mom and take a deep breath before I grab the office doorknob, turn, and push.

The smell hits me. Stale. Musty. Humid.

This is not how I remember Dad.

I hold my breath and look around, trying to recall the distinct way he smelled. This used to be Dad's office. Now it's a stagnant room full of useless things. Things we're going to get rid of. All his books and papers and desk toppers. Junk crammed onto a six-foot desk and packed into a room that is little bigger than a walk in closet.

Mom pats me on the back and I step inside. Letting out a breath with a whoosh, I tiptoe around piles of books on the floor and sit in the office chair. It creaks backwards. Mom stands in the middle of the room with her hands clasped tight together in front of her stomach. Thin streams of sunlight filter through the blinds, highlighting the dust motes in the air.

Bluster noses his way into the room, waddling around to sniff at each pile of books and papers stacked on the floor. I bend down to pet him. Not only is it the anniversary of my father's death, but it's also the anniversary of the day we got Bluster. It's almost as if he came to replace Dad, arriving mere hours ahead of the incident at the restaurant. Bluster's stubby reddish brown tail beats at my thigh as I try to hold him down and hug him. Bluster's softness rubs against my bare legs. I can hear his heartbeat pattering and his breath wheezing as he struggles to get out of my grip. He smells like a dog should, musty wet from his recent bath. I breathe deep, the smell overpowering the staleness of the office around us.

When Dad brought home Bluster five years ago, I was thrilled. Corgi pups are divine and I was absolutely smitten with the little guy. I'm certain it was the reason boys never interested me until later. From the first tail-wag, mess on the floor, and sharp bark, I was in love.

Mom only shook her head and sighed. Dad was forever surprising both of us with shenanigans. He usually got away with them, too. I dropped hints for years about wanting a dog, but Mom always said no. It was much harder to say "no" to the dog's face.

Bluster and I bonded the minute Dad set him into my arms. No matter how much Mom didn't want a dog, she couldn't take him away from me because Bluster was the last present Dad ever gave me.

Shoes tap in the main part of the house on our wood floors and my best friend Nichole appears in the doorway. She glances at Mom and then locks eyes with me, looking down at me from her model height of 5'8". She hesitates outside the door, still holding my gaze with her own brown eyes. She twirls a slender finger through her shoulder length brown hair with blonde highlights and chews on her lip.

"Are you sure that it's okay for me to be here?" Nichole asks.

I nod and she steps inside, her heels tapping on the wood floor without rhythm as she takes tentative steps.

"Thank you for coming. Of course it's okay. Vanessa and I very much appreciate you helping out," Mom says.

I frown. "We don't have to do this."

Nichole says at the same time, "It's okay, I wanted to help."

We look at each other. Normally we're more in sync, but today everyone's rhythm is off.

"Thanks, Nichole," I sigh.

She remains silent, waiting for Mom to be the parent and say something helpful.

Mom shakes her head. "It's time." She sighs heavily and

unclasps her hands. Mom wears no makeup and her eyelids droop. Her lips are a thin, pale line without lipstick. I have Mom's hair, at least when she was younger, but I don't have to dye mine to keep its dark brunette color.

Nichole purses her lips and I internally roll my eyes at Mom's lack of parental guidance. At the very least, she usually gives me the canned therapy version of sympathy and support, but today is hard for her too.

Mom sweeps her hair over her shoulders, out of her pale face, revealing the too-large ears I inherited. She steps back into the hall to pick up the cleaning supplies we'd forgotten outside the room. Bluster looks up at me and whines. I pet him and he settles down onto the floor.

Touching Dad's precious books and trinkets makes his presence feel closer than it has felt in years, like he could walk in and tell us the corgi bobblehead doesn't belong in a box, but front and center on his desk next to his donut patterned mouse pad. Putting his stuff in a box is like putting him and my memories of him into a box. I don't want to forget Dad, but both Mom and my therapist agreed it's time to donate the books and clean out the office. That it has to be done. In a single story house with three bedrooms and an office, we sure don't need the space. I don't understand why today, of all days it has to be done, but it isn't my choice. Mom wants to get it over with. She has plans tomorrow. I don't have enough energy to object.

"So," Nichole says into the silence. "I'm glad you have the air-conditioning on, it's hot out there." She wipes the back of her hand over her forehead. Her cheeks are sun-tanned, slightly darker than her normal olive skin tone. We're both of mixed European heritage, but Nichole got genes for tanning and I didn't.

"It's Florida in the summer. Of course it's hot," I say. I get up out of the office chair, releasing a puff of dust.

Mom starts with the pictures. Photos clutter Dad's desk and windowsill, overlapping with smiles and memories. My heart constricts tighter and tighter with every photo placed face down in one of the medium-sized boxes Mom dragged in. I don't want to cry in front of Nichole. If I'm too much of a bother, she might leave and hang out with her other friends, doing something more fun.

The sun creates shadows through the dusty blinds, striping on the box like a jail cell. I apologize silently to Dad's memory as I nestle in each new photo.

"Do you want to keep any, Vanessa?" Mom asks.

I look at the collection of bobble heads on his desk, the Rubik's cubes and desktop puzzles, the office toys. They don't remind me of Dad the way Bluster does. They don't mean more than my memories of him. I shake my head at Mom and she tilts her head, regarding me, before settling back into the routine of placing odds and ends from the desk into boxes.

Then I see the last photograph.

It's a larger picture, printed at home and tacked onto the corkboard in a hurry. On Dad's last day alive, after he'd surprised me with the dog, he took us to Sarasota's only dog park. Bluster was six months old, still small enough for me to hold him tight to my chest without his legs falling out of my arms, but old enough to mingle with the park's smaller dogs. We'd gone to the dog park to let Bluster socialize and Dad was going to break the world record for most powdered donuts eaten in three minutes. After Bluster wore himself out, we put him back on the leash and left the dog area to find ourselves a secluded picnic table.

The picture was taken after Dad failed. Powdered sugar coated Dad's beard, the top of Bluster's head, even dusting the park bench and floating to the ground below. Mom kept trying to wipe powdered sugar off Dad's beard.

Dad had no qualms asking a stranger to take our photo. It was frustrating that I couldn't even remember if the stranger had been a man or a woman.

I remember Dad.

Dad was an inch or two above average height, about 6 feet tall, and had the regular dad paunch that signifies the presence of children who never finish their own dinner and give leftovers to Dad to eat. He was always trying to talk or wave to strangers.

Everyone always recognized Dad for his friendliness. I wonder if it was to show me that good people exist in the world. That I could be one of them.

I reach up to pull the photo off the corkboard, but my hand stops halfway. I can't do it. This is still Dad's office, in some way, and the picture belongs here.

Mom smiles at the picture, but her eyes still droop and her lips are so thin they almost disappear into her mouth.

"It'll get better," Mom says.

"You still have each other," Nichole offers. "And you have me," she adds.

"I know."

"This is really hard for both of us." Mom looks away. "I've scheduled you with Dr. Bryan later today while I'm out with Walter."

"Your new boyfriend, right?" Nichole asks.

Mom won't meet my gaze. I know this is hard for her, too. I try to give her a break for setting up a dating profile online. For abandoning me on the hardest weekend of the year for a date. I'm mad at her for being so open about dating again, for telling me about it and expecting me to accept that she's moved on when I haven't.

"Walter has been helping me get through this, too."

Nichole looks at me for an explanation, but I don't want to get into the argument about Mom dating again right now.

"I'm kind of hungry, Mrs. S.," Nichole says, sensing our discomfort.

Mom nods absently.

"How 'bout a snack Mrs. Smith," Nichole says louder.

Mom shakes her head as if to clear away her thoughts. "Sure, be right back girls."

Nichole waits until Mom's out of the room to start shoving books into another larger box.

"Hey," I say.

Nichole pauses and stands up straight to regard me. "What?

You're dragging this out and it's not going to get easier the longer you do it. Let's get it over with."

Nichole walks over to me, reaches up to grab the photograph off the wall and I slap her arm away.

"Seriously? Come on Vanessa."

"Don't you dare. You can't just walk in here and throw his stuff into boxes like it's junk."

Nichole raises her eyebrows and takes a step back.

"That's not what I-"

"I'm going to leave this one," I say with a scowl.

Nichole holds up her hands in surrender.

"Fine," she says.

I reach up to touch the photograph, fingering one of the loose corners at the bottom. Peripherally I see Nichole take another step back, watching the wall and my finger.

She trips over a stack of books on the floor. I don't think. Swiveling to help her, my finger is still hooked around the edge of the picture. It rips as I leap sideways to grab at Nichole's flailing arms. She backpedals over the stack of books. I yank her back to the open floor and let go of her arm. The ripped corner of the photo clutched in my fingers flutters to the ground.

Nichole sucks in a breath as I turn to face the ruined picture. Something flutters behind the missing corner and I lift the stiff paper to peer behind it.

Something is there.

Nichole and I both jump at the sound of a crash from the front of the house.

"Mom!" I yell.

I'm wound up from being in Dad's office, from remembering our last day together, to the finality of packing up his stuff that I go into panic mode and run toward the door. Nichole bumps into me in our haste to make sure Mom's okay and we both fall to the floor. My world turns upside down and I bang my head against Nichole's knee. I'm panting and scrambling to disentangle my limbs from Nichole's. Mom still hasn't answered.

We run out to see what happened. Mom's in the kitchen, her hands braced on opposite sides of the sink. For a moment I'm immensely angry that she didn't answer when I called, scaring the bejesus out of Nichole and me, but then I notice she's crying. Shame at my anger crashes down on my shoulders.

"Give us a minute?" I ask Nichole.

She nods and heads back to the office. I wince at the sounds of books smacking into one other as Nichole throws them into boxes.

"Mom?"

"It just slipped," she says without looking up.

Several large pieces of one of our flowered yellow and green plates are on the ground next to Mom. We've never broken any of the plates before.

Thankfully, I'm wearing my favorite pair of Crocs, and I don't have to leave Mom alone right now to go get shoes. I can see smaller pieces of the ceramic littering the floor in between tufts of Bluster's fur and crumbs from our last meal.

"It's okay, Mom."

I bend in to hug her and she turns to me with shaking shoulders, sniffling and blinking to stop her tears.

"It'll get easier," I tell her, patting her on the back.

"Grief is a funny thing. It's never the same and it's always a tough upward climb, but you'll get there. It won't be easy, but you're strong and you'll get through it," Mom assures me, turning back into the parent.

Ugh. There's the canned therapy talk. At least she's feeling more like herself, even if I don't.

I notice she doesn't include herself in the statement.

"Don't you miss him?"

"Of course I miss him; he was your father." She sighs out.

The anger knots tight, pressed up against the agony and emptiness Dad left behind. He wasn't just my father; he was Mom's husband. He had friends. He was a part of my world and now he's pictures and mementos and everything I still remember about him, and more that I can't.

I don't want to replace Dad, but I want to move on. I put on a brave face, masking my emotions as best I can and say, "Nichole and I can take care of the rest of Dad's stuff."

"Thank you, Vanessa," Mom agrees.

Dad wouldn't have wanted me to get upset at Mom, especially since she's also sad today. I grab her shoes for her. She smiles at me with another sigh.

"You go ahead with Nichole. I'm going to clean this up first. Here." Mom hands me a bag of carrots and some homemade hummus. "For Nichole and for you if you get hungry." She glances at my stomach tight against my shirt and I suck in reflexively. Even on this bad day, she has to remind me that I'm overweight.

I take the snack and walk back to the office. Nichole sits in the chair, using her feet to swivel herself back and forth as she holds something in her hands.

"What, break time already?" I ask. The anger knots tighter.

Nichole drops the piece of paper onto the desk and I watch as it flutters back and forth and settles off-kilter on the edge.

"What does it say?" I ask.

"I don't know." Nichole hands it to me. It's a lined notebook paper with a bunch of scribbles. Sorrow hits me. I don't recognize the handwriting, but it has his name at the top, under the date.

The numbers blur as I hold back the tears. I've forgotten another part of my memories of Dad.

I read through the scribbles and turn to Nichole in confusion. I show her the note.

July 22, 2002

1. ~~Get a dog~~
2. Win a food challenge.
3. Shoot a gun.
4. Ride a motorcycle.
5. Skydive.
6. Perform a kind deed without expecting anything in return.

"It's a bucket list," she explains.

"But why?"

"What do you mean, why? Most people have them," Nichole says.

"Not my dad. He would have told me."

Nichole gives me a funny look. "Seems like your dad though. I mean, c'mon, win a food challenge?"

"Yeah, it does kind of sound like him. But only one has been crossed out." I frown, thinking of everything Dad never got a chance to accomplish. Did he even get a chance to try half of these things? "The day he died." I gulp and close my eyes for a long blink. "The day he died, he was trying to beat the world record for most donuts eaten in three minutes. I remember that day. Almost every detail. Why isn't that on this list, why the generic food challenge?"

Nichole doesn't answer and I continue. "He took us, Mom, Bluster and I to the dog park. He was always into getting things done. A dog and donuts on the same day, in the same place. I remember he let me hold the timer. It made me feel important."

Nichole nods.

"He wasn't very good at eating donuts fast, but he made us laugh. He was covered in powdered sugar and it made me think of Christmas snow. I was proud and embarrassed for Dad at the same time. He was so fun, but he was always doing weird things."

Nichole inclines her head at my words and gets out of the office chair. She paces the room twice and then starts methodically and carefully putting books into boxes.

"I remember I could taste the powdered sugar. He was eating so fast that it was poofing everywhere. Bluster kept winding his leash under his legs as he watched us. Mom and I both laughed at Dad. He managed to swallow the first donut and was already stuffing the second one into his mouth."

I stop my story and sigh. Nichole looks up at me.

"I'm listening," she says.

"There was no way he was going to beat the record and I teased him the rest of the day for failing. Now, I wish I hadn't." I look down at my hands, Dad's bucket list clenched in them.

"You should do it," Nichole declares.

"What?"

"You should do his bucket list."

"What? No way."

Mom appears in the doorway. I slide the paper under a stack of folders on the desk.

"Everything alright?" she asks.

Nichole looks at me and I shrug.

"Here, I'll take the boxes out to the car," she offers.

She lifts one of the heavier, book-filled boxes and staggers out. I'm glad we're donating his books, but I'm sad to see them go. The room is empty without them.

"Are you going to tell her about the list?" Nichole asks.

I consider it. "No. I don't think so." I don't want to share this piece of Dad with anyone else. Mom would make me share it with my therapist. She would minimize it and then disappear on a date.

"Well, I'm pooped. Do you want me to stick around?" Nichole asks.

"Ugh no, Mom scheduled a session for me later this afternoon. Why can't she just pull me out of class like all the other parents so I can at least skip school?" The humor sounds foreign to my ears because I'm still reeling from cleaning out Dad's office and having to comfort Mom.

I retrieve the list from under the files and walk up to take down the photograph from the corkboard. I want to move on. Nichole ushers me out of the room, clutching the unopened bag of carrots, Bluster following behind us. I clutch both the bucket list and the ripped photograph in my hands as she shuts the door firmly behind us.

CHAPTER TWO - SMOKE MEMORIES

Therapy sucked the first session and still does after four years. The fish hardly move in their tanks. The magazines in the waiting area are over a month old. Even the therapist, Dr. Bryan, wears the same drab and dark button down shirts every time I see him.

"I know it wasn't my fault," I repeat the words for the umpteenth time.

Dr. Bryan's expression doesn't change, but we both know it's a lie.

"I know it wasn't anyone's fault."

Another lie. He uncrosses and re-crosses his legs, his notepad resting on his leg, his pen slack in his hand as he listens.

I was the one who made us go to that particular restaurant on that particular day. I was the one who whined about wanting carbonara and then ordered spaghetti.

Dad was the one who didn't stay safe outside the burning building. Dad was the one who rushed into the smoke and the sounds of sirens, screams, and the crackling of flames to save a dumb kid.

It was the dumb kid, Ben, who killed my father. Officially, the fire was caused by a faulty electrical connection, but I just know Ben started the fire. I saw him in my dad's arms, right before my favorite person in the whole world collapsed onto the pavement from smoke inhalation. I saw the kid's eyes and it was unmistakable what I saw there.

Guilt.

I wish I'd seen my dad's eyes. Everything in my world in that moment was focused on the kid. Who was he and why did my dad save him? Would Dad have gone back into the burning building if he knew he'd never see me again? I can never truly hate the kid my dad sacrificed everything for, but how can I ever forgive my dad or Ben?

"Do you have to forgive the boy to move on?" Dr. Bryan asks, echoing my thoughts.

His words pull me out of the memory and I'm startled to see the blank walls of his office, a few certificates breaking up the monotony of the gray paint.

"Sometimes, I don't know if I want to move on."

"Tell me more about Ben."

"I don't want to talk about him."

"We don't have to talk about him today."

"No, you don't have to talk about him. You don't even know him. You don't know my dad. You don't know me. You don't even know my mom," I say.

Dr. Bryan blinks slowly.

Screw you, Dad. I think back to Dad's secret bucket list and the last item on it. *Make a difference in someone's life or do something for them that they can't do themselves.* Some pay it forward bullshit and here I am in therapy.

"Shall we go back to the fire, then?"

I half growl, half sigh. I spent my first therapy sessions trying to make Dr. Bryan rise to my own level of anger. I cried. I yelled. I even yanked one of his certificates off the wall and smashed it against his desk.

That was years ago.

"What about the fire?" I say.

"Do you want to talk about your phobia?"

"It's not a phobia."

"Lighters, matches, images of fire, the smell of burning toast. These are all triggers you've told me about."

"Yeah, so?" I snort.

"You blame your father for your fear of fire?"

"What? Why would I blame Dad for that? He didn't start the fire. Ben did."

"We've been over this, Vanessa. Ben didn't have anything to

do with the fire. Granted, he wasn't supposed to be in the kitchen at his age, but he didn't start the fire. There was an electrical malfunction. Pair that with a greasy restaurant kitchen and you have a fire no one could stop," he says levelly.

"Yeah, I know."

Dr. Bryan squints at me and I make my face into stone, concealing the emotions that tangle together inside of me.

"I can't be angry at a dead man. Least of all a hero," I add.

"But you are angry at your father. He chose to save Ben. You've felt like he chose Ben over you."

"Dad loved me. He's a hero. Besides, everybody's afraid of something."

I don't want to let Dr. Bryan know that he's right, that I'm still upset at Dad. That I do blame him for my fears. That I can't touch matches. That Mom had to buy a stove without gas burners. That whenever someone lights up a cigarette I freak out and have to move away and count to ten. Yeah, thanks a lot Dad.

CHAPTER THREE - SCHOOL

We never sold Dad's car after he died. It sat in our yard, getting rusty, with tires steadily losing air until I got my permit. Now, I drive his Honda.

I jingle the keys in Nichole's sleepy face and she bats at my hand. I'm usually more awake before school than she is. Another reason why I get to drive. That, and I'm the one with the car. We both get in and Nichole instantly goes for the radio, tuning to find a song she likes. I back carefully out of my driveway, avoiding the ditch on both sides and drive us to school.

Dad's Honda drives smoothly under my direction. I've driven us to Booker High School so many times I know the route by heart. It didn't take me too long to get used to the car's quirks either, like the seat belt that requires extra force to snap into the buckle or the door that you have to close just right. Mom cried for days before getting a new battery and starting Dad's car up for the first time in years. The first thing I did was swap the old, cardboard smelling Little Trees air fresheners for fresh ones. The combination of Peachy Peach and Strawberry scents the car like it did when Dad drove.

Nichole turns down the punky rock song when we're almost there. She puts her arms across her chest and rubs her lip gloss between her lips and then pops them open with a distinct 'poh' sound. "You've been sulking since school started this year."

"Have not," I automatically reply.

She points a finger at me, her lips opening with a smacking sound from all the gloss. "You're no fun to be around. All you do is school and homework. When can we have fun again?"

"That's not true. Last weekend we saw that movie."

"That was two weeks ago and I had to drag you out of the house."

I try not to press down on the accelerator, but I can't help the tightening of my fingers on the steering wheel and the gritting together of my teeth. "What do you want from me, Nichole?"

"I want you to be happy."

I pull into the student lot and find my assigned place. I'm upset enough that I have to back out and angle in twice to park. The girl who has the assigned space next to me always parks so close to the line, I have to be extra careful when I pull in.

"I'm just saying we used to do things all the time and now it's all about school." Nichole slams her door and I do the same.

"We're seniors. We have to focus now."

Nichole shakes her head and starts walking away. I follow her, jogging to catch up.

"I'll see you at lunch, I have to get a book from the library before class," I say.

"See!" Nichole says with a smirk on her face.

"What? It's true. Besides, I like Miss Copeland."

"Yeah, I know. Sometimes I think you're better friends with the librarian than you are with me," Nichole says.

"What, worried I'm going to become best friends with an old lady, tell her all your secrets, and forget all about you? Come on, Nichole, we're best friends forevs."

"I don't have any secrets," she teases.

"Oh, I'm sure she'd love to hear all about how you sneak off campus to go to McDonalds."

"She's the librarian, she wouldn't care, besides that is so vanilla. Whatever, go have fun pretending you're more adult than I am. Enjoy your conversations about arthritis and the latest political scandal."

I laugh and wave exaggeratedly, my hand slicing waves through the air. I don't get why she's upset that I have other people I talk to, especially when they're not even our age. Sometimes, she's just doesn't get me and I need to talk to an adult that isn't my mom or therapist.

Miss Copeland greets me with a wave. Besides Nichole, I'm friends with the librarian and my guidance counselor. Loner to the core, I know, but I'm busy. Homework and classes and projects and attempting to keep up with Nichole. We've been best friends for so long, I'm not sure what I'd do without her.

I check out a few new books and head to first period. In AP chemistry, I sit behind Kenny.

He's Jamaican. His accent is so slight, it only comes in now and then on a strong syllable, cutting its way through my mind every time I hear it. He's one of those tall, lanky black boys that everyone expects to play a sport or something, but he doesn't. He never got over the awkwardness of puberty and continuously bumps into everyone and everything.

I finish the morning worksheet and pull out a new book to read, with a sly peek to the front to make sure Mr. Poole can't see what I'm doing.

A thin, folded sheet of notebook paper falls out of the book and lands on my desk. I jump up, but my knees hit the desk and I fall back on my butt in the seat as I squeal. I set the book aside with a thump, glance sharply toward the front, and grab the paper, hiding it under my palm.

"Something the matter Miss Smith?" Mr. Poole asks.

I take a deep breath. Everyone's looking at me! Kenny stares into my eyes and I clear my throat and blink a few times.

"Nothing, just thought I saw a bee," I say quickly, frantically trying to calm down my hot, red cheeks. Hopefully Kenny will think I'm embarrassed at the attention and not because he's looking at me.

"I don't like bees either," Kenny says quietly.

My blush deepens and I look down at my desktop and start reading my worksheet furiously until Kenny turns around. The rest of the class settles back into scuffling and filling out worksheets around me. I slide the paper back in front of me and unfold it carefully. I slowly read it.

You can do anything.

I glance around the classroom, but everyone is focused on their worksheets. Mr. Poole grades papers. I glance back down at the note, smoothing out the creases. The bell rings, interrupting my scrutiny. I snatch the sheet of paper, tucking it back into the book.

I wait impatiently until lunch and race up to Nichole in the food line.

There are three places to get lunch at school: the regular disgusting cafeteria, the food cart outside the courtyard, and the food stand outside the cafeteria. The food cart and food stand sell the same stuff – pizza, candy, and chips. I would eat it every day if I could get away with it. Mom packs my lunch, unfortunately, and she'd have a fit if I spent her money on pizza. I don't like quinoa tofu weird salads, but I don't want everybody to see me eating pizza for lunch every day, judging me because I'm a little overweight. Becky never says snide things to Nichole about the pizza, but the one time I bought a slice with my birthday money, Becky mentioned how many calories were in one slice of pizza really loudly. She's such a bitch.

"Check out what I found in my library book," I say, bouncing up and down.

Nichole tilts her head and smirks. "Again with the books, give it a rest." She gets two slices of pizza and I follow her to our usual spot outside in the courtyard. We sit at one of the picnic tables.

"This is different," I protest as I pull out the book.

Nichole rolls her eyes. "Alright, fine, tell me all about this new book you love," she smiles knowingly at me.

She picks up her pizza and eats down the side of it like it's a piece of corn. It doesn't matter that she's not giving me her full attention, at least she's sort of listening, so I go on.

"Not the book. Look what was inside."

I find the loose page and pull the sheet out, holding it up for Nichole. She reaches out to grab it and I pull it away.

"Greasy fingers," I tell her.

She shrugs and leans in to read it.

"So what's the big deal?" she asks.

"Isn't it cool?"

"So?" she repeats.

I set the paper back down with a shrug, my enthusiasm dying.

Becky and Anja, Nichole's other friends sit down with us. I turn away so Nichole won't see my disgruntled look as I resettle on the bench to make room. Anja is more overweight than I am, but it only adds to her beauty. She has the most inviting heart shaped face I've ever seen and she carries her weight in womanly curves. It helps that she's taller than I am so the weight is better distributed. Becky is the powerhouse tanned white girl that nobody wants to piss off. She is so athletic she almost joined the football team, but opted for jiujutsu instead when there was a scheduling conflict. Nichole turns to talk with Becky and I fidget.

"Aren't you going to eat?" Anja asks me.

I sit on my hands to stop them from moving and shake my head.

"I'm not really hungry," I lie.

She nods like she understands, but she doesn't. None of them do. If I start eating right now I might never stop. Another thank you to Dad. If I'm not angry, I'm hungry and I have to be careful with my self-control. Not that I never eat… I just don't want to eat junk in front of Nichole's judgmental friends.

Nichole offers me her other slice of pizza.

"No thanks, I'm good," I say, trying not to lick my lips at the hint of fresh dough scent that lingers in the air.

Becky waves to someone walking up to the table. He steps forward, and suddenly all my attention is on him.

With burn scars bubbling up his neck and cheeks, everybody at the table pays attention to the new guy. He looks down at the table and scuffs a toe in the pavement, his tray of cafeteria food wobbling in his hands. I try to figure out what's wrong with his left hand and it takes me a moment to realize that he's missing two fingers. The remaining fingers are misshapen and swollen-looking.

Nichole gets up beside me. "Becky," she says, her voice trailing off, as she just stands there. She glances beside Becky pointedly and wrinkles her nose slightly, before turning back to Becky.

"This is my younger brother, Ben," Becky says.

My mind rushes through the memory of That Day and settles

on the face of the child Dad held in his arms. It was Ben then and it's Ben now. I know everything about him and nothing at all. Suddenly, I have no appetite.

Anja scowls at Becky. Nichole looks everywhere but at Ben. I am the only one that stares at him. His eyes meet mine for a split second and he sucks in a breath before saying something to Becky, too quiet to hear, and sitting down at the end of the table on Becky's side.

"Ninth graders." Becky shrugs her shoulders and sits down.

It's so quiet I can hear Anja whisper to Nichole, "What's his deal?"

"Hey Becky, can I have some of your goldfish?" Nichole asks loudly.

Becky hands Nichole her small packet of goldfish. "Thanks, pizza is great, but sometimes I need more cheese."

"Ugh, if that's what burn scars look like, I would totally get plastic surgery," Anja says, loud enough for Becky to hear.

Nichole frowns. Becky glowers at Anja. I fidget in my seat as I pretend not to listen. A mild headache pushes against my forehead, right above my eyes.

It's not like it's that much of a surprise that Ben goes to the same school as his sister, but why haven't we seen him since the beginning of the school year?

"What gives, Becky? Why'd you invite him here?" Nichole asks finally.

We all turn to look at Ben, but again I'm the only one who openly stares at his scars. Anja and Nichole both flit their eyes right back to Becky, as if they're not supposed to see Ben at all. As if he shouldn't be here.

Becky frowns. "He's been homeschooled and wanted to go to public school. I told Mom I'd look out for him. He's my little brother, so be cool."

Anja snorts and trades a look with Becky.

"Yeah, this is a girl's only table," Nichole says.

Ben stands up from the table, looking nervously down at his

feet. He picks up his lunch tray and walks off.

"Aren't you the one who never says no to her friends? Well, I'm asking for you to let Ben hang out with us, at least until he gets settled. I mean, come on," Becky says.

Will a boy who looks like that ever settle in at public school? No wonder I didn't hear about this if he just started. It would have been better for all of us if he just stayed at home.

I'm not sure what to think. My thoughts are muddled. The sounds of the other girls talking fades. Their words laugh and echo around my mind, bending and twisting and distracting.

"Vanessa?"

"Vanessa?"

Anja and Nichole are looking at me.

"What?" I shove away from the table and stand up stiffly. I shake my head to clear it.

"You okay?" Nichole asks.

"Fine."

The bell rings, thankfully, cutting the awkwardness short.

"See you after. Don't leave without me," Nichole says.

I don't know how I'll be able to concentrate on the rest of my classes, knowing that Ben is so close.

Those scars. Ben's high-collared shirt had no hope of covering the tendrils of white, ropy skin that trailed up his cheeks. I almost feel sorry for him, but my empathy disappears when I remember how he got those scars.

CHAPTER FOUR – BEACH BBQ

"Nessa! Nichole's here for you!" Mom yells from the kitchen.

"In a minute, Mom. I'm getting dressed," I shout back from my room.

Bluster watches me from his favorite spot on the floor as I hunt through my closet. It's the same dilemma. What fits after my weight gain last summer? I hold up a shirt and then another. Sometimes I wish the mirror would lie about my size. I wish I could give back all those comfort food donuts I ate. They only made me feel better for the time it took to eat them and then all I felt was guilt.

I don't even want to go to the beach. My room, my bed calls to me. Gravity pulls on me with extra vigor. I can't imagine trying to walk through the sand.

Nichole bursts into my room and a little surge of adrenaline flies through me at the noise and intrusion.

"Oh my God, you know it scares me when you do that," I say, words fast like my beating heart.

"For the love of God, take those off," Nichole says, pointing to my feet.

I rub the insides of my feet against my favorite pair of Crocs self-consciously. We have wood floors and Bluster is forever shedding, so I wear shoes inside.

"They're all the rage," I say with an eye roll.

"Yeah, for small children that don't know any better, and old people who don't give a flying smack." Nichole says with a head shake. "Every time you wear those God awful things, a panda dies."

"And every time you tell me to take them off, um, a puppy chokes on a gumball."

"That's sick. Fine, you win this round. But, for the love of everything fashionable, put something else on."

I'm glad she doesn't mention my oversized shirt.

"I wasn't going to wear them to school," I grumble and slip off the shoes, kicking them in the corner of the room. My victory over winning our game doesn't last long.

Nichole turns to the rest of my ensemble. "Capris, really? The shirt is hot, even though it's a bit too baggy. I'm not totally feeling the color combinations, but I guess they'll work. Now, you just need some accessories."

I pout at her. "C'mon. This is good enough. Let's just go."

I tug at the sides of my shirt. It is too large for my frame, but it hides the extra fat around my waist.

I notice she's wearing a mini skirt with pleated ruffles up the sides and a tight top with tiny sleeves that accentuate her thin arms. Nichole's taller and thinner and has a smile that can only turn into a laugh. I wish I could wear mini-skirts, but my butt flares too far out and my thighs are too thick. I would look like a tree trunk, not a cute teenager.

She pulls me by the arm to the bathroom. I almost trip over the glass scale. I shove it between the toilet and sink with a snarl.

"This is for your own good," she says. "Stop pulling on your shirt, you'll stretch it out even more. You look fine."

"I look fat," I say as I stand in front of the bathroom mirror.

"You're not fat, just pudgy in the wrong places. If you were to wear makeup, people might not even notice."

"Fine," I say grudgingly.

Nichole's eyes light up and she sets her purse down on the counter to dig through it. She pulls out mascara, eye liner, and a four color eyeshadow palette. Within five minutes, she's applied all three.

"Not bad," I admit.

Opening the drawer with all my hair ties, Nichole pulls one out the same color as my pale salmon colored shirt. She holds it up to my shoulder.

"Hm. I think this one. But if not, you can always wear the black one," she says.

"Black goes with everything," we say at the same time.

I giggle and she tosses her shoulder length brown hair over her shoulders in a practiced motion, blonde highlights flashing in the bright bathroom lights. My own dark, mousy brown hair is somehow frizzy and flat at the same time.

"Should I get a perm?"

"Ness, we've been over this. Your hair looks fine, besides a perm will do more damage than good for your hair."

"You got a perm," I point out.

"That was in ninth grade and look at my hair now. Dry and dead. Yours is still so soft and natural. Don't ruin it." Nichole runs a hand through my hair, tickling my shoulders with the stray hairs.

"Today's going to be so much fun," Nichole says.

I pull a brush through my hair before looping it twice through the hair tie and into my signature low ponytail.

"Don't give me that look."

"I wasn't," I protest.

"I know you better than you know yourself. You're pouting. Just relax. If you lighten up and stop being so uptight, I promise you'll have fun."

I make a face at her and she frowns before waving me off and bustling out from behind me and into the hallway that connects the two bedrooms, silent, empty office, and guest bathroom. I hurry after her out into the living room and toward the kitchen that wings outward from the open space we use as both living room and dining room.

"Hi, Nessa's mom!" Nichole crows and skips up to my mom, giving her a side hug. "I'm taking Nessa for the day."

I roll my eyes.

"Wonderful. What are you girls up to then? Movie? Bowling?" Mom asks, completely ignoring me.

"Not at all. We're going to Siesta Beach."

"What a lovely idea. Vanessa hasn't been to the beach since you took her at the beginning of the summer."

I don't want to go to the beach. Sand everywhere. Sunburns. I never tan, just turn red and blotchy. Blech. Mom and Nichole jabber about the beach and I tune them out until Mom mentions that she and Walter recently went. She doesn't take me to the beach!

"I changed my mind. I'm not going," I say.

"You shouldn't stay here by yourself. Dr. Bryan said you shouldn't be alone," Mom says.

"You'll be here," I protest. Not that I want to talk to Mom.

She hesitates and Nichole picks up the argument, "The beach. Ten minutes. No discussion."

"I can't," I whine.

Nichole pulls me into the living room until we're out of earshot and sight of Mom.

"Just because you're mad at your mom, doesn't mean you have to take it out on me. Let it go," she whispers fiercely.

"I don't like your tone."

"And I don't like your lame, pathetic excuses. Man up."

Mom walks out of the kitchen and stops when she sees us still in the living room.

"I have a test Monday," I say in my normal voice in a move of brilliant improvisation.

Nichole huffs and wrinkles her nose. Mom sniffs the air and looks mystified.

"What class?" Nichole grills me.

"Chemistry," I answer without missing a beat.

"What's it on?"

"Chapter fourteen."

"Oh, you're good. Too good. Fine. At least I'll have Becky while you live your life from your room."

"Wait, you invited Becky?"

Exasperated, Nichole flips her hand at me. "It's a barbecue. You're not the only one invited." She turns and walks toward the door.

"Wait," I call after her.

She turns with a grin on her face.

"I'll think about it."

Nichole's grin fades and she shakes her head. I don't stop her as she walks out the front door. Mom clears her throat and puts her hands on her hips.

"Test? Vanessa, you need to get out more, have some fun. This is going to be your last year in school before you go to college and become an adult with responsibilities. It's only going to get harder from here on out. You spend too much time studying and you'll regret it later."

Another canned parental response, but it still makes me want to respond negatively, to contradict her. "Not all of us can just move on," I grumble.

"That was uncalled for."

"So. Just because you were always too busy with your job when Dad was around, doesn't mean you have to take it out on me now."

She holds up her hands in defeat and turns back to what she's cooking. Sometimes, I wish Mom would push me, argue back, like Nichole does.

Mom stirs the pot on the stove. Whatever it is smells terrible, like boiled plastic gloves and rotting fruit, which is most likely a combination of the newest super fruit and some grain nobody in this country eats but is good for your complexion and stress levels. I can't wait until Mom gets a new hobby. I go back to my room and pull out my latest novel and a handful of Jolly Ranchers I have stashed in my jewelry box.

I'm getting really into the book, sucking on my last watermelon Jolly Rancher, when a knock at my window startles me. I fling the book down in a flutter of pages. Curtains cover the window, but I can see the outline of a person. I creep over to the window and carefully peel back the curtains, swallowing the lump in my throat.

It's Nichole. I let out the breath I'd been holding and place a hand over my heart and close my eyes for a moment as I compose myself.

"Back already?" I manage to say once I've calmed down.

I look over at my clock. She must've been gone at least a half hour already. Why'd she come back? I hope she can't see what I've been doing. I glance over my shoulder and try to decipher if the book is visible from the window. A trashy novel is a far cry from studying for a chemistry test. Crap. She can probably see my bookshelf from the window, where all my textbooks are lined up neatly, the names of my classes written in large bold font on the spines. She never comes back to check on me once I've made up my mind to stay behind, so what gives?

I hurriedly trash the rest of the Jolly Rancher, stuffing it between two pieces of discarded notebook paper in my trashcan. A moment later Nichole glares at me from my doorway. Bluster peeks from behind her legs and I wave my hands in the air and call his name in a high pitched voice. It only takes two calls before he waddles over to me and flops on the ground. I lean way over the side of the bed to let him nudge my hand with his nose. I give Bluster my full attention, lean over more until my hands can reach the floor and tickle his doggy armpits.

"Cut the crap, Vanessa." Nichole stoops down to pick up the paperback, distracting Bluster. "You would choose this over a fun day with me at the beach? On a Saturday?" she scoffs and tosses it onto the bed. "This isn't a staycation."

I harrumph and she slaps her hand beside me on the bed to get my attention.

"I don't want to go to the beach," I say.

"Don't you want to do anything?"

"I want to be left alone."

"No, you don't. Every time I leave you alone I have to put you back together afterwards. You fall apart. I'm not letting you do that anymore. You're coming with me. Your mom told me-"

"You talked with my mom?" I interrupt her.

"You're being kicked out. Reverse grounding," Mom says as she appears in the doorway behind Nichole. "Here, boy!"

Bluster, traitor that he is, wriggles from beneath my hand and rushes over to Mom, butt waggling in excitement.

"Did you do this?" I narrow my eyes at Mom.

"This was all Nichole's idea, but we think you need the diversion. I trust you to act appropriately. Here." She reaches into a pocket and pulls out a crumpled $10 bill. "For your adventures."

Instead of handing it to me, she walks over and slips it into Nichole's empty hand.

"Thanks Mrs. S., I'll be sure to take good care of your daughter and have her home in time for curfew," Nichole says with a smirk.

Mom laughs. She doesn't even get that Nichole's making fun of her.

"There's no curfew in this house. Never needed one." Mom walks out of my room, shutting the door behind her, further illustrating the point that she's too preoccupied to really care about me.

"I have a curfew," Nichole mutters before shoving the money into a pocket and pointing toward the hallway.

"You don't have a curfew. You get home past midnight sometimes."

"Yeah, you think I don't get in trouble for that?"

"Wish my mom would bother herself to notice if I got home late," I say.

"One. You never get home late and two you don't want your mom to be up on your ass all the time about being perfect. Now, stop frowning and come on."

Nichole reaches for my arm, but I scamper away to my dresser.

"Can't forget my phone." I throw the phone into a purse and grab my Chapstick, to Nichole's chagrin. I toss in my wallet for good measure even though it only has my license and off we go.

Mom waves from the kitchen, her phone in hand. Nichole whisks me out the door before I can say goodbye. I'm secretly relieved. I don't want to be stuck with Mom when Walter arrives.

Jason Gregory leans against a Dodge Charger in the driveway. I hesitate, ducking my head and willing my blush to disappear.

Jason is the guy everyone knows, but never goes out with. He's soft and cuddly looking, like he could be everybody's older brother. Protective. Caring. He's from farther south and moved up here last year. He's adorable and I'm sure I'm not the only one who thinks so.

Nichole slides into the car's backseat. Jason gives me a once over and I resist the urge to cross my arms over my chest. I can't, however, stop the blush that overtakes my face at the sight of him.

Oh my God. The Jason Gregory. I want to stare at him, but I don't want him to see my face so I rush over to the car and scoot in after Nichole into the backseat.

"I can't believe Jason is here," I whisper.

"Duh, I invited him and he was only too happy to drive us, I might add." She grins at me wickedly. I stare her down with my mouth in a thin, hard line.

"Oh come on. You've had a crush on him for what, like three years? He only lives five blocks away."

"Sh!" I quiet her as Jason gets into the front and turns to look at us.

"Hey, Vanessa, you can sit up front if you want," he greets me.

"I'm fine back here," I say in a voice that belongs to a Muppet.

I resist clapping my hands over my face. He doesn't seem to notice my red cheeks or weird voice because he shrugs, smiles and turns to face the front again. I breathe a sigh of relief and hope to God Nichole doesn't continue talking.

I look longingly toward my own car before buckling my seatbelt and glaring at Nichole until she puts hers on. I would rather have my own car so I can leave the beach if and when I want, but I can't argue in front of Jason. I'm stuck now.

As soon as we leave the neighborhood, Jason asks, "So how come I don't see you anymore at school, Vanessa?"

Nichole grins at me and wags her eyebrows, prompting me to answer him.

"I'm in AP classes?" I squeak out.

"Oh, that's cool," he says and falls silent.

After another few minutes of silence he turns on the radio to a Ben Folds ballad.

"I like this one, can you turn it up?" I ask in one breath.

The music gets louder and I turn to Nichole. She's staring out the window and I have to tap on her shoulder to get her attention.

"Hey. You didn't tell me you invited Jason?" I whisper.

"You never would have come," she says.

"You're so devious. I can't believe you'd do this, you know how nervous he makes me," I mutter, rolling my eyes and looking out the window behind her.

"Moi? You're always too busy studying or reading or getting ready for school that you hardly have any time for me anymore. Remember when we went to the dollar theater, watching double, sometimes triple features? You've changed, Nessa. Ninth grade was so much fun, but ever since you started all your AP classes," Nichole makes finger quotes around the word, "you've been no fun at all."

"I can't do nothing with my life."

"Are you saying my life is nothing? I have friends and I'm happy."

I frown and open my mouth to protest that I'm happy too, but it would be a lie and Nichole's not done berating me. I glance to the front of the car, but Jason is bouncing to the upbeat piano tune and mouthing along with the words, oblivious to the come-to-Jesus speech in the back, thank God.

"I wanted to be there for you, but you turned away from me. You hide in your house and make up excuses for why you can't go out. I know your mom doesn't keep you home, even if you do have homework."

"That's not fair, don't bring my mom into this," I protest lamely.

Nichole swoops in for the kill. "Newsflash, you're always blaming her for holding you back. You're the one without a curfew and your mom doesn't care if you get bad grades. That's all you."

"Burn," Jason says under his breath.

"Shut up!" we both yell.

"Remember the day we met?" Nichole asks after a pause.

"Yes. First day of high school. I'll never forget."

"You marched up to me on the bus, stared me in the eyes and said 'I'm sitting next to you'."

"And then you stuck gum in my hair," I say.

"Yeah, well you deserved it." She tosses her hair.

"You told me it was an accident!"

"Well, the bus did hit a bump but you were such a dweeb." Nichole says.

"Geez, will you ever let it go that I had a roller backpack? Sheesh."

"You thought you could get away with a roller backpack? In high school? You thought you were the center of the world and everyone would just let you be a dork."

"It wasn't confidence, but yeah, you did make me feel terrible and uber unwelcome," I mutter.

"Don't be an idiot. You're older and wiser and I make sure you don't pull any fashion faux pas. You can be confident."

I sigh. "It's not so easy for me."

"Of course not, you think this all comes easy to me? I have to work at being a bitch." Nichole winks at me.

"So who else will be at the beach?" I ask, nonchalant.

"All my friends, of course." Nichole starts to count on her fingers in a bored voice. "Jason here, Anja, Jekendra, Becky, Victor, Kellen and anyone else that gets invited I guess."

I listen, but my heart's racing and there's a whooshing sound in my ears. I can be cool and calm around Kenny, at least most of the time, because he comes from another country and is polite and aloof, but Jason is another matter entirely.

My hands start to sweat before we even arrive and Jason hasn't said a word. He pulls into the giant parking lot at Siesta Beach and takes the first available parking spot. We get out and Nichole slings her arm through mine. It's reassuring to have her so close and we walk to the food area.

"Are you hungry?" I ask.

"Naw, Becky said she'd meet me here and show us where

they've set up."

Of course. I don't mind Jason being at the barbecue, but with all Nichole's friends here, I'll end up a forgotten wallflower pretending to be involved by picking up trash or building a sandcastle by myself. I follow silently behind Nichole as she traverses around beach goers munching on over-priced, under-fried food. The smell makes me want to stuff my face with salty fries and vomit at the same time. I take off my flip flops and wiggle sand between my toes.

"Hey, girlfriend!" Becky spots us and walks over to hug Nichole. "Glad you still came," she says with a sidelong glance at me.

"Yeah, just had to get my ride," Nichole says smoothly, hitching a thumb back at Jason, who dawdles behind us.

"What's up, Jason?" Becky calls and he walks forward to our circle.

"You look nice," he says.

"Thanks, just picked this out."

Becky's two piece is a deep pink, almost red, contrasting distractingly with her deep tan. The top is a spaghetti strap triangle that accentuates her muscular shoulders and the bottom is so far below her dangling belly button ring that everyone can see she has 'v' shaped lower abdominal muscles.

Becky leads the way. Nichole falls into step beside her.

"Where'd you get that swimsuit, it's totes hot," Nichole says.

Jason walks beside me as I let Nichole and Becky get a few feet ahead of us.

"Did you bring your suit?" Jason asks.

I gulp and shake my head hurriedly.

"Not a fan of swimming?"

"Not really," I say.

We walk onto the sand away from the snack shack area and I squint at the glaring overhead sun. Jason pulls sunglasses from his pocket and puts them on. Nichole laughs ahead of us, the sound fading into the too-loud conversations of tourists all around us walking toward the snack shack. The water is clear glass, reflecting the sun into my eyes and I look down at my feet. Even the sand is too bright. I peer ahead. Nichole and Becky are getting farther and farther ahead of us down the beach as my steps drag and I slow down. Maybe I could get Jason to take me back?

"There they are," Jason says and quickens his step, pulling away from me.

Nichole's group of friends stand around one of the few barbecue grills up the beach away from the water. Nobody waits for me to get there, they're too busy grabbing sodas from coolers and greeting one another. When I walk into their area, nobody says hello. Hot dogs sizzle on the grating of the barbecue. I lick my lips and glance at Nichole.

She laughs with Anja and Becky, digging her toes into the sand. I toss my flip flops onto the sand and walk up to the water, alone.

Maybe I should just walk away. Nobody would notice. I glance back at the party in time to see Ben walk up to the grill. I stomp back up toward Nichole, who hasn't seen the new arrival yet.

"I thought this was a seniors' party?" I snarl, my shyness back at the water's edge.

"Hm?" Anja asks.

I turn and shove my pointer finger toward Becky and Ben so vehemently my elbow pops. Anja laughs, but it's half as loud as it should be and dies off fast.

"Don't worry about it. Hey, want to take a walk with us?" Nichole asks.

"Sure." Anything to get away from Ben.

Ben doesn't move to follow, thank goodness. I don't want to see him anymore. It's not even the scars that bother me, or the way he looks. It's the fact that he's alive. I want to yell in his face.

We don't walk that far before Nichole turns to walk up the beach and into the resort area.

"Shouldn't we go back to the public beach area?" I ask Nichole, peering anxiously at the random people wandering to and from the large cabanas and umbrellas lining the private resort. It screams exclusive and we weren't invited.

"This is exactly where I want to be. I want to go swimming."

Becky giggles beside Nichole and I frown.

"The beach is back that way," I point toward the water on the horizon and Nichole shakes her head. She laces arms with Becky and flounces past the large cabana and into the pool area.

I hesitate, but don't want to be left behind now. I might lose Nichole as a best friend.

Nichole strides ahead and turns sharply onto a walkway leading to the largest and most presumptuous looking cabana. Tanned, long-legged women and buff, sunglass-wearing guys lounge outside a pristine pool. The place is noticeably bereft of children and teenagers. I don't want to make a scene. I walk haltingly behind Nichole, Becky, and Anja. I have to wipe my sweating hands on my capris.

"Chin up. Look like you belong. And don't slouch your shoulders like that," Nichole tells me when I catch up to them.

I blush as the other girls look at me with a hint of disdain in their fake nice smiles. I want to punch Becky in the face, but she's five foot six of badass. Becky is, like, a state champion at jujitsu. I don't want to get on her bad side.

I straighten my shoulders and walk with long measured strides, my shoulders back and chest leading the way. I match Nichole's lengthy strides as best I can with my shorter legs. She's the tall, blonde-highlighted, beautiful one. She fits perfectly in a resort setting, with her movie star attractiveness. I look like I should be carrying her towel. I keep my eyes trained on the ground. *Don't look at me. Don't look at me.*

Nichole doesn't stop when we get to the pool or the rows of lounge chairs. She throws the door open and walks into the building. I step in just as the door closes silently behind us and I'm assaulted by the over-air conditioned lobby and my hands start to sweat because I'm cold. I try not to shiver, but goosebumps erupt all over my bare arms. The gleaming tiles under my feet sparkle with cleanliness. I hope I'm not leaving a trail of dirt and sand in my wake. I glance behind to check and Nichole yanks on my arm. I almost stumble and open my mouth to protest when she halts several feet in front of the front desk and speaks loudly to the concierge, whose back is turned to her. He's dressed in silky maroon slacks with a long sleeved black button down shirt and matching, pristine maroon vest. I should have put my shoes on. I feel homeless in this spotless hotel and wish I was wearing a new bathing suit like Becky instead of my worn out capris that hang almost to my ankles like ill-fitting pants.

"Atten-hut!" Nichole shouts and the startlingly young-looking concierge is so stunned he drops what he's holding and whips around, spotting Nichole immediately. She would stand out in any crowd, but we are the only ones in the lobby at the moment. Thank God.

He pulls on his too-large pants, hiking them higher over his hips.

"Nikki! And you brought your friends. How nice!"

His acne-riddled cheeks barely move with the shallow smile he gives Nichole. His dark eyes narrow.

"Jose." Nichole's smile is so large; I know it's fake. She wants something from this guy. I wonder if he goes to our school or if Nichole just knows him from somewhere. He doesn't look a day over sixteen.

Nichole leans onto the desk and gazes up at Jose. "So, how about that roof key?" Nichole bats her eyes at him.

"Uh." Jose looks from each teen girl to the next and rubs his left hand on his upper thigh.

"Come on Jose," Anja pronounces his name like an exotic flower she can't wait to touch.

Becky leans over, her cleavage spilling over her bikini top. Panic shines in Jose's eyes and he looks at me with relief.

"I can't do that," he says.

"But Jose," Nichole whines. "You're always saying how you can do things for me at school. Time to deliver."

Jose makes an odd high pitched sound and then looks right and left before deftly flinging open a drawer and handing over a lanyard with several keys attached. Nichole blows him a kiss and turns toward the stairs.

Jose blinks five times in rapid succession and stares at me. I mouth "sorry" to him and scamper after the group, already pounding up the stairs.

The roof itself is not accessible. The key opens a small viewing room at the top of the stairs. We sit and watch the ocean.

After about thirty seconds Anja says, "This is boring. Does that key open anything else?"

"Let's check," Nichole says with a twinkle in her eye.

I'm the last to leave the viewing area and follow a few feet behind the huddle of the others. Nichole fits the key into the first lock we come to, room 862, and it opens.

Anja giggles as Nichole steps inside. The room is hotel pristine, bed made and floor empty. Anja walks over to peer out the balcony window. Nichole opens the mini bar and takes out a Snickers bar.

"What are you doing?" I say in a loud whisper.

Becky raises her eyebrows at me and walks up to the mini bar and takes out a small Grey Goose bottle, her eyes on me the whole time.

"Cheers," Becky says to Nichole.

Anja steps back from the window and strides up to the others.

"What else is in there?" she asks.

"Put those back!" I say to them, slightly louder than a whisper.

Nichole slaps her Snickers bar against the glass Grey Goose bottle as Anja roots around and pulls out a bottle of champagne with another giggle.

I glance toward the open door and take a step toward it. If they won't listen to me, then I'll just leave. Not that Mom would care if I got into trouble. Or would she? I take a step back toward the mini bar.

"Where ya' going to put that?" Nichole asks Anja.

Anja pinches her floral patterned two-piece swimsuit and sighs, setting the bottle back into the mini bar.

"Vanessa has baggy clothes," Becky points out.

I start at the sound of my name on her lips. She acknowledges me now? When she wants something from me? I scowl at her and cross my arms.

"We can take the vodka," Nichole says, eyeing me.

Becky rolls her eyes and grabs the other Grey Goose, handing it to Anja. They shuffle past me, hands only half covering the vodka bottles. Someone will see the alcohol.

"Fine. Give them to me," I say, hands out.

Becky passes her bottle to me and I put it in my pocket. Anja regards me thoughtfully before handing hers to me and I place it in my other pocket. I make sure my shirt covers the bottle tops sticking out of my pockets and nod to Nichole.

I can't believe I just did that! Now I'm the one carrying stolen alcohol. My back starts to itch as we get into the elevator, Nichole twirling the key around her finger. I almost scream when the doors open on the third floor, thinking we've been found out, but a bathing suit clad couple stands outside the elevator. We move over in the elevator and they get in, their eyes locked on each other.

I want to wipe away the moisture gathering on my upper lip, but I'm afraid to let go of the bottles I'm pressing into my thigh. Finally, the elevator stops on the first floor and the couple get out and walk toward the front door as Nichole waltzes over to the front desk and drops the key with a loud clunk onto the desk.

"Thanks, Jose," she says with a suggestive smile.

I practically cling to Nichole when we get back to the barbecue area. I hand both bottles of vodka over to Becky who pops the top off the first and hands it to Anja before opening the second and taking a large sip. She doesn't even flinch as I gawk at her and back away.

Ben flips burgers by himself on the grill. Becky and Anja go down to the water to join the growing group in the waves.

"Why don't you go swim or something?" Nichole says as I follow her up to the cooler.

"I'm getting a soda," I explain. I grab a Mountain Dew right after she grabs a Coke.

"Should you be drinking liquid calories?" she asks.

I shrug, but take a small sip in defiance before setting it down, the bubbles clawing at my throat as I swallow.

"Am I bothering you?" I ask.

"What? I'm worried about your health." She eyes my midsection and I suck in my gut.

"Okay, Mom," I say, drawing my voice out and lowering it.

"Your mom isn't that bad."

"My mom is insane when it comes to food. You've been to my house."

"Not during mealtimes," Nichole says.

"She's been getting worse, even since she met Walter. Not only is he gluten-free, sugar-free, blah blah blah. He's also a vegan."

"At least your mom tries. Most of the time I eat cereal for dinner."

"What I wouldn't give for some cereal. The kind with those tiny marshmallows that melt on your tongue."

I take a hearty swig of the soda again and Nichole frowns at me.

"Burger?" Ben says.

Nichole ignores him, looking out toward the water. I stare at him, but don't answer. He looks down at the grill, moving each patty back and forth.

"Becky told me about this cool beach. Has all these dead trees in it. If you're really too stuck up to be cool with my friends, maybe we could have fun if we went there. Jason can drive us back to your house first so you can drive the Honda." Nichole says over the top of her soda.

I'm not sure if I should be mad at her for saying I'm stuck up or grateful that she suggested we go somewhere without her friends and without Jason. So I simply shrug and squint against the sun.

"Jesus, when will you relax?" Nichole turns to me in a huff.

"I went to the resort with you guys," I protest.

Nichole rolls her eyes.

"I'm here now," I add.

"Sure, but you can't just fake it all the time. I can tell you're not feeling it, so can everyone else. It makes people uncomfortable. Look, see, everyone else is having fun."

My eyes flit to Ben, alone against the backdrop of shrieks and hollers from the water's edge.

"Let's go then. Right now," I say, my voice warbling only a little,

That's the spirit!" Nichole crows and claps me on the back.

CHAPTER FIVE – TREE BEACH

Private property. We stare down the end of a dead end drive, ending in a small cul-de-sac. Large houses. Definitely private property.

"Nichole?"

She ignores me and hops out of the Honda. I shove aside fast food wrappers and scamper after her. She's already moving past the sign. I regretted telling her that I'd take us to the dead tree beach as soon as Jason dropped us off at my house. I'm not feeling any better about it now.

"Why would there be a path if we're not supposed to use it?" Nichole says in her innocent voice. We skirt a thick chain that crosses the packed dirt path. I glance at the nearest mansion by the side of the path, set back a hundred feet to accommodate their wraparound driveway.

"But…"

"No buts, no thinking, just do. Remember the gum."

Nichole grabs my hand and pulls me along. I try to keep up. We emerge from the lightly wooded path onto the beach, the dirt and pine needles turning rapidly into cloudy sand full of broken sun-bleached shells under our feet. This sand is not the fine sugar white sand of Siesta Key Beach we just left behind. The water is still far away from this upper beach area and the spindly trees we walked through to get to this open space thin out so I can see clearly up ahead.

I stop and stare.

"Don't make me call in backup!" Nichole says over her shoulder at me.

"What is this place?" I'm in awe. I shake my head and blink my eyes. My vision doesn't waver. It's beautiful here. Twisting trees, branches bending into impossible shapes, poke out of the sand, their dead roots buried far beneath the sand. The trees are a medium brown color and have been skinned by the water and smoothed by the wind.

"Yup. Told ya'." Nichole runs ahead.

I follow her out into the sun-filled wonder. We meander along the beach, pausing at the unique piles of driftwood to take pictures. I kick off my shoes and drag my toes in the sand. Nichole is a ray of chatting sunshine now that I've done what she asked.

"See! Jason told me about this beach, isn't it amazing?"

"When did you talk to Jason?" I ask.

"When you were sulking at the beach, but don't worry. I got your back. I told him all about how great you can be when you're comfortable."

"You did what?!"

"Calm down. He likes you."

"What exactly did you say to him?" I ask, leaning over to touch the smooth wood of a nearby dead tree.

"I just told him that you were conscientious and loyal and stubborn to a fault."

I guess that isn't that bad. It seems I'm back on her good side. I have her full attention. I'm glad I agreed to come.

"So, about the bucket list," Nichole says, leaning up against one of the scarred trees. "Have you given it any more thought?"

"Hm?" The drift wood trees remind me of Ben and I didn't hear Nichole.

"Your dad's note, will you do it?"

She's excited, giddy, her face alight. How can I say no to her?

"I don't know." I kick my toe into the sand.

"What all was on it, again, do you remember?"

I read the list so many times I have every curve of every letter memorized.

"Win a food challenge. Shoot a gun. Ride a motorcycle. Skydive. Perform a kind deed without expecting anything in return."

"That's it?" she asks.

"Yeah, but that's a hard list. The last one isn't even specific. Can we skydive as minors? Where do we find a gun or a motorcycle?"

"Google it," Nichole responds.

I bury my toes in the sand and wiggle them around, letting granules stick between my toes, like sandpaper.

"I would help you. Think about it." Nichole claps her hands and springs off the tree. "Hey, there's a geocache around here, want to find it before we go?" Nichole asks.

"Sure," I answer. "What's a geocache?"

I don't want Nichole to lose interest in hanging out with me. I just hope geocaching isn't worse than what we did at the resort. I don't want to get in trouble. We were lucky we weren't caught.

"It's something you can do with your phone. You find hidden treasure boxes using clues from a website."

That doesn't seem dangerous at all. I smile back at Nichole. "Let's do it!"

Nichole pulls out her phone and brings up the information we need to find the nearby geocache. I grab my phone as well and notice a text from my mom.

"Dammit," I mutter.

Nichole stops reading and looks at me.

"Mom's on another date."

"So?"

"So, she's been on two this week already."

"So?"

"I just don't like it, okay? I wish she would just stay home like your mom. She's always going out."

"You're out. You should give your mom a break."

"Yeah, whatever, did you figure it out yet?" I say through clenched teeth.

She shrugs and holds the phone up to her face to read it. Nichole points up the beach and I follow. We walk in silence until we get to a crude hut made out of smoothed tree branches. It's only about five feet long and four feet deep, so we have to duck to enter. The sand is cooler under our feet and the sun is nearly blocked by the crisscrossed tree branch roof above us.

Nichole reads off the description. "A lovely little hut found on one of the secret beaches most often visited by boat, this little hooked beach is often called Beer Can Island. The geocache is a camo'd mint tin."

I notice some leaves by the corner of the hut and push one aside. My hand brushes against something cool and metallic.

"Like this?" I point to the corner.

"Nichole pulls the leaf down. There's Velcro on the back and Velcro attached to the corner branch of the hut. The small mint tin is also attached to the back of the leaf with Velcro where it is out of sight.

The mint case looks ratty and old, as if someone has painted all over it with cheap spray paint.

"Mint?" Nichole holds out the container and I take it from her. It's rusted shut so I have to grip the tin hard to open it. I have to pull and twist at the same time before I get it to pop open. Several small items fall to the ground.

"Those aren't mints," I say stupidly, half bent over to pick up the stuff.

I stop, my hand partway to the ground. The dead trees fade from my vision as I stare down at the dark packet surrounded by sand. Matches.

The panic surfaces. Threatening to overtake me. *Oh no. Oh no. Oh no.* My knees wobble and I drop to the ground, heart hammering. There's a bright red, plastic basket with smudgy little containers of herbs inside. I'm mixing the herbs together on a plate. The smell comes to me. Burnt pizza. Sweet, acrid dough burning into charcoal in the next room. The air starts to haze. I rub my eyes with my hands, clenching them tightly closed.

"Make it stop. Put it out."

"Oh God! I'm so sorry, Ness. I had no idea what was inside."

I know she's stooping to the ground and shoving matches back into the mint tin. I can hear the snap as she shuts it. I slowly uncover my eyes and take a cautious sniff. Salty breeze. Nichole's pushing the leaf with the mint tin back onto its corner of the hut. She sinks back down next to me. But my heart doesn't slow down and I can't get enough air.

"It's fine, Ness. There isn't a strike stripe."

"I can't breathe," I say between small gasps.

Nichole grabs my arm and pulls me up and out of the enclosed hut.

"Open air, see you're outside. We're on the beach. Breathe, Vanessa!"

Nichole thumps me on the back and I choke on the next gasp and pull in a breath of salty air. She walks around so she's in front of me and mimes breathing, her hand pushing nothing toward her mouth and she gulps forward like she's a fish. It would be comical if I wasn't already distracted by memories. All I can think about is that evening.

Smoke billowed into Estefano's and we raced toward the hostess stand. She had disappeared. The other customers had left. Dad opened the first entrance door and shoved me through. I coughed. I had inhaled smoke. Mom opened the second entrance door and pulled me through. I shrugged off her hands. My throat itched. Clawing at it, I coughed some more.

I saw the hostess pacing back and forth on the grass under the sign for Estefano's. *Specials every night.* A few people wandering around outside and some of them were pointing back at the building. I coughed again and turned to look.

The first front entrance door flew open. Stefan, the old man who owned the restaurant, staggered out. One hand was holding his shirt collar over his mouth, the other was holding up a woman. She dropped to the ground. Stefan swiveled to face the restaurant. Hacking, he bent over, hands on his knees.

Smoke blackened the air above the restaurant. I wasn't afraid until that moment. The situation was under control until then. Too much smoke filled the sky. I knew something bad would happen.

I scrape my teeth across the top of my tongue to clear it of the acrid taste of smoke. My tongue is heavy in my mouth, but I don't taste anything. I blink a few times and notice Nichole in front of me. She wasn't there that day. I'm backing away from my memories, letting them dissipate into bright sand and dark blue ocean. I push this particular memory as far back and away from the present as I can and focus on Nichole.

"There's mustard on your arm," I tell her.

She chuckles nervously. "Thank God. Were the memories bad this time? Are you okay now?" she asks.

I breathe out and in.

"No," I say weakly.

My throat feels raw and my breaths too shallow. My head feels fuzzy from lack of oxygen and I just want to lie down.

Nichole's eyes get wide and she stares at me.

"Should I call your mom?" she asks.

I nod and look at the ground, at the sand I'm sitting on. When did I sit down?

It takes over an hour for my mom to arrive. Walter dropped her off. The fact that I interrupted her date makes me tired. Nichole helps me to my feet.

"Are you okay, Pumpkin?" Mom asks, hugging me.

I shrug into her and take a deep breath. I'm exhausted and all I want to do is sleep. I notice the worried looks Nichole and Mom exchange when they think I'm not looking.

Mom walks me to the car.

"Keys?" she asks as I stand stupidly near the passenger's side.

"Oh." I dig them out of my pocket, cringing at the moisture inside my pocket that reminds me of the Grey Goose. I hand Mom the keys. Nichole stands by the private property sign, one arm holding the other.

"Aren't you coming?" I ask.

She shakes her head. "Anja's gonna pick me up and bring me back to Siesta."

I wilt further. Nichole waves as Mom starts the car and we drive away. I slump to the side of the car so Mom won't try to talk to me, and thankfully she doesn't. Not yet, that is.

CHAPTER SIX – FAT BOY RUN

"Nichole told me about the bucket list," Mom says.

"What?" I stop pretending to eat my cucumber sandwich, setting it carefully back down on the plate.

Mom swirls her spoon through her made-from-scratch minestrone soup, not looking at me.

"They're re-opening the restaurant and we've been invited as special guests."

My mouth drops open. She can only be referring to one restaurant. The restaurant.

"Estefano's," I say stupidly, in shock.

She frowns into her soup and nods with a sigh. She picks up her spoon and sets it back down, pushing the full bowl away from her and setting her elbows on the table.

Bluster thumps into my seat and I absently pick off a piece of crust and drop it to the floor as I consider this new piece of information. Mom frowns.

"Bluster, away from the table," she says.

He looks up at her and lets his tongue loll out of his mouth.

"Shoo!" Mom says in a commanding tone of voice.

Bluster whimpers and waddles away from the table and sits staring at us from the living room.

I'm trying to decide if I'm angry at Nichole for telling Mom about Dad's note or if I'm angrier at the restaurant for coming back to life. Why would Nichole tell Mom? What has Stefano been doing for the last five years?

"Vanessa?" Mom asks, her voice cutting through my thoughts.

"When?" I say.

"Nichole told me after you got home from the beach."

"No, when did you find out the restaurant was re-opening?"

"A few weeks ago."

Mom picks up her spoon again, but puts it back down.

"I'm sorry I didn't tell you right away, but we were going through the office and I didn't want to burden you."

"Is that what the therapist told you to do?" I snap.

Mom's head jerks up from the table and her eyes bore holes into mine.

"That was uncalled for, Vanessa."

I hang my head to hide my eye roll. "Sorry," I murmur, keeping my voice level.

"The restaurant opening will be on the news. They're hosting a food challenge."

I get what Mom's trying to do. Dad's bucket list had a food challenge and the restaurant has a food challenge.

"I don't want to go."

"Pumpkin, why not?"

"Why should I go?"

"I think this could be good for you," Mom protests.

"No." I push out of my chair, letting it scrape the floor as I get up, hoping it leaves scratch marks in the wood floor Mom's so proud of. Mom gets up too and walks around the table to hug me. I stiffen in her arms and don't hug her back.

She whispers into my ear, using her baby voice. "Everything will be alright."

I push myself out of her hug. "I'm not a little kid anymore," I tell her.

She stares at me, her eyes searching my face as if waiting for an apology or explanation for my behavior.

"Are you sure you don't want to go?"

"Yes, Mom. I'm sure."

"Do you want me to stay with you today?" she asks.

"Don't you have a date?" I narrow my eyes.

"I don't have to go; I can stay with you."

"You don't have to sacrifice for me. I already have plans with Nichole."

Mom looks both relieved and disappointed, her face twitching, the left side of her cheek moving and she opens and closes her mouth. Dr. Bryan must have told her to comfort me. She's hugging me more and trying to have heart-to-heart conversations after one of her sessions.

"Well, have fun," Mom says.

"You too," I echo, but then add, "have fun abandoning your responsibilities."

"Vanessa, you just told me you had plans," Mom says with a helpless sigh.

"Whatever."

I don't want to argue; I just want to get away from Mom. So I stop talking and head to my room and slam the door, but not too loudly.

I text Nichole, telling her to meet me at my house in ten minutes and fling myself down on my bed. *I won't cry.* I wait, listening intently for Mom to knock on my door, but she doesn't. I hold my phone up in the air while I'm lying down and scroll through my message log from Nichole while I wait.

She texts me back twenty minutes later to tell me my door is locked.

I toss my phone onto the bed and get up to open the door for her.

"Why was your door locked?" she asks, stepping into my room.

I shrug.

"So what do you want to do today?" she asks.

"I dunno."

"You told me to come over," she prompts.

I huff out a breath. All I want to do right now is take a nap, but Nichole's staring at me like she expects a response.

"So you knew about the restaurant opening?" I ask Nichole, changing the subject instead.

"Yeah," she says, elongating the word.

"And about the food challenge?"

She looks at me sidelong.

"Duh."

"Why'd you tell Mom about Dad's bucket list? I told you it was personal," I say, guarded.

"She's your mom. I thought she should know."

I jab a finger at her. "That's *my* business."

She holds up her arms. "Sorry, Nessa, I thought you would appreciate me telling her for you. I guess I didn't realize."

"No, you didn't."

"You're in a mood."

"Shut up."

Nichole's lip curls up and she huffs out a breath. "Did you want to hang out or just be a bitch?"

"I'm not..." I start to say, but at Nichole's raised eyebrows I relent.

"Sorry. I'm still getting over the beach thing."

"Yeah, okay, but don't be a smack."

I think about Nichole leaving me so she can hang out with Anja or Becky. I can't lose Nichole; I'll have nothing left. *Stop it. Just stop it I tell myself.*

"Okay, I'm better now," I lie.

Nichole grins. "Good. Now that that's settled, let's get out of her, your room is depressing. Let's do the Fat Boy Run."

"The what?" I say.

"You love food, right?"

"Yeah," I say slowly.

"And you loved your dad, right?"

My nose twitches and I stare at Nichole without answering.

"Naturally, you'll want to do the food challenge, even if you don't do the other things from his bucket list, right?" Nichole asks.

"Maybe."

"Well, then you have to train. Anja told me about the Fat Boy Run and I want to do it."

"But what is it?" I ask.

"It's where you get something to eat from the value menu from each of the fast food places in one area, get it?"

"And what happened to staying away from liquid sugar? So it's okay to eat fast food, but not drink soda?" I argue.

"Do you or do you not want French fries?"

Is this a trick question? I always want French fries, but I don't understand what that has to do with a food challenge.

"Of course I want French fries, Mom made banana buckwheat pancakes with vegan sausage for breakfast. Not to mention the cucumber sandwiches and weird homemade soup for lunch."

"Then let's go. Got your keys?" Nichole asks.

I grab them from my dresser and lead Nichole out of the house. Mom's talking on the phone, her words fast and excited. I shut the door louder than necessary behind us as we leave.

"Walter?" Nichole asks.

"Yeah, when she's not with him, she's talking to him on the phone. He even showed her how to text and now she won't stop."

"Parents. When my mom was still dating she was such a pain. She kept taking my shoes without asking," Nichole shakes her head in sympathy.

"Your mom is weird. I can't believe she would wear your shoes. That's so gross."

"Don't talk smack about my mom." Nichole smiles.

"And don't get me started on Lewis," I say.

"I could go on about Lewis," Nichole replies.

We're already in front of the queue at the first fast food place. "Are you sure about this?" I ask as we idle behind a tan van in the drive thru lane.

"Absolutely. Besides, vegan sausage? What does that even mean?"

That makes me laugh.

"They're not that bad." I say.

"Sausage means pork or meat or something, like literally."

"Mom's trying out the vegan thing."

"Walter's a tree hugger?" Nichole guesses.

I laugh again, louder this time, letting it out naturally and filling the space within the car.

The tan van pulls forward and I roll up to the menu board to order.

"Ah. Here we are. Stop numero uno. This one's my treat, you get to order one item off the value menu," Nichole says

"Yay," I say unenthusiastically as I push the button to power down my window.

One item? I'm too hungry for one little item. I'm upset and the smell that wafts into the car when the window is fully open overtakes my stomach and it demands comfort fried food.

"What do you want?" Nichole asks me.

"I don't know. Fries." I pretend unfamiliarity with this particular establishment's menu, but truthfully, I know their value menu by heart.

Nichole instructs me through each drive thru and the bags pile up, their scents mixing together in a cacophony of grease and delicious salts. I look at Nichole sheepishly.

"I shouldn't." My protest is lighthearted and Nichole shrugs it off.

Nichole divvies the items up between us. I munch on a fry, letting the salt soak into my tongue and the guilt of eating junk food distract from my enjoyment. Mom tries so hard to get me to eat healthy and here I am gorging on junk. What would Mom say if she saw me? What would Dad say?

CHAPTER SEVEN – HOLDING A GRUDGE

Nobody knows about my secret stash of candy, not even Nichole. It's one secret I'll never tell. I don't want anyone to know how bad my addiction to sugar has gotten. I don't keep any evidence in the glovebox. Too obvious. I store all my goodies in a special compartment in the trunk of the Honda.

I want a Jolly Rancher before class, but Nichole doesn't leave me alone. I wish I'd put some candy in my backpack this morning because I ate the last one in chemistry class.

"You're always ditching me in the morning. You don't have to go to the library right now, do you?" Nichole says.

I shrug, but I glance toward the trunk of the car. Nichole pushes her back against the Honda's door and crosses her arms, pouting out her bottom lip. I roll my eyes and grin at her.

"We spent all day yesterday hanging out," I argue.

"And everything was for you. I wanted to go to the mall with Becky, but I took you out instead. I was helping you get ready for the food challenge. It's not like it's a good idea to eat junk all the time."

"It's for a good cause," I say.

"Duh, that's what I said."

"Fine, I don't need to go to the library, but I really don't want to hang out with your friends. If they're not ignoring me, they're making fun of me."

"They don't make fun of you."

"Yes, they do, you're just so oblivious," I say.

"Fine, I'll make sure they don't make fun of you, now let's go."

Nichole pushes herself off the car and giggles as she hops forward. "Come on, time's a wasting." She grabs my book bag, but drops it almost as soon as she picks it up. "Jesus, what the hell do you have in here?"

She unzips the large pocket and pulls out my books one by

one, reading their titles and shaking her head.

"I knew you were in advanced classes and stuff, but seriously? Nerd."

She shoves the other books back in my bag and hands it to me. I lift my backpack over my shoulder, groaning at the weight. Nichole raises an eyebrow but doesn't comment. Nichole slings hers over one shoulder.

"That's bad for your back," I say at the same time that Nichole says, "Are you sure you're up for the food challenge?"

She frowns at me, but puts the other shoulder strap on.

"Food challenge I can do, but I'm not so sure about those other things. I mean, shoot a gun? That sounds stupid and dangerous."

"True that, but are you sure you're going to be okay doing it in the same place he died?"

"Technically, he died later at the hospital. He was unconscious at Estefano's."

The casual way we're talking about this makes my heart thud. I'm trying to keep my voice steady, to hold in my screams of pent up frustration. Nichole peers at me, probably trying to figure out why I'm not outwardly upset at the mention of Dad, but then the bell rings. I breathe out a sigh I didn't realize I was holding. Becky and Anja walk up to us as Nichole side hugs me.

"See ya' later," I say in a chipper voice that sounds like it belongs to someone else.

Nichole waves to me and walks away between Becky and Anja. We're only in a couple of classes together. Nichole doesn't take AP classes.

After my morning classes, I hurry to the library before lunch to return a few of the books Nichole made fun of this morning. I really did want to go to the library before class.

Nichole's waiting for me in line at the food cart. She grabs a Snickers bar from the display rack and points to a larger slice of pizza.

I follow her to our usual table and Nichole's friends trickle in to sit down around us. Becky sets down her bento box and unpacks its contents, pulling out a shiny silver chopstick set that has a pink ornamental flower to match. Anja got the pizza, but she pulls off the crust and sets it beside her plate with satisfaction. Becky nods her head approvingly at the move.

"Did you talk to Kenny today?" Nichole asks, digging into her pizza.

"Huh?" I ask.

I'm trying to figure out what the heck is in my lunch bag.

The other girls perk up at the mention of a boy's name. I blush and pull the items out of my bag in rapid succession. Celery. Sardines. A Ziploc baggie full of misshapen crackers. The girls stare at my lunch in fascination. I peer into my bag as if something more appetizing might be stuck at the bottom.

"No. I had to return some of those books," I say.

"One of these days you're going to have to talk to Kenny, and not just about a lab project or a Spanish assignment. You can't hide behind your books." Nichole laughs, taking smaller bites of her pizza slice, up the side. I've never met anyone who eats pizza like corn the way Nichole does.

"Besides, lots of people write notes in books."

"Did you rob a Whole Foods?" Anja interrupts.

I look down at my assortment of lunch items.

"No. It wasn't written in the book, it was a note inside the book," I clarify and glare, not at Anja, but at Nichole. She said she'd have my back.

Becky snickers and shares a look with Anja.

"Never mind. Are those sardines?" Nichole asks, squinting at the table in front of me.

I hold up the unopened package of sardines. The other girls eye it warily. A phone beeps and Becky pulls out her cell.

"Don't worry, I'm not going to open it," I say to the table.

I actually like sardines, but not enough to be the table pariah who brings smelly fish to eat. There aren't enough Tic Tacs in the world to fix sardine breath. I push the package to the side and open the crackers. I pull one out and hold it up to the light. It's dense and filled with flattened seeds of all colors and shapes. I take a bite of one cracker and it half crumbles into my lap. It tastes like bad tofu and flavorless vegan cheese, but I'm hungry. Mom must be trying out a new recipe. I pop another one whole into my mouth, letting it crumble into dry flakes of cardboard that stick to the back of my tongue. Mom didn't pack any drinks for me and I try to swallow the rest of the cracker dry.

The other girls talk about some boy or movie or something. Becky gets up. "Be right back," she says.

Anja shrugs and takes a picture of her nails using her phone. Nichole turns to me, opening her Snickers bar. She hands me a piece and I take it, popping it into my mouth and savoring the chocolate.

Nichole stares off into the distance behind Anja. Becky walks up to the table, Ben in tow.

Why can't Ben sit with his own friends? I grind my teeth together in frustration. It would be easier if I could forget he ever existed.

"Becky, can you get me a soda?" Nichole asks.

"Uh, sure, Pepsi?"

Nichole nods and hands Becky a dollar.

Becky walks off with her Ben shadow.

"We need to instate a rule that no freshmen are allowed at this table," Anja says as soon as the siblings are out of sight.

"Ugh, right?" Nichole agrees with a disgusted sound in her throat.

I remain silent.

"Hey, want to go to that new movie this weekend?" Anja asks, perking up as she turns to Nichole for approval.

"Can't. Sorry, chica. I'm taking Vanessa out."

Anja's eyebrows shoot up and she barks out a laugh.

"Not like that," I protest. "Where are you taking me?"

"I got special tickets to the new restaurant opening. Allen Williams will be filming his show there. The local news channel is going to be there."

"And we're not invited?" Anja asks.

"Sorry, they sold out of seats."

"Sold out of what seats?" Becky asks as she sets down a perspiring can of soda in front of Nichole.

Nichole stares at the soda can. Ben hovers at the end of the table as Becky sits down.

"Some restaurant opening and a food challenge. Isn't Allen Williams that guy who does the *Been There Ate That* show?" Anja says.

"Yup," Nichole corroborates.

"Wait, you mean my parents' restaurant? The one they're re-opening as a bar and grill?" Becky asks.

Anja looks at Becky and then turns to look at Nichole and I.

"Yeah," Nichole says.

"Stay away," Ben says, his voice deeper than I expected. The other girls look at him, but Nichole doesn't budge in her stare at Becky.

"We're going," I declare.

Anger rises in my throat, bubbling out through words I've wanted to say to Ben for years. "You have no right to tell me what to do, you little shit."

"What the hell, Vanessa!" Becky stands up and glares at me.

I stand up and before I can think about what I'm doing; I shove her with a finger. She takes a big step back, as if my one finger actually pushed her. She turns to Ben and grabs his shoulder to pull him with her, her shoulders up to her ears and her eyes wide. "Let's go," she mutters to him. "Can't you teach your dog to heel?" She spits the final words at Nichole.

"What did you just call me?" My voice continues to rise as Nichole grabs hold of my shirt and I lean toward the retreating Becky. "Don't you dare call me that." I throw a stalk of celery at her receding back, but it falls short.

I'm panting, don't know when I lost my breath. Nichole yanks me down onto the bench and holds me at arms' length.

"Listen to me, Vanessa, you need to calm down."

"So these are the people you want to be friends with?" I ask.

"Hey now," Anja protests from the other side of the table.

I'd forgotten about Anja.

"She didn't mean that," Nichole says to her.

"Yeah, whatever, see you in class," Anja says. She wanders out of the courtyard, leaving me alone with Nichole and my seething anger.

CHAPTER EIGHT - GRAND RE-OPENING

Nichole holds my arm like we're on a date, hers slung through mine. She continuously pulls me forward as she walks faster than me to my car.

My phone buzzes in my pocket and I hold it up with my free hand, stumbling as I walk.

"Is it your mom?" Nichole asks, letting go of my arm.

Be home before 8. Love you.

"Oh, now she wants me home at a certain time?" I say, my face heating up.

"Let me see."

Nichole tilts my arm toward her and looks down at the text. "She means that she'll be home before 8. You're so lucky you still don't have a curfew."

"You're lucky your mom cares," I mumble.

"So she's on a date, big deal."

"I'm going to eat so many burger patties and fries." My voice is hard and determined.

"I'm just glad the restaurant re-opening buffet is only $15 each and that your mom is paying," Nichole teases.

I glower and open the driver's side door to slide in. I can't believe Mom gave Nichole money for us to eat fatty fried foods for dinner.

"I wish she didn't."

"Why?" Nichole asks as she settles into her seat and clicks her seatbelt buckle.

"She's the biggest health nut and she wants us to eat junk food? She's so obvious."

"Appreciate it while you can, she'll be back to her usual healthiness before you know it."

I turn on the car and back out of the driveway. The back right side of the car dips ominously toward the ditch as I think about Mom and food. I switch to drive to pull forward and back out again. Nichole doesn't say anything, but turns on the radio and scans for a station we both like. She settles on 105.9 fm and the sounds of Led Zeppelin fill the car.

"This is going to be epic. Fat Boy Run was good and all, but a buffet for drive thru foods is going to be awesome," Nichole says when the song changes to an old rock ballad.

"You hardly even eat that much greasy food. You're more into the boxed and canned variety."

"I may have grown up on store-bought boxed macaroni and cheese and have had intimate encounters with Hamburger Helper, but I seem to recall someone's rather unhealthy obsession with a certain sub-dollar snack, also known as –" her voice drops to a whisper, "ramen."

"Ha-ha, very funny."

"Turn left up here," Nichole directs.

I smirk at her and take a left, the Honda's blinker pattering softly in my ear.

"After this turn, you'll go straight past two lights and then make a right," Nichole tells me.

I know this route. My heart speeds up as I pass the first light.

"And a right up here."

I slow to make the right hand turn, barely flinging my blinker on before I'm in the turn.

"Wait a minute." I don't accelerate but slow down. My breathing speeds up to match my runaway heartbeat. I don't see the road or other cars. My memories explode in a cloud of smoke and sirens. I press forcefully on the brake as I shut my eyes tight and I'm flung forward against the seatbelt. My head flies back and I wince.

"Ness, there's people behind you. Open your eyes," Nichole prompts.

"But-"

The memory continues. Dad smiling at me across the booth. Mom laughing at something Dad said. The first hint of the fire tickling our nostrils. Biting into the free bread.

A car honks behind me, the sound disappearing into the night ahead of us.

"Just go, it's up ahead on the right," she prompts.

I hesitate. The back of my head aches where I hit it and my eyes burn when I open them to slits. I stomp on the accelerator, jerking us forward and turn the wheel hard to the right to pull into a side street.

I will not go there.

The next time I blink, I can't open my eyes, like they're glued together. The memory forces itself down on me and I see myself that last time we went to Estefano's.

I raced ahead of my parents to open the first door. At twelve, I was still excited to be around my parents. Mom almost always cooked so it was special for us to eat out. Estefano's had two doors to get inside, one after the other. I liked standing in the hallway between the doors. It made me feel like I was outside of Sarasota, somewhere foreign and different.

Dad opened the door and Mom stepped in. I scooted forward and opened the next door, graciously holding it open for both Mom and Dad.

Italian landscapes sprawled along each of the restaurant's walls, partially covered by racks of wine. The hostess led us to one of the corner booths.

I sat down on the end of the booth's sagging seat and rearranged the spices in the bright red plastic condiment caddy. It was a ritual every time we ate dinner at Estefano's.

"Vanessa? Are you okay?" Nichole puts a hand on my arm, clearing the memory away.

"I just. You know what happened. We can't."

"It's time. I can't imagine what you're going through, what you've been through. But if you ever want to move on you have to do this. You told me you were ready. Do you need me to drive?" she makes a move as if to slide over the gear shift.

I didn't realize I was crying. I wipe my sleeve across my eyes and stare down at the shifter knob.

"No," I whisper.

"Listen to me," Nichole says. "This is easy. There are no matches, there are no fires. It's just a building. If you can't do this, we can go home. Fine."

I can't help the tears, but I wipe them away, digging the back of my hand across my face. I put the car into reverse and back out. I'm not ready to see the restaurant again, but I can't stop this forward momentum. I pull back out onto the road carefully, breathing deep, and watch the sign edge closer and closer. The words blur together and I can't read them. I look away as I pull into the lot. There are only a few spots available and I pull into one of the last spaces. Nichole hops out of the car. I remain rigid in the seat, hands shaking in my lap.

"I don't think I can," I say to myself.

But we're here and Nichole's opening my door, reaching across my chest to unbuckle my seatbelt, and pulling me out of the car. She grabs the keys and locks the door, pocketing them herself. I can't move.

"This will be good for you. I promise." Her voice is compassionate and understanding, but I can't help resenting her for bringing me here, for convincing me I was ready and could do it.

"No," I say, planting my heels like an insolent child.

"Please? We're already here."

"No!" I say louder.

Nichole grabs my arm and drags me away from the car. I want to clutch it for dear life, but instead I drift after Nichole, her hand firmly gripped on mine. I try to avoid looking at the large sign, but the bright glow of the letters glares straight into my eyes, creating a migraine and all the words haze together.

"Neat, huh?" Nichole asks.

I don't know what she's talking about, but I nod anyways and continue to stumble forwards.

Nichole pushes me inside the main hallway. There's only one other person in this area, waiting for space to open up inside the restaurant beyond the second door.

"Is she okay?" the guy asks.

"I'm fine," I snap, echoing the past. I hate it when people ask me if I'm all right. Friends and family, even strangers, did that when Dad died. People still do it now. Anger fills my chest every time, like I'm always on a medium boil inside. I hate it so much.

"Look, I know this is hard for you, but remember your dad's bucket list. You can do this."

"It's just a piece of paper," I say. My knees are wobbly and my vision is clouding at the edges.

"It's a bucket list, it's special," Nichole says. "I think if you did them for your dad, it might help you feel closure or something. Right? You wanted to do it before, don't chicken out now." Her words are sharp and pointed.

I close my eyes and breathe. When I open them again, I stare down at the floor. The shiny new off white laminate looks like tiles where before it was made of wood. I brush the back of my sneakers against it to create a dirty scuff mark.

I squeeze my eyes tight and open them, seeing spots. I've had enough. I turn to go. Nichole hasn't let go of my arm and yanks me back. I fall to my knees, giving in to their unsteady wobbling, tears trickling down my cheeks.

She leans over to look me in the eyes. I notice several other people inside the restaurant staring at us through the second and inner door as they wait for the host to seat them.

I look up at the ceiling so I can't see any people, but my eyes fall on a framed newspaper article, dated just a week before. I gasp and jump to my feet, leaning against the wall for a better look. It's my dad. His face beams out at me. I'm horrified as I recognize the picture from the dog park, Mom and I cropped out so just my dad is left. There was never a picture before in the news. They never showed Dad's smile or wacky humor. It was always words, words, words.

"Where did they get that picture?" I demand of the article.

"I sent it in." Nichole's voice is small beside me. "Your mom told me about the restaurant re-opening and I thought it would be nice if everyone could really see your dad."

His smile is an exact replica of the one that hid his bucket list, that tore in half, that sits taped and slightly bent on top of my dresser.

"You went into his office?" I turn away from the article to stare daggers at Nichole.

"I thought that, well, I just." Nichole falls silent and I turn with slow deliberation away from her, back to the wall.

I take in the rest of the newspaper article. September 9th, 2007. Less than a week ago. "Local Restaurant Rebuilds After Hero Saved Owner's Family." I stop reading after the title.

The floor is shiny laminate, newer while the walls are the same off white grey. Wine racks are hidden in all the nooks and crannies. It is the same as I remember, only newer, shinier, and buzzing with people and noise.

"It's cool they renamed the place," Nichole remarks.

Why would they change the name?

"What's this place called?" I demand.

"You didn't see the sign? You were looking right at it," Nichole says.

I turn to face the outer door and squint through the thick glass to see the large sign. Hero's Bar and Grill. Nichole's smile is encouraging and I turn away.

I sink back down to the floor. For my father who died saving Stefan's family. I glance back around to the picture of my dad and pound a fist against the wall with a hollow thump. My head follows and I bang it again and again just below the framed article.

Nichole drags me off the wall, but I sink to the ground, thumping my butt against the laminate flooring, sending a jolt up my body as I bury my head in my hands.

Nichole hugs me and whispers soothing words that I can't make out because there's a thunderstorm in my ears and the rushing sound blocks out all the noises around me. I can't close my eyes and between my splayed fingers I see an empty frame next to my dad's article. Above the frame it says "Hero's Challenge."

"I think it's time you faced what happened. All these people came to honor your dad and what he did. I thought your mom told you about it. The restaurant owner created a challenge in your dad's name. They're donating the proceeds to the local fire department."

"Oh." My voice is small. Inadequate. "Why didn't Mom say anything?" My hands clench into fists and I scream in my head, the sound dying into a hiccup on its way out. I yank my phone from my pocket. No messages. I dial Mom's number. It rings and rings and goes to voicemail.

Mom knew I was going to this event. She knew how hard this was going to be and yet she's not here. Again.

"Probably on a date," I say darkly.

"Focus, Ness. Food challenge. This is for your dad."

I nod and stare up at the picture of him.

"A food challenge," Nichole prompts, "and this is their opening night. They have that guy from the food channel here to run the challenge and get media support. I thought you'd want to be a part of it." Nichole's voice falters when she says 'you' as if she's unsure of her decision.

She grabs my hand, more gently than before. "If you want to leave, we can."

"Why didn't she tell me?"

"She did tell you. And I told you," Nichole says.

"No. I didn't know about," my voice trails off and I look down at my hands. My right hand shakes and I grab it with my left hand, holding it forcefully against my thigh.

"Do you want to go?" Nichole asks again. "I can drop you off at home."

"And leave me there?" My voice rises. "No."

"You told me your dad was all about weird things," she says. My heart rate spikes at the words, but she goes on as if she didn't just insult my dad. "Wouldn't he have wanted to bring all these people here for something so ridiculous as watching some guy eat his brains out on burgers and fries? Wouldn't he have liked a buffet of junk food?"

I nod, but there's a frog in my throat and I don't speak.

"Listen, I know you miss him and how your life used to be, but I think you'll really enjoy this. It'll be good for you."

"How come I didn't get an invitation?" I sniffle.

"Um. Your mom didn't think you'd want the attention. We're just regular people here tonight, nothing special. I even got us a small table in the corner, I think."

"It's. So. Hard." The words come out slow and thick like brownie batter. My nose burns as I hold in a heaving sob.

"Keep it together, Ness." Nichole looks away from me.

"I'm sorry I'm so embarrassing."

Nichole sighs. "Are we staying or going?"

"Okay."

"Okay to stay?"

I wipe at my eyes, rubbing them and blinking away the spots at the edge of my vision.

"Stay," I say weakly.

She smiles and we go through the final set of doors into the main part of the restaurant.

The place reeks of body odor and perfume. People are everywhere, standing around and sitting in every seat. Waiters and waitresses run in between and around people. A film crew crouches in one corner and a man in the other corner sings softly into a microphone. There are large landscape paintings on the walls and the lights are dimmed. The bar is off to our left, and people crowd across its entire length, upside down wine glasses hanging over their heads. The hostess, who can't be older than us, leads us to two seats we hadn't seen from the entrance. The table is hardly larger than the two chairs on either side of it and it's tucked into a corner up against a wall. The hostess explains the buffet, but I'm not listening. I'm watching the restaurant. It's alive and throbbing with human life.

Nichole says something and I shake my head and point to my ear. I didn't hear her over the sound of all the people talking. It's like an ocean in here, so many people talking and laughing. There's a speaker next to our table that blasts me with Frank Sinatra.

"Let's hit the buffet," she says, her voice breaking through the cacophony of sounds, and we join the line. In celebration of the food challenge and the restaurant's opening, they have a buffet instead of the usual table service. I don't want a buffet. I want to complete the food challenge right now, not wait until after some T.V. dude tries it for the first time.

"There's too many people here."

"Breathe, Vanessa," Nichole tells me. She puts both her hands on my shoulders and stares into my eyes. I breathe and count to ten. "All better?" she asks.

"I think so; even thoughts are triggers."

"Then don't think about it. Enjoy yourself. Oh, look! There's the camera guys and they're setting up at that table over there. Do you think we'll be in the camera shot?" Nichole asks.

I turn to look. The restaurant is an 'L' shape and we're in the middle with the buffet, facing out at both long sides where tables and chairs and people are scattered all around. Our table is on the side with the camera crew. Great. This means I won't have Nichole's full attention during the spectacle. My shoulders sag as I sigh out and I think the chaotic restaurant noises cover my annoyance, but Nichole stares at me with a scowl.

I can smell the cooking oil grease in the air, like bacon and potato perfume. Comfort foods. We're close enough that I can see most of the spread. I stand on tip-toe so I can see better.

A long table covered in a starched white restaurant tablecloth features an immense chocolate fountain. The chocolate's metallic shine glints in the light. It towers over the other platters. When I finally look away, I'm awed by the amount of food. Platters are stacked somewhat precariously with steaming burger patties, mounds and mounds of crinkle-cut French fries, long thin sweet potato fries, greasy onion rings, and mozzarella sticks.

My mouth remembers lightly salted fries that have just the right crunch and pillow softness in the middle and I lick my lips in anticipation.

Nichole reaches the beginning of the buffet line first and grabs a plate off the pile. Surprisingly, she hands it to me and reaches for another.

"Thanks."

She holds a hand out, indicating that I get the honor of going first. I'm reaching for the first burger patties when a voice breaks through the clattering of dishes and smattering of voices.

"Thank you all for coming to the Hero's Bar and Grill for our Opening Weekend. Our roots were Italian, but we've decided that Sarasota needs a good burger bar and so here we are. But we haven't completely lost our roots, Wednesday nights will be all you can eat spaghetti." Stefan pauses as several customers laugh. "It is my great pleasure to announce the Hero's Challenge in honor of a local hero. Some of you may already know this, but for those of you who do not, tonight we also have the honor of hosting *Been There Ate That's* Allen Williams to help us kick off our celebration!"

Nichole and I both lean out from behind the buffet line to glimpse what's going on, but I haven't forgotten that voice. The owner, Stefan, has a deep and booming voice, even when he's right next to you. I strain to see beyond the sea of heads.

The din drops to a low hush of clinks and the soft whisper of waiter feet as they whoosh around the over-crowded restaurant. Then applause breaks out and I join in without thinking, clapping with the crowd. The noise is deafening.

"Now." Stefan, the speaker, tries to break through the noise. He tries several more times before the clapping subsides and we can hear him speaking. I spot him over by the camera crew at the table where some beefy guy with a goatee and dark hair is prepping a napkin bib for himself.

"This man is going to be the first to ever attempt the Hero's Challenge. What is the Hero Challenge and why have we created it, you might ask? Well, this is the first food challenge in Sarasota.

Any contender has 20 minutes to finish all of the following dishes: onion rings, sweet potato fries, French fries, burger patties, and mozzarella sticks. Doesn't sound hard, but don't be fooled. There's over six pounds of food and all of it must be consumed within the allotted time period for the contender to be victorious."

"Woohoo!"

I cringe as a table near the buffet line, full of college-aged boys with Billabong shirts, board shorts, and frayed flip flops, hollers and several people turn to look at our area. I bunch up closer to Nichole, hunching my shoulders up to my ears. The line parts just enough for me to see Stefan.

His face looks younger, pudgier than I remember, but his hair is peppered grey and bronze and recedes further beyond his brow than before. He appears shorter and I'm surprised that he's shorter than the waiters who stand like tall willows beside him. He was always so tall, but now I see him for how he really is – a short, pudgy, middle-aged business owner with a radio personality and a booming voice.

Stefan continues to speak. "The first person to beat the Hero's Challenge will win a $100 certificate to the Hero's Bar and Grill and will be featured in our menu and on our wall of fame."

He points to a wall in the middle of the restaurant. It features a large garish sign with bold comic sans font with underlines and alternating bright pink and bright blue colors with the name of the challenge and the bullet points to victory.

When will Stefan mention Dad?

As if he heard my thoughts Stefan says, in a more solemn voice, "We are here today because of the heroic efforts of one man. Several years ago there was a kitchen fire and this man, Aaron Smith, risked his life to save my wife and son."

He pulls Ben up next to him. Ben wears sunglasses, a frown, and crossed arms. But his sullen teenager act doesn't distract the crowd from his bunched neck skin that is a white river of scars leading up to a blotchy patch of red and white scars and embarrassment on his face. He's wearing a long sleeved shirt and shuffles from foot to foot. Even from in the back I can tell he's sweating from his flushed cheeks.

Stefan's wife, a round-faced woman who is pudgier than him, comes up behind Ben and holds his shoulders proudly, her double chin tilted outward to the crowd. I can't help but scowl. Ben. I stare him down as if he can see me amidst the sea of faces in the restaurant. Nichole only has eyes for her plate of food.

"You didn't tell me Ben would be here," I say.

"Becky said he wasn't going to go, I'm sorry."

My gaze finally leaves Ben's scarred face. His dull brown hair is ruffled in a deliberate manner as if it can hide the scars or the acne, but he needs a haircut and all his facial flaws are still apparent. He's wearing his stupid pants below his waist to show several inches of plaid blue brown boxers and the ineffectiveness of a studded silver belt. The long sleeved forest green shirt hangs above the belt. If his skin wasn't so pale and the scars weren't so visible and disturbing, he might look like a regular teenage boy.

The owner continues, "I may have lost my restaurant that day, but I didn't lose my family. Unfortunately, Aaron, our hero, didn't make it. And so today we reopen our restaurant in honor of his actions that day and half of all proceeds tonight will benefit Sarasota County Fire Department Station 17."

The crowd hushes in respect. I turn around to look at the people around us. Do they really care? They're here for cheap food, the *Been There Ate That* guy, and a sense of community. They don't care about my dad, only his story. My anger rises. Stefan isn't finished.

"And so, our friend Allen Williams will attempt the Hero's Challenge, starting in half an hour. I ask that you please remain in your seats, unless getting refills from the buffet. Also, happy hour today includes a special $4 margarita for those of you who are over 21. Thank you and enjoy the food."

Another smattering of applause sounds, but it trickles to a few more enthusiastic patrons before disappearing into the cacophony of voices and the sounds of the singer starting an upbeat Frank Sinatra tune. The line moves forward. Nichole and I make it to the end, our plates full of more fatty, greased up food than I've ever tried to eat in one sitting, Fat Boy Run notwithstanding. And we can always get more. My temper dissipates with the heady aroma of perfectly fried potatoes and the promise of salt and comfort. Ben is nowhere in sight.

We meander through the crowd to our seats. I notice our area is more full of people than the rest of the restaurant as customers try to get a glimpse of the challenger or get into a camera shot. Allen Williams is talking and gesturing and I wonder if they've started filming. Nichole already has a smile ready. We sit and I dig in.

I'm shoveling down my plateful of food when I smell something burning. My stomach drops like I'm on a roller coaster and nausea takes hold of me. Is it just me or is the air hazy? The food settles heavily in my stomach, especially the burger patties, and I think I'm going to vomit.

Mom and Dad agreed to split a plate of eggplant parmesan on That Night. They usually shared a meal, but let me order whatever I wanted. I wanted a half-portion of spaghetti bolognaise.

The busboy brought us our bread and I poured oil, oregano flakes, and cheese onto each of the three plates, swirling a piece of bread through the mix and handing one to Mom and one to Dad.

"Do you smell that?" Mom asked.

Dad looked up at the ceiling and inhaled a few times. He shrugged and dug into the bread.

Mom set down her bread and pointed toward the kitchen. I straightened in alarm. Ragged black clouds rose from the door jam. Mom shot out of her chair, the bread in her hands falling to the floor. Dad grabbed my arm.

The fire alarm erupted in a shrill yell. I clamped my hands over my ears. I wanted to shut my eyes. But I didn't. Dad shouted something at me. I couldn't hear him over the alarm. He yanked me from the booth.

The food challenge guy is still waiting for his food. I think I'm going to throw up. Looking around, nobody else is sniffing the air or getting up to ask questions. Is the smell just in my head? *I can do this. Everything is okay.*

I see Stefan himself carrying a large serving tray with several plates stacked high with the burgers and fries and other challenge items. I sniff the air again, but the mysterious scent is gone. It's too loud in the restaurant to hear what Stefan is saying this time, but I imagine he's describing all the components of the food challenge as he sets plate after plate on the table in front of Allen Williams. With the last plate down, Stefan bows like a butler, smiles to the camera, says one last thing, and disappears behind a cluster of waiters who guide him to the nearest computer.

"Hello, earth to Nessa. Are you even listening to me?"

"Yes..." I say.

"Ben's apparently a waiter here," she says, pointing toward the buffet line.

Ben crouches down on his knees, running his hands through his hair, and standing back up to stare at the computer screen with pursed lips. A waitress shoves him aside to use the computer and he says something to her and she jabs the air near his face. He takes a step back as she wrinkles her nose and says something that makes Ben's eyes narrow. She stalks off, her chin high in the air and he taps away at the computer.

"Are you done?" Nichole asks.

"Huh?" I've completely forgotten we're eating. "Maybe."

A bell dings one long solitary note and we both turn at the same time to watch Allen Williams. There's an overly large plastic timer on the side of the table, marking the time and we're close enough and at the right angle to see it counting down from ten minutes. He's shoving fries into his mouth like he's stuffing a turkey. Nichole's mouth drops open. There's a piece of something dark stuck between her teeth.

"Ew, and people watch that in HD on their television? There are fry bits falling out of his mouth," Nichole mutters.

"He's under a time limit," I say in his defense.

It is really gross. Crushed potato and breading are all over the lower half of his face and he shoves so much into his mouth at once that he can't close it all the way to chew. Nichole looks away.

She doesn't see as Allen Williams leans over the side of his table and barfs.

"Oh my God!" I say, a gag rising in my own throat and I cough to clear the feeling. On my next inhale I breathe in smoke and my eyes bulge.

"What!" Nichole looks at me and I point and avert my face from the disaster, willing the smell to go away.

"That's so gross," Nichole says. "Guess he failed. So, question, if you finish the challenge and then puke it all up, do you win or lose?" Nichole asks.

I breathe in tiny breaths to keep from being overwhelmed by the slight acrid scent in the air that tickles my nostrils.

"I think you probably have to at least keep it down for, like, an hour. Plus, he didn't even finish in the first place," I say.

My head is heavy and I can't help but gulp down a large breath of air. It makes my nose ache and I gasp at the strength of the burnt toast smell.

"Yeah… I think I'm done," Nichole says.

I tilt my head to look at the ceiling and then down to the floor. Nothing alarming is in the air, but I can't get rid of the scent that invades my nostrils. It gets stronger, like rotten perfume mixed with fast food oil that hasn't been cleaned out in a week. I pinch my nose together and breathe through my mouth for a minute, trying to clear my head. All I can think is, get out, but my feet don't move and my butt is glued to the chair.

The fire alarm blares, waking me out of my stupor and I stumble to my feet, head reeling. Sound echoes in my ears and the singing is replaced by the insistence of the fire alarm. *Go. Go. Go*, it tells me. Two Nichole's and two tables and four plates of crumbs hover in front of me. I grab at Nichole's arm and miss, my arm flopping against the back of her chair.

Both Nichole's look at me and say something, the words a whisper against the blaring siren between my ears.

"What?" I mouth.

Why isn't anyone panicking or moving or trying to save themselves? I grab for Nichole's arm again and am surprised when

I feel her smooth hand in my own clammy one. I drag her away from our table, toward the door, but my feet move like they're in butter and I slip on something wet.

Nichole can't stop my fall and our arms stretch as I fall down. She doesn't let go. I bump my knee mercilessly on the hard floor and my scream is so loud as it erupts that I hurt my own ears. The sounds blur together and there's only a ringing in my ears as the memories come crashing down on me.

"Mom, I'm scared."

Mom bent down, level with me. "Everything will be alright."

"I love you, Pumpkin," Dad said to me and raced past Stefan into the building.

I jumped up in terror. "No!" I screamed.

Mom held me and I squirmed in her grip. Fires were dangerous. In just 30 seconds, a small flame could grow completely out of control. I remembered the demonstration when the firemen came to school. The video they showed of the couch going up in flame from a cigarette and the whole house burning down was the scariest thing I had ever seen.

Dad emerged, helping a woman limp to safety. Stefan's wife. She wailed and coughed and struggled in Dad's arms. Stefan helped her to her feet and she screamed Ben's name, looking back toward Estefano's front door.

Nichole grabs my arms and I push against her. I have to save these people. I have to help them. Tell them. Get them to move. I pant faster and faster.

"Vanessa!"

I recognize my name on her lips, but no sound reaches my ears. There's a rushing sound and then the alarm disappears and all I hear is the warble of the singer holding a long high note, laughter, and a million voices talking at once.

"Is she okay?" A man with short salt and pepper hair and a business suit leans over me with his hands on his knees.

"Fire," I squeak out, completely out of breath.

"Let's take a look at that knee," the man says.

I heave myself up and push him away weakly. Where's Nichole? I blink and see her again, standing behind the man. She comes forward.

"You screamed so loud. Did you break something?" she asks.

"Have to get out," I say in between breaths.

Nichole looks back and forth, confusion pulling her brows down.

"There's no fire, Vanessa. It's okay."

She reaches out and I latch onto her arm. She leads me around the restaurant toward the front. I don't smell anything wrong. I only see people eating and talking.

"See?" she asks. "Here, let's get some fresh air."

But we can't get out because Ben is in our way, blocking the door with a tray of drinks as he waits for people to move.

The only thing holding me back is Nichole's tight grip on my arms. I'm not sure if she's holding me or I'm holding her, but I want to hit Ben. I want to knock the tray from his hands and then whack him with it.

"It's okay, Nessa. It was just a false alarm. The firemen took care of it."

Stefan is speaking. The noise level decreases. I continue panting and staring at Ben. He doesn't look away.

"Let's just get back to our table," Nichole tells me.

She pulls me back to our little table. We see Allen Williams walk by, camera crew in tow. People applaud as he walks by each table, stopping now and then to say hi as he makes his way around the restaurant and back to his own table. Stefan presents him with a bill the size of a regular sheet of paper. Allen Williams, with his own flourish, pulls out his wallet and throws some bills down on the paper. The owner takes them and scuttles off. I can't catch my breath.

Nichole sits back down. We're done eating, our plates shoved aside and forgotten. A lone fly buzzes back and forth between the morsels left on my plate and the crumbs on Nichole's.

I want to close my eyes and lie down in the corner, pull my knees up to my chest and hug myself.

Ben appears. Him. He's rushing towards our table and before

I can think of what I'm doing I've shot out my leg. I'm mad the fire alarm went off, that this stupid restaurant exists, and my anger takes over.

He topples onto his chin and the half-empty plates he's carrying scatter crumbs all over the carpet.

"Vanessa!" Nichole cries.

"What!"

"Don't you want to come back here?" she says under her breath.

"Duh, I want to do the Hero's Challenge. It's on the bucket list."

"And?"

"That was an accident." Pride creeps into my voice and I look off innocently.

Nichole shakes her head, but neither of us get out of our seats to help Ben clean up the mess.

CHAPTER NINE - THE MOVIES

It's Saturday again, a week after we saw Allen Williams fail to complete the Hero's Challenge. Nichole and I have plans. We're going to see a movie and then attempt the Hero's Challenge. We just parked the car on the top floor of the parking garage downtown near the cinema. We walk to the stairs and start the long way down. I take the first corner too sharply and the edge of my shirt catches on the railing and stretches out, pulling me back with it.

"Dammit," I mutter. "This was my favorite."

"I told you not to wear such baggy shirts."

"I like baggy shirts," I grumble and continue walking down the stairs, careful to stay away from the sides.

"So," Nichole says after another two flights of stairs. "Can we have a snack with the movie?"

"Huh?" It takes me a moment to realize she's talking about the food challenge. I turn to look at her, my feet slowing down so I don't accidentally trip.

The corner of her lip is upturned and her eyes squint. The dimple in her cheek appears as the sly smile grows and grows until she's laughing at me.

"Come on, no eating at all?" she asks between laughs.

"Nope." I bite down on my lower lip to hold my smile back.

"Won't you lose your appetite if you don't eat all day?" Nichole asks.

"Good point, but no. For this first attempt, we will fast all day in preparation. We need our entire digestive system to be empty and waiting."

She shakes her head at me, but then stops. "Wait. You said first attempt?"

"If we don't succeed now…" I hold up my hands, palms up and shrug.

"Now hold on a minute. I'm not doing this more than once, even in camaraderie!" Nichole puts her hands on her hips. A hint of a smile sneaks up the corner of her lip and her dimple rises in response. I give her my best impression of puppy dog eyes.

"Fine. I'll do the first attempt."

"Will you eat the hot pepper?" I ask.

"What hot peppers?" Her voice rises and I squint at her. "You know I don't like spicy foods."

"It's a hot pepper, not hot sauce. And I saw that they just announced-" I begin.

"Who announced?"

"No interruptions!" I clear my throat. "The Hero Bar and Grill just announced that they're upping the stakes and increasing the rewards with their Hero's Challenge."

"No way!" Nichole interrupts sarcastically.

"As I was saying before I was so rudely interrupted. Again. Every month the challenge goes unconquered, one new element will be added and the prize will increase by fifty bucks."

"I can tell you're getting obsessed over this. How'd you even find out about it?"

I glance away.

"Never mind," she says. "Are they still donating-?"

"Half the proceeds, yes."

"Well, I'm still up for it, but there's no way I'm eating the hot pepper unless I'm going to finish," she says.

"Great and my plans exactly."

We finally reach the bottom of the stairs and walk out of the stairwell through the back alley area past the bathrooms toward the front of the movie theatre.

"Now, it's time for some movie-hopping madness. You still game?" Nichole asks.

"Wait, movie-hopping? What does that mean?" A blanket of foreboding smothers me and as we turn the corner I see Anja and Becky. My heart plummets through my stomach.

Anja and Becky stand to the side of the ticket line, huddled together like conniving penguins. I think I've got heartburn or I'm going to have a heart attack my chest is so tight.

"What are-?"

"Nikki!" Becky calls, interrupting me, even as Nichole's already walking faster to leave me behind and greet the other girls.

I make a face and walk slowly up to their group. Anja crosses her arms and glares at me sourly.

I ignore Anja's stare and walk up to Nichole. She turns to me. "What's up?"

"Can I talk to you for a second?"

She raises an eyebrow, but lets me hook an arm through hers to lead her away from Becky, who smirks at me. I pull her towards the wall, in front of the movie posters. Brad Pitt stares down at us.

"Why'd you invite them?" I ask.

"What do you mean? They invited us."

They invited Nichole. I'm just her tagalong. Her attachment. Ugh.

"Maybe this was a bad idea."

"Oh my God, stop being such a smack. Just deal with it, okay. Just because Becky's brother works at the theatre doesn't mean you can't come here and see a movie."

Wait. Ben works here? How come I didn't know that about Ben? I swallow my surprise and kick myself again for not keeping tabs on him.

"Don't back out on me now, Smith."

"I'm not," I say. I bite my lip. "What's movie-hopping?"

"Becky told me about it. We're going to have Ben get us tickets and then we're going to watch a couple movies in a row. It's going to be fun."

Is she trying to convince me? I glance back toward the parking garage.

"Hey, I'm going to go with you to the Hero's Bar and Grill. I'm doing the damn challenge. Can't you do this for me? Don't you want to hang out with us?"

"I want to hang out with you," I protest. I don't want to hang out with them. I don't want to get into trouble.

"Great!" Nichole says.

She grabs my arm and drags me over to Anja and Becky. Nichole waves us on toward the ticket counter with a triumphant smile.

I clench my hands into fists without meaning to at the sight of Ben. I uncurl my fingers slowly as we wait behind several couples before it's our turn at the window. Nichole lets Becky go up to the counter first. Becky sets her elbows on the counter and gestures behind her. We're a few feet away and I can't quite make out the garbled words coming through the little window speaker.

Becky looks back at us, peering intently at Nichole and me before turning back to Ben and gesturing more with her hands. Nichole stares at the movie posters along the opposite wall.

Finally, Becky takes a few slips of paper from Ben and walks triumphantly back to us. We meander toward the front doors and away from Ben's unrelenting gaze.

Becky hands us each a ticket.

"See, that wasn't so hard," Nichole says.

Becky glowers. "I hope you're happy."

Nobody answers her. Becky stalks up to the concession stand and gets popcorn. Anja follows her lead, asking for her popcorn without butter.

"Can we get some popcorn?" Nichole asks.

"No!" I say, louder than needed.

I'm still angry at her for bringing her friends and getting us free tickets at the expense of using Ben. I don't want to ever feel like I owe him anything. I mean, at least I have the decency to look him in the eyes.

The movie is lame and all I can think about is the scent of salt on Becky's popcorn.

As soon as the credits start rolling I pop up out of my chair. None of the others get up and since I'm on the very outside of the row I wait for a moment and pretend to stretch before sitting down and rooting around under my seat as if I can't find my phone.

"We always stay for the whole movie," Anja tells me when they finally get up to leave. I lead them toward the bathroom, looking back over my shoulder every few moments to make sure they're still following me.

We enter the bathroom in our four-person group and hover near the mirrors. Becky pulls out a tube of lipstick to reapply a shining red coat to her lips.

"That's a great color," Nichole comments.

"Want to try?"

"Sure, thanks."

Nichole grabs the tube and layers it over her own pink lipstick.

"That color looks great on you too," Becky says.

I scowl and look away.

"You can keep that one, I have another," Becky says a bit louder.

"Thanks Bey, I never have enough lipstick."

When has Nichole ever called Becky 'Bey?'

"What's next?" Anja asks the question before I can.

"Well, let's check the times." Nichole pulls out a sheet of movie times.

Becky peers over Nichole's left shoulder and Anja over her right shoulder. I shuffle forward, but can't see the list so I peer at myself in the mirror as if all I wanted to do in the bathroom is fix my hair.

My lips are pale and thin. I rub down my hair, trying to get it to lie flat at the top where it frizzes up. There's a red spot on my forehead and I lean in close to see a zit forming. Great.

"It's just after 2, so here are our options." Nichole says, but I can't see what she's pointing at and she doesn't elaborate out loud for my benefit. I press on the pre-zit and the skin around it darkens.

"If we check out this one, that'll leave us a 15 minute break before this one starts," Becky says.

"The less time between them the better," Nichole says as she crumples the paper back into her pocket. Her eyes meet mine in the mirror and she smiles. I stop touching my forehead and turn around slowly.

"Let's go," Becky says.

Anja opens the door and the two of them stroll out of the bathroom, Nichole following close behind. She forgets to hold the door and it bangs shut. I stare at the grey door with darker scratches over it. I could just stay here and they'd forget I even came. Nichole would get a ride home with Becky and Anja and forget all about me. My lips quiver and I blink to hold back the tears. My nose burns and I sniffle.

The door bangs open and Nichole walks in and stops when she sees me standing there beside the mirrors.

"What are you doing?" she asks.

"Nothing," I sniffle.

"Are you okay?"

"It's just," I say. But I can't say the words. "A zit."

Nichole laughs. "That's it? That's easy. Come here." She walks up to the mirror and pulls out a compact from her purse. "It's a little dark for your skin tone, but we can do your whole face and nobody will notice."

I tilt my head up and close my eyes. She rubs something soft around my cheeks and dabs it delicately across my forehead. When I open my eyes I see a tanned Vanessa with an even skin tone.

"Perfect," Nichole says.

Nichole leads me to the next theater. It's dark already and the screen shows a preview of an action thriller, the colors bright and then dark in an instant as cars crash during a high speed chase. Nichole pauses just inside the theater and holds a hand up to her forehead to look for the girls.

She pulls on my arm and we walk all the way up to the back and join the others. I sit on the outside again.

This movie is a romantic comedy. I freak out when an ill-uniformed, pimply-faced teen holding a dull flashlight walks into the theater and stands under the exit sign. Is she counting people in the seats? Does she know we didn't pay for this movie? My heart skips a beat.

"Relax," Nichole whispers to me.

I slump into my seat and am only able to relax when the pimply-faced teenage worker leaves.

"Told ya."

I smile at her and we settle in to enjoy the rom-com, but I'm distracted by my stomach. Pangs of hunger push at my insides. Mom's going to be furious when she finds out that I haven't eaten all day. She'll be extra furious when she finds out what I'm going to eat for dinner.

We shuffle out of the theater with the crowd and head directly for the bathroom on the other side of the theater. I check the time on my phone after the second movie and notice Mom left me a text. *Out tonight with Walt. There's a gluten-free veggie casserole in the fridge.* "Who the hell makes a veggie casserole that's gluten free," I say out loud.

"What?" Nichole asks.

"Nothing."

Becky fixes her makeup in the mirror and Anja scrolls through her phone, openly ignoring me.

The last movie is a two-hour, action-packed thriller. The chase scenes are unbelievable and distracting. I forget about the other girls and my hunger until the movie credits roll. I stand up and sit down immediately, remembering that the others won't leave until the last credit is done and the house lights come on.

"So good," Anja says.

"Jason Statham is so hot," I say.

"Ew, he's so old," Anja says.

"I like Liam Neeson," Nichole adds with a smile in my direction.

"You're weird. I think Chris Evans or Tobey Maguire's hot, but not old guys," Anja says.

"Not even Brad Pitt? He's like 40," Nichole argues

"A classic and good looking, I'll give you that," Becky concedes.

I don't say anything else and wait for the others to stand up before I do as well and then I let them walk ahead of me out of the movie theater and follow a few steps behind. The sunshine outside is so bright, I squint and am momentarily blinded. My momentum carries me straight into the back of someone and I stumble to the side, scrambling and say a hurried, "Sorry."

Ben turns around. After a hesitant moment he smiles at me, but his eyes are panicking.

"Don't touch me!" I shout. I yank my arm back and glower at him. I stand up as straight as possible and open my mouth to really let him have it when Nichole pulls me backwards and I stumble, biting my tongue in the process. I shrug off Nichole's hands and step back up until I'm inches from Ben. It surprises me that I'm almost as tall as he is and I'm so close to him that I can see how the pinky-white flesh of his neck scar branch up like a tree.

"Do you like playing with matches or was it just a mistake?" I say to him before Nichole can stop me. "Murderer, you bastard," I add. What am I saying? I take a step back and cross my arms, waiting for him to respond, to deny it, to hit me. Anything. He stands there until someone calls his name and he just walks away, pulling his collar further up his neck. I crunch my guilt under my tongue and walk toward the parking garage.

Nichole runs up behind me and taps on my shoulder. I shrug off her finger and keep walking.

"What the eff, Vanessa."

"Leave me alone."

"I can't you leave you alone because you keep running your mouth. Can't you just be normal?"

I stop fast and turn to her. "It's the truth."

"That doesn't make it okay."

"Ugh, you think I don't know that!"

Nichole pulls out her phone and bites her lip as she stares at the screen.

"What?" I ask.

"Becky. She thinks you should be nicer to Ben."

"Is that what she said?"

"More or less," Nichole says.

"You don't like him either, do you?"

"Eh." Nichole shrugs noncommittally. "At least he won't be at the restaurant right now, since he's working at the cinema."

"I didn't think of that. Thank God!"

Nichole's phone buzzes, but she shoves it back into her pocket without looking at it.

"Okay, just you and me now. I promise."

"Finally," I say.

"We're best friends."

"Yes. Yes, we are."

We walk side by side to my car.

"To the Hero's Bar and Grill, Driver," Nichole says.

"Why of course ma'am," I answer.

We both giggle as I start up the car and head out of the parking garage, a buzz of anticipation spreading outward from my empty stomach.

CHAPTER TEN - FIRST ATTEMPT

By the time we get to the Hero Bar and Grill, it's almost 7:30 at night. I'm roaring hungry and antsy with worry and excitement and anger at myself for being such a bitch earlier. At least Ben won't be here.

Inside the restaurant for the second time, I shiver as a memory of That Day takes over.

Seconds ticked by like hours. Dad went back inside the restaurant. The building creaked and groaned like a giant walking down rickety stairs. I put my hands over my ears, rocking back and forth on the ground. Mom held me tight.

My hands clamped over my ears, I could still hear the sound of sirens. I turned toward them. A fire truck and an ambulance pulled up next to the sidewalk. The firemen came into view. The owner gesticulated wildly to them and the restaurant. The firemen were thick and heavy looking under their gear as they jogged into the building. I relaxed. They would help Dad. But they didn't come out. The restaurant creaked louder.

"For two?" The hostess asks, hand on her hip. Her eyes are narrow and she breathes out her nose.

"Sorry, yes. For two."

She leads us to a booth in the middle of the restaurant, two overly large menus clutched under her armpit.

"Your server will be right with you," she assures us as she sets the menus down.

Our waiter is held up by a table of guys next to us. By the time he arrives, I can tell even Nichole is out of patience. Before she can say anything I cut Nichole off.

"Two for the Hero's Challenge, please." I smile.

He's a 20-something hottie with broad shoulders and a chin cleft that would put Superman to shame. His hair is slicked back and his eyes are the bluest I've ever seen on someone with brown hair. I know what's going to happen next. Nichole leans over the table, resting on her elbows and looks up at our waiter with large eyes. She flutters her eyelashes and gives him a moment to admire her before putting in her request. "And two waters, please."

He smiles at her as he stuffs his writing pad back into his waiter's apron. He turns to the kitchen and shouts, "two Challengers!"

I hear the kitchen echo back, "two Challengers!" and the guys at the next table laugh and then talk amongst themselves, their murmurs settling into the general buzz filtering through the restaurant.

"Not even sexy girls can win," one of the guys says loud enough to rise over the other sounds between our table and theirs.

"Too bad I prefer men to boys," Nichole says casually.

I suck in a breath and hold it. Our waiter smiles at her for a second longer, winks at me, and walks off. I glance at the boys' table and see a stack of tens sitting beside their short salt and pepper shakers. One of the other boys slaps a ten on the table and then catches me watching him. He gives me an encouraging nod. His eyes are the darkest brown I've ever seen. He winks at me and I look away.

Nichole says, "How old do you think our gorgeous waiter is?"

"Too old for you, Miss I Prefer Men To Boys."

She ignores my joke and licks her lips. "Doubt it. I bet he's only 22 or 23. Don't you think he's cute?"

"For someone who works in a diner slash bar, sure," I shoot back with a smirk.

"You've always got to come up with a reason to criticize a boy. Such a pessimist." She holds up her pointer finger. "This one doesn't do his homework." She pops up another finger. "He obviously just wants the V." She giggles and pops up a third finger. "And this little piggy---"

"Stop it! They'll hear you." I glance at the boys' table next to us out of the corner of my eye.

One of the boys is laughing so hard I can see a crown on his back tooth. The other boys are staring at the boy and shouting to each other. The pile of tens is untouched in a haphazard, distracting pile in the center of the table.

I bite my lip at Nichole and have an idea.

"Hey, they just bet that we can't finish half the challenge."

"Hm. Which ones?"

"Does it matter?" I ask. I peek at the dark-eyed boy again.

"Not really," she says in an offhand manner, pretending to inspect her cuticles.

She hops up from her seat.

"Are you thinking what I'm thinking?" I ask.

"We're going to win that money," she says.

"Exactly, but-"

Her eyes are set on the boys' table and she saunters up to them, her skirt swishing against her thighs with every step. I spring out of my seat and join her. The guys stare at us.

"Can we help you?" Dark-Eyes asks.

"Yes, yes you can. My friend Vanessa here has a proposition for you." She turns to me.

"Um. Yes. Yes. We have a proposition for you." I stall and turn to Nichole.

"We bet you," Nichole says and puts a finger on the pile of $10s to drag it around the table with her manicured finger. "That we will finish half the challenge."

I put my hand on my hip, mimicking Nichole.

"It's a bet!" Dark-Eyes says.

I loop my arm through Nichole's and we walk with even steps back to our table.

"At least one of them has a chance," I hear one of the guys say.

Was he talking about me?

"Whatever. We got this," Nichole says.

"Uh, we better because that's a fucking lot of money," I say flatly.

"I thought you wanted to bet them?"

"Yeah, but not with money. I don't have enough to cover that."

"What were you thinking then?"

"I don't know. Something else. I hadn't thought that far."

"We'll just have to win, then."

"Duh, that's what I was planning on doing anyways."

"Don't be mad at me. It was your idea," she says. "Besides, it's not like we're going to finish this anyways."

"Yes we are. What are you talking about? This is important. My dad's bucket list, remember?"

"I thought you weren't going to do those things?"

"That's not true!" I insist, my whisper squeaking at the end. "I will do this challenge and I will beat it and then I'm going to maybe do those other things."

"That's the Vanessa I know! Half-committed and overly stubborn!"

I slam my fist lightly on the table and smile at Nichole. The waiter calls out "Challengers!" He sets down a large tray beside the table on a stand and we marvel at the plates. One of the betting guys gets up and stares down at the food.

"As if." He goes back to his table and says to them. "Eat up boys, dinner is on them."

Onion rings that are perfectly round and heavily breaded. Sweet potato fries lined up like fence posts next to shoestring French fries. Moist burger patties that are well-done and stacked up like pancakes. Mozzarella sticks with a side of marinara. A small plate with a wrinkled, soft yellow-green pepper.

I swallow and breathe in the smells of comfort.

"And the timer," the waiter says, holding the timer aloft so everyone nearby can take a look.

Out of the corner of my eye, I can see the guys' table is watching us.

"Remember, now. Every single item in 20 minutes. Are you ready, Challengers?"

Nichole nods and unfolds her napkin, placing it delicately in her lap. I follow suit and nod at the waiter.

"Hero's Challengers, on your marks. Get set, go!" the waiter shouts for all to hear as he presses down on the timer and sets it in front of us on the table.

Nichole starts with the onion rings and I go for the fries. Our waiter smiles at us, bows extravagantly, then rushes off to fulfill his other duties. The guys next to us laugh and I hear one chanting, "Eat, eat, eat."

I chew madly through my fries, setting the hot pepper aside for last. I've never actually eaten a raw jalapeno. I finish up half of the fries – both crinkle and sweet potato varieties and take a hasty sip of my water. Nichole is most of the way through her onion rings, but stops to pick up her own water. We hold our glasses aloft, turn to look at the guys, clink our glasses together and take a sip.

I only slow down when I get to the meat patties. They're soaked in grease and I try to scrape off some of the excess oil. We only have seven minutes give or take a few seconds left. I haven't even touched my onion rings or mozzarella sticks. Where did all the time go? Nichole has only finished her onion rings and some of her French fries. We're not going to make it. Can we still get halfway through the food? I try to chew faster, but only succeed in choking on a piece of burger and have to waste time slugging water. I usually like burgers, but this one is well-done and I'm beginning to hate meat.

Our waiter rushes back over as the guys count down, "ten, nine, eight, seven, six, five, four, three, TWO, ONE!" One of the guys makes the sound of a buzzer dinging and Nichole and I slam our hands down on the table and swallow what we have in our mouths.

The waiter shakes his head and clucks. "You girls hardly made a dent. Guess I have to bring you your bill."

"Wait!" cries one of the guys. "Bring out a kitchen scale."

The waiter protests until we explain our purpose and he disappears to bring us back a kitchen scale. We weigh each of our plates and figure out how much is left.

"And subtracting the plate itself, that's… 3.3 pounds for…?" guy in the orange smiles at Nichole and she prompts him with her name. "Nichole. Right, and 3.2 pounds for Vanessa."

He remembered my name. Dark-Eyes gets up and swipes the $10s off the table. Nichole's arm starts to rise, but Dark-Eyes reaches over and hands the pile of $10s to me.

My stomach gurgles and I put a hand to my belly. I ate so much I can't suck in my gut without feeling ready to burst. I hope my loose shirt hides my full belly.

"Thanks," I tell Dark-Eyes.

He winks at me.

I fan out the $10s and wave them at the table and then walk over to our own, Nichole in tow.

We let the busser load up our leftovers in a to go box, even though I know Mom will most certainly throw it all out when she sees it in the fridge.

"How much did they say it was when you lost?" Nichole asks.

"Ugh, $30."

"Wow, pricey!"

"Well, it's free if you win," I counter.

"Whatever, at least we can cover it with this." She points to the money. There are only enough bills to cover the food and a tip without any leftover. I hand the money to Hottie waiter when he gives us our bill.

I groan, wanting to lie down, my stomach rumbling in protest. Nichole grabs both our doggy boxes.

"See ya', boys." Nichole blows the neighboring table a kiss as we walk out the door, our heads held high. One of them whistles again. Dark-Eyes jumps out of his chair and hands me a slip of paper. My face gets red again as I pocket the phone number and try to look anywhere but at him or the other guys.

Hero's Challenge, winning at a food challenge is not a check. Dad only listed five items and I can't even do one of them. I crush the phone number into my pocket. I don't care about the stupid boy.

CHAPTER ELEVEN - PICTURE HUNT

"Get out of bed, Ness. I have plans for the whole day," Nichole says from the doorway of my room.

"But it's still early," I whine.

Nichole walks into the room with arms crossed over her low-necked t-shirt. The pockets of her short shorts sway back and forth as she moves, the frayed ends float back and forth.

I put Dad's bucket list into the historical fiction book I've been reading as a bookmark. I set the book down gently on the nightstand.

"You're using it as a bookmark, but you won't do it?" she asks, pointing to my book.

"It's the last thing my dad wrote," I say. "I'm going to do the food challenge and that's all that matters. Speaking of, I want to try the food challenge today."

"It hasn't even been a week, just wait until tomorrow, okay?"

"You always choose what we do."

"Uh, no I don't," Nichole says.

"Fine. What do you have planned?"

"That wasn't too hard to convince you for once," Nichole says. "See, you actually like doing new things. You'll love what I have planned. I did it all for you."

I bite my lip as I root around in my closet for a decent pair of flip flops. My baggy shirt flops off one shoulder and down my arm like a shawl, revealing too much of the top of my cleavage. I pull the shirt from the back to even it out between my shoulders.

"Just wear the strappy blue ones. They look great with your pale skin tone."

"Um, thanks?"

"It's a compliment. I know you don't tan."

She pulls out her phone and taps a few buttons as I put on my blue sandals. Mom's already gone for the day so I don't bother being quiet as I shut my door after Nichole and tromp down the hall past the bathroom to the main living room.

Nichole walks around me in the opposite direction of the front door, toward the kitchen.

"You won't find anything you like in there," I warn.

"I like healthy things."

She pulls open the fridge and frowns.

"What is this shit?"

"Juice cleanse."

"But there's no food in here," Nichole says.

"I told you."

"What do you eat?"

I walk out into the dining room and drag a chair into the kitchen. Opening the cupboard above the oven, I root around behind a teapot we never use and some plates that we never threw out from an old set. I pull out a tin of coffee triumphantly and dangle it over Nichole's head.

"It's not coffee," I tell her.

She grabs the tin and opens it. "Nice." She pulls out a sleeve of Ritz crackers and an individually wrapped oatmeal cookie with white frosting on top. "Not very healthy, though."

"That's an oatmeal cookie," I protest.

She raises her eyebrows at me and I grab the tin away from her and put on the lid, shoving the container far behind everything in the cupboard before climbing off the chair and putting it back.

Nichole opens the Ritz cracker sleeve and pops one into her mouth and closes her eyes.

"Want one?"

"No, thanks. I don't really eat those much," I lie.

"Suite yourself." She pops another Ritz into her mouth and I look away. If she left right now I'd devour that entire sleeve of Ritz and want more besides.

Nichole snacks on Ritz as I lock the house and unlock the car.

"Okay, where to?" I ask when we're both in the car and buckled.

"Back out of this driveway."

"Really?"

"I'm joking, just take Desoto to 301. I know you know how to get out of your own neighborhood."

"You're so full of it," I say with a chuckle and press down on the accelerator to rev the engine before pulling out of the driveway.

Nichole directs me to downtown Sarasota and we pull up in the temporary parking area in front of the Regal Cinemas movie theater. I keep my foot on the brake and the car in neutral, ready to go park. Three people stand near the bench out front. Nichole rolls down her window.

Three guys turn to look at us. Three familiar faces. I blink. Nichole could not be so stupid.

"What are you doing?" I hiss so hard spit flies into the air.

My breath quickens and I huff in and out through my nose. Nichole doesn't respond to the question. My face burns and I look away from the guys. I wish I could disappear. They don't know it, but Nichole and I both know that standing outside my car are Jason and Kenny: my two crushes, and Ben.

I look for Ben's shadow, Becky. Or would Ben be Becky's shadow at this point? For once, the girls are nowhere in sight.

What are my two crushes and Ben doing here? Nichole is behind it all. When exactly has she set all this in motion? So much for having a nice day and hanging out with Nichole.

"This will take your mind off everything," Nichole says to me proudly.

I slam the car into park and yank open my door. I leap out and stalk around the car and up to Nichole.

"What the fuck is this!" I whisper-shout in her face.

"Calm down."

"Whatever this is, just stop."

Nichole glances behind me at the three guys. I turn my head

and see them shuffling back and forth, staring at the sidewalk and the shops across the street.

"Don't embarrass yourself."

"You're the one who should be embarrassed," I hiss at her.

Someone honks behind us and I jump.

"Listen. I think this will be good for you-"

"I don't understand what this is!" I shout, no more pretense of whispering.

"Hey Nikki!"

I whip around and see Becky, Anja, and Jekendra getting out of the car that honked at us. Nichole waves at them with a large smile on her face and then turns to me and says in a clipped low voice, "back out now if you want, but don't make me look stupid, okay? It wasn't easy getting everyone together today. I hardly even know Jason and I've never even talked to Kenny."

"And Ben?" I say his name like it's a disease, emphasizing the first letter.

"You need to let it go."

"No, you need to stop letting Becky tell you what to do. Is Becky your best friend or am I? What am I, a joke?"

"I'm not trying to make fun of you. This is a photo scavenger hunt, you and the boys versus me and the girls." Nichole's voice drops so low I have to lean in to hear her. "I'm including you and giving you a chance to be with some hot guys and maybe reconcile a few things with Ben."

"You don't know what I want!" I clench my fists, digging my nails into my palms.

"We're best friends, okay. I did this for you," she repeats.

"Is she okay?" Jekendra asks.

"I'm fine!" I shout.

"You two gonna fight?" Becky asks, pointing to my clenched fists.

The skin on my knuckles is pale white. I unclench them. Four red dashes form across my palm from my nails. I look at Nichole's friends.

"I'm fine. We were just discussing how I'm going to beat you skanks."

Becky looks at Nichole and bursts into laughter. "You and them? Please." She points to Ben, Jason, and Kenny.

"Bring it, bitch. I can win all by myself," I say, taking a step toward her.

"Whoa, whoa. No solo teams. Vanessa, Jason, Kenny, and Ben are on a team and I'm on a team with the gals," Nichole says.

"No!"

Nichole glares at me. My hands shake. Nichole is going to leave me alone with these guys. I can't even look at them. My face is so flushed; I can feel the heat radiating from my skin.

"Here you go," Nichole hands me a thin sheet of paper.

Jason and Kenny lean over until our heads are close to touching. I hold the paper out so they don't have to get so close, but they don't move away. Ben stands a few feet off to the side staring out at the movie theater. He reminds me of myself when Nichole and her friends ignore me. I shake my head to clear away the thread of sympathy and read the paper. It's full of bullet points.

- Kiss by the famous statue
- A pregnant lady
- On a slide
- A man with a mustache
- Flipping off a stranger
- Walking a dog
- With a set of twins
- In an elevator
- With a mannequin
- Eating a donut with a police officer
- A sign with one of your names on it
- The funniest thing
- Bathroom graffiti
- Eating ice cream

"What kind of a competition is this?" I let the paper flop down.

"The first group has to get pictures of at least ten items from this list," Nichole says. She pulls out another sheet of paper and waves it at us. "Wins."

"Wins what?" Ben asks, his voice low and measured.

"Wins a date with one of us girls."

Nichole doesn't mention what I win. She winks at me.

"That's enough prize for me," Jason says, eyes on Anja's miniskirt. I glower at Nichole but she's too busy waving goodbye and walking off to her car full of friends to care. When I turn back to the guys, Kenny is scrutinizing the list.

"What's the famous statue?" he asks.

If Nichole wants to play dirty, then we'll play dirty. I can't believe she would pair me with Ben, but I'll play her game. Ben be damned. I'll do this for Dad and I'm going to win.

"We can't win if we go down the list in order. We need to plan it out. There's a store that sells donuts near the statue. In fact, I think most of these can be completed near the statue. Let's go!"

"What's the famous statue and why kissing?" Kenny asks

Looks like Kenny's going to slow us down. I guess Jason is my best bet for winning.

"We need to go to the peninsula where Unconditional Surrender is," I say.

The boys hesitate outside my car.

"Just get in," I tell them.

Ben gets into the back with Kenny and Jason takes the front. I pull smoothly away from the curb.

"Here's the plan. Let's divide and conquer, okay?"

The boys nod their heads. Palm trees and buildings fly past us through the car windows

"Here's the deal. I'm assigning the mustache man and someone with a dog to Jason, set of twins and sign with one of our names on it to Ben, and bathroom graffiti and something funny to Kenny. Everyone be on the lookout for a pregnant woman. The others are probably too difficult to do in time so don't worry about them unless you see them. Got it?"

Nobody responds and I check the backseat in my rearview window. They're all looking at me.

"What?"

"I just never heard you say that much before," Jason says.

"Oh."

Am I not supposed talk? Or tell them what to do? Is Jason looking at me weird? Did I forget to brush my hair? *Breathe. Just breathe.*

A bright ping comes from Jason's pocket. He flips out his phone and stares at it.

"Whoa!" Jason says.

"What?" Kenny asks.

"They got the pregnant lady," Jason informs us.

Shoot. I press down on the accelerator and we fly up Bayfront Drive. I wait impatiently to make the left hand turn into the Marina Plaza parking lot and zip down the road to park in the row of grass parking spots near the infamous Unconditional Surrender statue.

Cars drive by on Bayfront Drive to and from the beach. We have to wait for a couple to finish taking a photo under the statue before we can have our turn. We wait by the information sign and I skim the details. Seward Johnson was the artist, but he based the statue on a photograph someone else took. Blah.

Jason's phone pings again and we huddle up to check it. The picture is of a large cop with a donut and the rest of the gals with donuts in their hands. Dang it!

The couple leaves and it's our turn to take command of the statue. I need to choose who kisses whom.

"Kenny, um, you can kiss me and Jason can take the picture. Right? Okay."

Kenny stares at me, unblinking.

"It only makes sense for Jason to take the picture since the phone with the camera belongs to him. It'll look really neat for you to be in the picture because, um, you're so tall. Right." My bright, flaming cheeks must betray me because Kenny and Jason exchange looks.

"Are you sure?" Kenny asks, taking a step toward me.

I'm already underneath the 25-foot statue's shadow. It's larger than it looks in pictures. I put a hand on the girl's fiberglass leg and stare up her skirt. The statue is smooth and cool to the touch. Eyesore or commemoration, I'm still not sure, but it's a Sarasota landmark.

"Shall we?" Kenny holds out a hand, low enough to suggest I lean into it and imitate the pose of the couple in the statue.

My hands shake as I stare at Kenny's hand and then back up at the statue. The sailor dressed gentleman dips the girl in white dress over to kiss her passionately while keeping her from falling onto the ground. His hand is behind her back, supporting her in a couples dance show finale pose. What if Kenny drops me?

"Um, actually. Ben get over here. I think it would be much better with you here. Yes," I say.

Ben walks over at my prompt, but falters when he sees my face. He opens his mouth to speak and I'm sure he'll make some sort of protest.

"Nope. No questions," I say.

Nichole's tactic seems to work. Ben closes his mouth. I glare daggers at him and he looks away as he lowers himself down into Kenny's hands. I don't even know why he's listening to me. Kenny seems to want to pull his hands away, but I give him a cock-eyed glance and he solidifies his stance, careful only to touch Ben's clothes and not make contact with his skin. Just to be a bitch, I maneuver Ben slightly in Kenny's grasp and make a camera frame with my fingers. "Perfect."

"Roll away, Jason, they're ready. Okay boys, you're on."

Jason snickers and moves in for a close up. "Smile," he says, waiting for one of them to make a move.

Kenny looks at me, I give him the thumbs up, but he doesn't move.

"No way," he says.

"Do. It," I say.

Kenny grumbles something I can't understand and leans over.

"Wait, don't block the shot man," Jason says and Kenny leans his head away from camera. He puts lips to Ben's cheek, the one without any scars and both boys grimace. I feel guilty for putting Kenny through this as he hardly even knows Ben, but it's worth it for the discomfort that is clearly visible on Ben's face.

"Take the damn shot already, man. He's tickling my face," Ben mutters, trying not to move his lips.

Clicking commences. The previous couple stare at us, mouths scowling. The lady even has a hand on her hip.

"Hey Jason, take my picture. I'm about to give that couple the finger. Ready?" I'm gaining confidence in this whole scavenger hunt thing. He swivels to me, his finger at the ready near his phone.

I smile broadly at the couple and give them the best middle finger I have. The lady's jaw drops, which makes me giggle.

"Got it," Jason says.

"No time to waste, let's go," I tell them and take off at a sprint toward the peninsula. I slow down after a minute, before I start to pant with the effort. I walk fast and look behind me pointedly. The boys are walking toward me, each several feet away from the others. I gesture with my hand for them to catch up, but I'm glad they don't run after me. I'm too out of shape for running.

A small beach sits out on the peninsula and a children's playground with a slide. Jason's phone pings again. It's a picture with all the gals around some random guy and his wife. She is definitely pregnant and he has a mustache.

"Come on!" I yell back to Ben and Kenny.

We race down to the playground near the beach and I breathe through my nose so nobody can see me breathing hard through an opened mouth. I'm lightheaded and want to gasp in the air and stop running. Kenny tips his head to Jason and breaks away. I falter in my step. Should I ask what he's doing? I decide to keep heading for the slide, but slow my pace.

We have to wait for some kids to vacate the slide so we can get on it for the picture.

"What's Kenny doing?" I ask between silent pants.

"He went to do the things you told him, I guess," Jason responds.

Ben stands behind Jason, watching me. If I were him, I would leave. Nichole and Becky are probably behind his compliance.

"Closer Ben, you're cut off in the shot," Jason says.

Ben looks at me and I scowl at him, daring him to get too close to me. Ben scoots imperceptibly closer and looks to Jason. Ben inches his shoulders up toward his ears, his shirt collar creeping up to block more of his scars. The marks remain clearly visible.

"C'mon man, closer."

Ben moves closer, though still far enough apart we aren't touching.

"Touch me and I will burn you alive," I mutter under my breath, staring at him.

Ben's expression doesn't change, but I see his nostrils flare. He's above me on the slide and I'm sitting on the lip at the bottom. I turn to look forward for the picture. Jason scowls at us, but then his expression changes and suddenly Ben is slumping into my back. I hop up off the slide like a snake bit me. Kenny laughs a deep throated chuckle.

I whip my head around and see Ben covered in soda. I hop up from the slide and point a finger at Kenny.

"You?" I ask.

He nods his head, barely keeping from doubling over with mirth. Ben is grumbling something under his breath.

"Funniest thing and all y'all on the slide," Jason says, biting his lower lip and chuckling.

"You didn't!" Ben finally yelps, turning around and snatching at the air where Kenny used to be. Ben shakes his hands to rid himself of some of the soda that drips from all parts of him.

"Come on already, man. We had to do it. For the girls," Kenny says, holding the empty soda can aloft in apology.

"You're a dick, you know that?" Ben responds.

"Time to send some of these pictures," Jason says.

"Good, we're falling too far behind. None of you saw a mustache or pregnant lady?"

"Well, there was this one lady, but I'm not certain she was pregnant," Kenny says.

"I think, well, I'm sure we all think you've done your part in this. You can go home if you want," I suggest to Ben.

I kind of feel sorry for him and how we picked on him. His hair is matted to one side with soda and his nose is wrinkled in disgust. He won't look me in the eyes. He just shakes his head at us and walks off.

Good riddance. We head back toward the statue and our waiting car. We get all the way to the entryway to the peninsula and stop. Nichole and her gaggle of girls are under the statue. Jason checks his phone. No photo of kissing under the statue yet, but they're about to win. How did we fall so far behind?

Nichole spots us. She's the one holding the camera. Becky and Anja haven't posed yet. I jog over and hold out my hand for her to shake. She grins smugly and moves to grab my hand, but I snatch her phone from her other hand and turn on my heel so fast I make a divot in the grass with my sneaker and run back toward the boys.

"Go, go, go!" I yell at the approaching Kenny and Jason. They just point behind me. Becky has appeared and is holding a phone. I see a flash and then Jason's phone pings. Uh oh.

"You can give that back to me now," Nichole says, holding out a hand.

I stop running. Shoot. I retrace my steps and hand back her phone. Not only did we lose the scavenger hunt, but I lost my cool and Nichole abandoned me to this catastrophe to be with her other girlfriends.

"Have fun?" Nichole gloats.

"No."

"I'll let you in on a secret. Guess which boy has a motorcycle!"

"You didn't!"

Nichole indicates toward Jason with her eyes. I laugh.

"You're telling me this whole setup was so I can ride a motorcycle? Unbelievable."

"Not just about the motorcycle thing. I thought you had a crush on Jason."

"And Kenny," I add. "But why Ben?"

"Ugh, Becky insisted that he come. Such a loser, but I don't say no to my friends. Did you ask Jason out? I think he's much better looking than Kenny."

"No, why would I do that?"

"Oh my God, Ness, I set this all up for you. Give me a break."

"No promises on asking him out, but maybe I'll ask Jason for a ride."

I wink at her. She smiles and turns back to Becky for a high five. Anja holds up her phone to show Nichole all their pictures. I'm forgotten again.

I reach over to tap her on the shoulder when Jason says, "Hey, so Nichole told me you wanted a ride?"

I glare holes into Nichole's back and turn to Jason with a shrug. "Sure."

My heartbeat races and I'm acutely aware of blinking too much. I keep my eyes open and then slowly blink as I nonchalantly wipe my hands on my thighs.

"Great." He smiles and holds out his hand. I stare down at it in confusion. "Um, yeah, you'll have to take me back to the movie theater where I left her."

"Her?"

"My bike." He grins sheepishly.

"Um, okay."

He walks off.

"Told 'ya," Nichole says to me.

"Smack."

I follow after Jason. We get to my car and I drive us back to the cinema. My hands start to shake the closer we get to our destination. Thankfully, Jason stares out the window. I pull into the parking garage behind the movie theater and slowly start the upward drive to find an empty spot.

"I'm parked near the top," Jason says.

"Okay."

My throat is so dry, I sound like I'm a chain smoker. I clear it. Why don't I stash water in my car along with cookies and crackers?

"There." Jason points to a motorcycle. It looks like any motorcycle I've seen. Shiny and dark and small inside the parking space next to the cars.

I spot an empty parking spot farther up and pull so far in, I slam on the brakes so I don't hit the wall in front of me.

"S-sorry," I stutter. "My foot slipped."

I turn off the car and get out, slamming my door harder than I mean to and lock the car using my key fob when Jason shuts his door.

"Oh, do you have shoes?" He points to my feet.

I'm wearing my Nichole approved pair of sandals with straps behind, in front, and over the tops of my feet.

"Actually, yes."

I unlock the car and pop open the truck. I grab the small backpack of overnight supplies I stash next to my hidden food supply and pull out a pair of old sneakers. I put them on as fast as I can and nod to Jason.

I walk behind him toward his motorcycle, rubbing my hands on my thighs every few feet. Jason looks at me and I quickly shove my hands behind my back.

"You okay?" he asks.

"Perfect."

He stops and waits for me to catch up and we walk side by side.

"Nichole told me you wanted to ride a motorcycle to honor your dad or something?"

"Or something," I repeat.

The motorcycle is nothing. It's not like I'm going to shoot a gun or skydive. It's all about the food challenge. This is just an opportunity to hang out with Jason and do something fun. At least I keep telling myself that.

He shrugs and walks over to his motorcycle. I wait inside the rectangle of the parking spot a few feet away as if his motorcycle's a horse that might kick me.

"Here, I'll help you with the helmet."

Jason walks up to me and holds out a bulky helmet, much thicker than a bicycle helmet with more straps.

"It might be a little big for you," he says.

"Nobody ever says that to me," I joke.

He doesn't laugh.

"Ha. Ha. A joke," I say.

"You don't have to belittle yourself to get my attention. Here."

Jason sets the helmet down on my head delicately. Grasshoppers jump inside me and I gulp down on my feelings. The straps dangle by my ears and he reaches to one side of my head, his finger grazing my cheek to grab the strap. I hope he can't feel my blazing cheeks. He latches it with a click to the other side.

"See if that is tight enough."

I wiggle my head back and forth. The helmet slides around, but stays on my head.

"Good enough."

"I don't have an extra jacket, but I'm going to be very careful and we'll only go around the block or so."

He points to the motorcycle. "These are your footrests." He unfolds a thin metal bar that rests against the motorcycle and then repeats this process on the other side.

"How do I get on?" I ask.

"Easy, come here, I'll help you. You just climb on."

I take two half steps forward and touch the seat of the motorcycle. Padding juts out from the back pad of the same leathery material.

"You sit back here and you'll hold onto me. Tight, got it?"

"Yes."

He holds up a hand and I quickly wipe mine on my thigh again before grabbing his and swinging a leg over and onto the foot rest on the other side, trying as much as possible to keep my weight to myself. I adjust my butt against the cushioned seat and let out a quiet scream when the bike tilts a little. I yank down tight to Jason's hand and try not to move.

"It's okay. See? Not going to fall over."

I open my eyes. When did I close them? I take a deep breath and let go of Jason's hand and clutch the seat around my butt just in case. Jason undoes something to make the kickstand part fold up and hops on the bike. I grab his shirt with two hands. Jason reaches around and pulls my left arm around his waist. I reach around with my other hand and grab his shirt from the front.

"It helps to interlock your hands or to hold onto my sides, not my shirt."

"What about stopping or turning?" I intermingle my fingers, which makes me body lean forward until my front is touching him. I was sweating before, but now, touching him, I feel the heat from my body increase and sweat trickles down the middle of my back. My stomach hurts from how hard I'm trying to hold it in.

"Stay neutral for turns, don't lean. Don't worry about pressing into me if we brake or accelerate. Tap on my shoulder if we need to stop. It'll get loud out there."

I gulp and nod, my helmet banging into his shoulder. "Sorry," I yelp.

"It's okay, you ready?"

"Yes."

He backs out and I clutch my fingers together tightly as we tilt side to side. He pushes the motorcycle backwards, his feet on the ground. Then the motorcycle roars to life and we're coasting down the parking garage.

This isn't so bad.

As soon as we make the slowest turn ever onto the main street, Jason speeds up and my arms are pulled into his chest, still clenched to each other. After one more, slightly faster turn, he accelerates so fast my fingers pull apart from one another and I'm forced to clutch his sides. He slows down and readjusts my hands lower on his torso.

When he speeds up again, I feel the wind pushing against my cheeks. I lay my head near Jason's right shoulder so I don't bump my helmet against him. I close my eyes and feel the wind and the closeness of Jason and nothing else.

I keep my eyes closed through three more turns until we stop. "Where?" I open my eyes to Main Street in front of the movie theater.

Jason tilts his neck around and grins at me. "What'd you think?"

"Oh my God, that was awesome."

He puts the kickstand down and helps me off the bike. I walk bowlegged for a moment, my knees wobbling so much I have to concentrate to stay upright. I put both hands behind my lower back and lean back.

"It's a different feeling," Jason admits.

"Yeah, I think I'm going to walk it off for a minute."

Jason opens his mouth to say something, but his phone goes off and he pulls it from his pocket.

"Sorry, it's my job. Gotta take this."

I nod at him and he presses something on the phone and walks away from me. I unclasp my helmet successfully after several tries and watch him. He purses his lips and says something and then puts the phone back in his pocket and walks back up to me.

"I gotta go in to work. Someone called out of their shift. Come by sometime. I'll get you a discount. Tommy Bahama's on St. Armand's."

I hand him back his helmet. "Okay, thanks."

I'm jittery like I had too much coffee as I walk up Main Street instead of back to my car.

Several streets later, I see the "now hiring" sign in the front window of the downtown Menchie's frozen yogurt place.

"Why not?" I say out loud and walk in, the bell above the door tinkling to announce my entrance.

CHAPTER TWELVE - TIP, DON'T BUY

I'm browsing the shirts section at our favorite Goodwill, the one on 41st, looking for something exotic and adventure-safari like. Nichole is browsing for khakis. If you're going to sneak into a party uninvited and not get thrown out immediately, you have to look the part. We're planning on crashing a themed party at the local four year liberal arts college - New College - in a few weeks. The theme is Jurassic Park. This is all my idea. Jason told me about the party after our motorcycle ride together. I was happy to accept his invite. His brother goes to the college, so technically we won't be crashing.

"I'm surprised you don't already own like four pairs. They'd go great with your Crocs." Nichole holds up a pair of the ugliest khakis I've ever seen and I wrinkle my nose at them.

"Seriously, though, they look about your size," Nichole says, holding them up to her own waist and frowning when the pant legs dangle three inches above her sandals. "Ugh, totally not going to fit. They're too short for me," she adds and hands them to me.

I hold them up against my waist. Perfect length, and they might fit over my large ass and thighs.

"You're so good at finding the right size. I think we should get vests and safari hats."

"We're in luck," she says.

Nichole points across the room to where we can make out the hat rack. It's festooned with hats of all colors, shapes, and sizes, but towards the top I see two safari hats almost like Indiana Jones' fedora except for the colors. One is a horrid khaki color and another is a darker forest green.

"I call the green one," I say quickly.

Nichole sticks her tongue out at me and goes over to snag the hats. I keep perusing the shirt racks, looking for something that will match khaki and looks like it belongs to someone on safari.

Nichole comes up to me. I stifle a giggle and grab the green hat from Nichole's hands. The thought of germs and other people's nasty heads comes briefly to mind before I set the hat down delicately over my own dark locks so as not to frizz my hair out of my ponytail too much.

"Perfect, except for…" Nichole reaches behind me and up to the shelf and grabs something, clipping it on the brim of the hat. I can't see it, but it feels like a paperweight pulling the hat down on my forehead. I walk carefully over to the nearest mirror so as not to unsettle the object. It's a hummingbird toy. I smile broadly at Nichole and look for something to decorate her hat with. I scan the tops of the shelves at the toys section. Goodwill has a ton of junk, but no more bird toys.

"Too bad. Nothing for you," I lament.

"Did you find any shirts?" Nichole asks.

"Uh, no. They're all nice, stylish tops. I could only find one safari looking shirt, but it had some holes in it."

"Show me, maybe I can make it work."

I go back to the racks and pull out the one shirt that would match the khaki pants and hold it up for Nichole. Several holes dot the fabric. Nichole places a finger in one and pulls. The hole grows larger.

"Hey, I thought you wanted to salvage the shirt, not make it unusable," I cry.

"It'll be just the thing when I'm done. Find something similar and then we'll look for white shirts to wear underneath. Something like a wife beater, okay?"

Nichole doesn't wait for me to answer. She places a finger on the tips of sleeves sticking out from the too many shirts stuffed on the rack and trails her hand along until she reaches the end of the aisle and moves toward the shoes section. This is going to be a full ensemble. Good thing I'm starting a job soon. This trip will cost me the rest of my birthday money and Christmas money from last year.

I finally find another shirt decent enough for our purposes and pick out two wife beaters. I meet Nichole up front and stand in line to pay for our purchases.

"The question now is should we clean them?" I ask.

"Naw, we're only wearing them for one night," she says.

I nod in agreement.

"So. Jason."

I'm amazed she's waited this long to bring up Jason. I can't keep the grin off my face.

"Riding his motorcycle was amazing."

"The perfect buildup to skydiving."

"What?! No way. I told you that was off the list." I squirm.

"Tell me more. What was it like?" she asks.

"Fast and windy."

"No, stupid, tell me about Jason," she says. She leans in closer. "Did you kiss?" she whispers.

I back up a step and look around, my cheeks reddening. "One, I would have told you and two, no."

It's our turn at the checkout counter and I hand over the rest of my money to pay for my share.

"Lame," Nichole says as we walk out of the store.

"Not. It just didn't happen."

"Did you want it to?"

I pause. "I'm not sure."

Nichole regards me thoughtfully and then shrugs. "You better tell me if something happens." She hooks her thumbs in the front belt loops of her shorts. "What now?"

"I dunno," I say.

"Whatevs, let's get some froyo."

"I hear there's one around here, where all the college kids go."

"I'm down."

"Speaking of froyo, I didn't tell you yet but I got a job working at the Menchie's downtown."

"Congrats, Vanessa! Your first job. My mom would be so proud."

"My mom would tell me all the ways this will help me get better and forget stuff and move on and yadda yadda yadda," I say.

Nichole laughs. "I'm glad my mom's not a health nut."

"And I'm glad my mom knows how to use the garbage."

"Burn. My mom isn't that much of a pack rat," Nichole says.

"Your mom could be on T.V. with the amount of crap she never gets rid of."

"Okay, enough."

We meander through the parking lot to the Honda and get in. I drive us down to the Menchie's next to the Starbucks on University Parkway. The parking lot is littered with vehicles. People walk to and from the Starbucks.

We walk into the froyo shop. Two people work the counter, a young blonde behind the cash register and an aproned guy near the toppings counter. They look too old to be in high school and too normal to go to the super liberal arts New College. They probably go to Manatee Community College.

We walk up to the self-serve station on the wall. I keep my grin in check as I pick up a stack of paper sample soufflé cups. I find a guilty pleasure as I finger the rim of the little cups, biting my lip as I read up and down the displays of the eight stations. There are two flavors per station with a swirl option in between.

"I'm going to try all sixteen," I say to Nichole.

She tilts her head to look at me and then nods. "Me too," she says.

I smile as I tilt the first froyo lever and a smooth spat of yogurt lines my cup, coming to a point an inch above the cup's sides. I lick off the top, savoring the simple pleasure of the smooth coldness.

I'm back at Dairy Queen the first time my dad took me, licking off their signature top swirl.

"Like Alfalfa's cowlick," Dad says with a grin.

"What?"

"Little Rascals, the movie. We'll watch it when we get home."

Dad is laughing and trying to grab my ice cream. I was a bit chubby, even back then as a 12-year-old before the fire, but he always insisted I get my own ice cream.

I clear my head. Focus. My stomach gurgles. I finish off the first cup and fill another. Peaches and Cream. Another. Tart Original. Very Berry. Chocolate Mousse. Tiramisu.

Nichole follows right behind me. Filling cups and sampling. We work our way around to the other side. I don't hazard a glance toward the front counter. We're probably being watched by the apron guy.

One of the empty, sodden soufflé cups is dripping onto my fingers so I dump it in the trash and clean my sticky fingers with a napkin. Nichole dumps her used cup and stands next to me.

"There's one more." She tantalizes this fact and gives her head a mild nod toward the last bank of froyo machines on the end closest to the toppings and checkout counter.

"And that'll be the last, you good?"

"Yes. Then we make a cool break for it after that one."

The male employee walks out of sight into the back area. The girl glances up at us now and then as she straightens the napkins and moves around the spoons in their jar.

I march over to the last machine. It's hardly even froyo, it's the one non-dairy choice, lime. We each take a pass at it and I slurp up my sample. It's surprisingly good, not too sweet, but still very flavorful.

"Hm, that ain't bad." I toss the last soufflé cup in the trash and walk toward the counter.

"Thanks," I say to the girl, dropping my very last dollar into her tip jar.

She's straightening the spoons in their jars, separating out the blue and pink ones into different glasses. She looks up when I speak and the words, "Are you ready?" die on her lips as she sees I have nothing left in my hands. I hold them up for emphasis. "All good."

The guy must still be in the back. Too bad, I'm sure he would have said something. The only other customers, a little girl and her mother, watch us as we walk out the door.

We burst into the fresh air and I take a deep breath of freedom.

"That was awesome," Nichole says. "Do you think we could get away with doing it again?" she asks.

"Absolutely."

I drop Nichole off at her house and park in my own driveway.

Bluster greets me at the door, hampering my progress inside and I scoot him along the floor until I can close the door behind me.

"That you, Vanessa?" Mom calls from the front.

"You're home?" I answer.

Mom appears from the kitchen. "Of course I'm home." Walter walks up beside her.

I lean down to pet Bluster, ignoring Mom and Walter, who stands awkwardly beside Mom.

"We're making dinner. It'll be ready in twenty minutes."

"I'm not hungry," I say as I straighten and stare at the pair of them. My stomach rumbles and words are pushed out by my disappointment and lingering hunger. "Your food tastes like shit, anyways."

"Vanessa!" Mom states, spitting out the 's' like bullets.

"You ruined everything." I point at Walter and stomp through the living room to my room, slamming the door behind me.

Two seconds later Mom throws open the door with a disappointed look on her face.

"Did you spend your money on junk food again?"

"No." I hold up my shopping bag full of clothes and let it drop to the ground with a thunk. "I'm just not hungry for Walter's gluten-free vegan diarrhea."

Bluster pads in the open door and I reach down to rub his ears.

"You will not hide behind the dog. You will apologize to Walter."

"Why?"

I look down at Bluster and pretend not to see when Mom puts her hands on her hips. I keep my eyes on the dog as Mom continues to berate me. I try to tune her out but the words cut through me. The phrases, "gained weight," and "no allowance to spend on junk" make me stand up. The sudden rush to my head makes me wobbly, but my words don't waver.

"Fine. I don't care."

"If you keep acting like a sullen teenager, I'll treat you like one. You're welcome to eat with us when dinner is ready. Walter is a nice person, if you get to know him."

Mom turns on her heels and walks out, shutting the door firmly behind her.

I grab Bluster and pull him onto the bed. He cocks his head at me and whines.

"Yeah, I know. She doesn't understand at all," I tell him.

CHAPTER THIRTEEN - PUPPIES

It's three weeks until Christmas.

I dislike the smell of the cinnamon brooms that wafts through the doorways of all the local grocery stores. I dislike the Christmas music that runs on repeat in every single store and café, the odd Jewish or Kwanza song thrust in the mix for diversity. I dislike the lines of people and the songs and the upbeat, fake-cheery moods.

Mom puts more and more fruit on the table. First there were apples and then bananas. Now oranges and grapefruits and pomegranates grace the table too. She also found my stash in the cupboard above the stove. Mom didn't tell me she found it but the day after our fight I went to get a frosted oatmeal cookie and the tin was gone. Even the Soy Delicious ice cream, which I only eat when I'm desperate, disappeared from the freezer.

The more Mom tries to control me, the worse I get. I'm in charge of my body one moment and then I'm eating my way through an entire sleeve of Ritz crackers the next. I'm energized and ready to tackle Nichole's friends head on until I get to school and see Becky's ice cold stare.

Dad's voice is fading more and more from my memory. Even Bluster has ceased to cheer me up. I'm in a funk. It doesn't help that Mom is always hanging out with Walter. He doesn't come over for dinner any more, she always goes to his place.

She's gone now and I'm sitting on the couch reading *The Island of the Blue Dolphins* and wishing I'm on my own island off the coast of California.

Nichole waltzes through the door without knocking.

"Hey, Couch Potato," Nichole flashes me a smile.

She's up to something. She never holds her hands in fists, as if she's hiding something small in her hands.

I roll my eyes and hop up from the couch. It's time for a diversion. I need to get out of this house. I need to get out of myself somehow.

"You ready?" Nichole eyes my naked feet.

"Let me just grab my shoes and jacket." I sprint to my room and fly around the corner, using the doorframe as an anchor. I yank on my socks, shoes, and jacket. I hear the front door slam. As usual, Nichole didn't wait.

I run to catch up as soon as I'm outside. I shiver in the cold air. It's only 60 degrees. I should've brought a hat to protect my ears, since my hair is still swept up and away in its low ponytail, but it's too late to turn back. Nichole catches sight of me and sprints ahead so I have to run again to catch up with her.

"What's this secret plan?" I ask.

"I think we should change up the decorations around here," Nichole says.

"Er, what?"

I look over at the house beside us. Christmas lights string the entire house, along each window frame, and up each tree trunk in the yard. A Santa display leans precariously on the roof and several blow-up reindeer are arranged casually on the grass.

Nichole doesn't respond. Walking over to the nearest reindeer, she peers down at its tangled cords and then picks it up gently and moves it over to another reindeer. She set it down so that its belly is up against the other reindeer.

"Um. You sure you should be doing that in our own neighborhood?" I glance right and left down the street.

"You scared?" she taunts.

"Absolutely not. I think you're the wuss. You talk a big game, but never have a boyfriend or go beyond third base. You're friends with Becky, but you won't even look at her brother. Where's your follow through?"

"I'm so tired of your attitude." Nichole pauses, an elf in her arms, and looks at me. "You really think that's true?" She shakes her head and stalks over to the next house. She moves the elves into compromising positions.

"I still love you, but it's true." I jog over to her.

"Oh, sure. It's fine for you to criticize me, but look at yourself. I try to help you and make your life better. I've helped you with the food challenge. I invite you to everything I do. I set you up with Jason. All you do is resist and be a bitch to my friends."

I race after Nichole, but she's going too fast for me to catch up. She makes it all the way to her house, slamming the front door dramatically behind her. I pause outside her house. I hope her mom isn't home. I hesitate and then pound a couple knuckles into the wood. A dog barks a deep baritone. Lewis must be home.

I usually let myself in, but I hesitate outside the door. I glance at the familiar brown edged tape over their broken doorbell and the cracked window next to the door that also sports tape on the inside to keep bugs out. Maybe I have been selfish and self-centered. Nichole has problems too and I never ask her about them.

I knock lightly on the door. Nichole's mom opens the door and she's momentarily surprised to see me.

"Hi, Sharon."

Nichole's mom opens the door wider to let me in. "Nichole's in her room," Sharon calls after me.

I know where Nichole is. She almost never leaves her room at her house, but not for the same reason I never leave my room. Her house is full of junk and never anywhere to sit. If chairs do exist, they're buried under boxes of her great-grandmother's clothes and old sets of dishware or piles ready to go to Goodwill but never actually make it there.

I wend my way around a large pile of towels that's stacked up to my waist, several pieces of low to the ground furniture that house a multitude of half-open boxes, and a fake Christmas tree lying in the middle of the hallway. Nichole's room is not much better. She grew into her adult body at the age of ten and has never gotten rid of any of her clothes since. Growing taller only made her shirts trendier now that they show just a sliver of belly. If only we were the same size, I could wear half the crap that's piled on the floor. At least she has a large room.

"Hey," I say to Nichole.

She's slumped out on the top of her bunk bed, glaring at me. I spend a minute inspecting some figurines on the dresser. The line of them continues onto the windowsill, getting dustier and dustier by the piece.

I look for an empty chair. Nine chairs are barely visible in the room and each has at least five things piled on it. I go to the one with the least amount of stuff on top, shove it all onto the floor and sit down. I bunch up my knees and set my elbows on them, hands cupping my face and peer up at Nichole with my best puppy dog eyes – fluttering my lashes and sniffing pitifully.

"Knock it off," she says with narrowed eyes.

I grin and stretch out of my posture, getting up and pacing around piles of her clothes.

"I know what will cheer you up. I planned it all myself just for you."

"Good," Nichole spits.

"It has soft and irresistibly cute puppies."

"You're not talking about that puppy place on 301, are you?" Nichole jumps up from her slouch and bangs her head on the ceiling. "Ouch" she mouths and rubs the tender spot.

"Yes. Puppy Palace. The one. The only. The place where you can bask in a sea of puppies."

"That's not planning, that's just a trip to a store," she argues, but her eyes sparkle and a hint of a smile teases across her lips.

"We've never been. I've been saving this for you."

"Fine. You can take me, but this better be about me."

"Yes," I say slowly.

"What aren't you telling me?" she asks.

"Nothing, really," I assure her.

"I don't quite believe you. And I don't think this is enough to show you care about me. I want you to invite that guy from the Hero's Bar and Grill."

"Uh, why?"

"He gave you his number, right?"

"Yeah."

"To show how much you love me; I want you to invite that guy. I know how nervous you get around good looking guys."

"Fine." I grab my phone and scroll through my contacts. I had put Dark-Eyes' number in my phone as soon as I got home that day. I never called or texted it before. I send him a quick invite and a reminder of who I am.

"Done."

"Great, and I'm not finished," Nichole says. She hops down from her bunk and shoves a few piles of clothes further up against the walls. She pulls a few items from the pile. "You have to wear this."

"Oh no, I am not wearing that."

She raises her eyebrows and I sigh.

"That would be utterly humiliating, but since I love you..." I trail off at the pointed look Nichole gives me.

"It was too big for me so it will probably fit you."

"Too big when? I don't remember this costume."

The ears are pointed. The tail is made of wire and is moldable into any position.

"Wearing this dog costume, you won't be so nervous about talking to what's his name."

Nichole bites her lip to contain her smile, but I laugh and she lets loose, too. I snatch the costume from her and hold it up to me.

"You think this is going to fit?"

"Eh… Maybe? Anyways, the tighter the better, right?"

I step into the one-piece suit and pull it up over my pants.

"Can you help me with the zipper?"

Nichole steps behind me and pinches the suit at the top. It stretches over my chest as she pulls the zipper up with little starts and stops. I hold in my breath and let it out slowly. The costume gives a little, but constricts my ribs enough so I can't breathe too deeply.

"Yep, I knew you wanted me in a corset. Nice disguise," I turn around to find Nichole staring at my phone.

"He said yes! He's meeting us in half an hour so we gotta move it. You look fine."

She waves a hand at me to dismiss my comment. I look at myself in her mirror, the portion that isn't covered in shirts on hangers that no longer fit in the closet. For a spotted dog, I look rather good. The costume is hugging my hips and butt and makes me look curvier rather than overweight. I wouldn't be caught dead in this at school, but I wish I had clothes that accentuated my good parts and hid some of my flaws like this outfit.

"My butt doesn't look enormous in this."

"Nope, you look good."

Nichole laughs and we leave her room. Cigarette smoke wafts into my nostrils and I sneeze. I usher Nichole through her house as fast as I can. Neither Sharon nor Lewis catch sight of us and we're on our way.

We're spotted by several neighbors as we walk to my house to get my car. Some smile and wave. I blush and pull my shoulders up to my ears, trying to look like someone else.

I grab the tail and curl it up near my side so that it doesn't poke me in the back as I'm driving. We speed out of the neighborhood, shifting up through the gears. My palm on the gearshift grows increasingly damp. I wipe it on my white-spotted thigh.

"Don't be nervous. He was into you."

"Yeah, like three months ago. He probably forgot who I am entirely and thinks I'm actually you. He's going to be disappointed when he realizes his memory has let him down and I'm really the mousy, thick one next to the gorgeous brunette," I glower.

"Aw, c'mon. You're not that mousy."

I roll my eyes and Nichole laughs.

"And I'm not that gorgeous. Plus, I'm a blonde now."

I shake my head. Blonde as in highlights that cover half of her brunette locks.

I pat my car's dashboard as I climb out. Nichole just rolls her eyes and slams her door louder than necessary. She spots the guy, zeroing in on him like a trained flirt and waves frantically at him.

He doesn't even notice her, he's too busy eyeing me up and down.

"Why, hello there. I didn't realize this was a costume party," he says as he saunters up to us. He tilts his head up to acknowledge the car. "Nice Honda."

He likes my car? Most people are neutral on the silver run-of-the-mill Honda, except for a guy at school who once called it a shitbox.

I'm pleasantly surprised and extend my hand, but pull it back when I see the glisten of perspiration on my palm.

"You remember Nichole?" I say.

"Yes, of course. Nice to meet you again, Nichole."

"What was your name?" she asks.

"Bruce."

"So," I say.

"So," Nichole says.

"Yes?" Bruce asks.

Nichole snickers and I look down at my feet.

"Aren't you going to ask why Vanessa's wearing a costume?"

I kick at her shin.

"Why are you wearing a costume?" He turns to me to ask.

"It's a best friend thing," I say. "Let's go see some puppies."

He shrugs and smiles at us. We walk into Puppy Palace and through the divide from the pet store to the puppy palace area and the smell of wet dog, urine, and dog shampoo greets us. Nichole clasps her hands together in delight.

"No wonder you saved this one!" she squeaks with glee and rushes over to the nearest pen.

Leaning down, she stares at the five dogs in the pen. They look like Golden Retriever puppies with a perm.

"Goldendoodles, how funny," Nichole says.

We spend almost an hour wandering from enclosure to enclosure and petting all the puppies, letting them lick and chew on our fingers. Bruce has a great smile and I can't help but look at him every time we go to a new puppy pen. His face lights up at the puppies.

One of the attendants walks up to us. He eyes my costume. I stare back at him.

"Can I help you? Want to take one of them into a personal puppy pen?" He points to one of the cubbies against the far wall, where the enclosure sides are only a couple feet high. Each bench inside is occupied by one or two people, each complete with a roly-poly puppy.

"Yes, absolutely yes. Why do you even bother asking?" Nichole answers for us.

"That one," Bruce says and points to the German shepherd pup next to us.

The attendant, his nametag reads Personal Puppy Assistant Jon, reaches over and deftly picks up the dog and leads us into a personal puppy pen.

"Don't let him escape," Jon warns us, setting the puppy down and carefully letting himself out, latching the door behind him.

The puppy scampers between Nichole, Bruce, and I as we coo and pet it. This is the ultimate therapy.

After ten minutes of personal puppy play time, I think I'm ready for more embarrassment.

"I'm going in?" I say, turning to Nichole.

"In where? What are you talking about, Nessa?"

I turn to Bruce, "Have you had your fill?"

He shrugs and smiles at me. I guess that's a yes.

We get out of the pen and hand the puppy back to our attendant, who puts him back in his enclosure. The place is busy enough that most of the attendants are helping other potential customers.

This is my chance. I lead Nichole and Bruce over to a cage in the corner. I lean over and count the puppies. This is the biggest area and the least crowded with other people. Seven puppies scamper about, on, and over each other, bumping up against the two-and-half foot-tall wooden fencing material that forms a circle. I step over the side, glancing at the nearest attendant. She's busy holding onto a feisty pug that's desperately trying to escape her clutches. Good. I put my other foot over the side and two puppies jump on my feet. One tries to eat my shoelace. I sit down carefully so as not to squash any puppies and lean back in a yoga-esque pose, glad for the tight material keeping my stomach as flat is it ever is. I'm invaded by puppies. One hops onto my face and chews on my hair.

"This is the life," I say carefully around puppy butt to Nichole and Bruce. "You coming in?" I ask.

"I don't think so. Wouldn't want to get peed on."

Something warm trickles down my stomach. I'll definitely need to wash this costume before giving it back.

I bask in the sea of puppies, closing my eyes, and slowly fanning my arms like I'm making angel prints on the floor. My fingers swipe over a puppy tail and I smile languidly. This is the life.

"Hey! You can't be in the puppy pen. You need to get out of there!"

The voice brings me out of my reverie and I open my eyes. Puppies cry and bark around me at the harsh tones in Personal Puppy Assistant Jon's voice. He's standing over me, towering like a telephone pole.

"You're cute when you're angry," I say to him. The filter is gone and I can say whatever I want.

His jaw slackens, revealing teeth in desperate need of braces. I push myself into a sitting position, upsetting the pup attempting to lick my face. I pick up the nearest puppy and snuggle my face into its warm side.

Jon points a finger and repeats himself lamely, "you can't be in the puppy pen."

"You're making a scene, Jon," I tell him.

He sputters and blinks at me, his face reddening. I don't care. I'm in puppy heaven. My mood drifts out of the door ahead of us, light and floating on clouds.

Nichole giggles and reaches a hand over to me. I peer down at it. It's joined by a second hand, a large hand with long fingers. I look up into the face of Bruce and grab hold of both their hands. They pull me over the fence and we stumble out of Puppy Palace.

"Hey! Hey!" Jon yells at us, finding his voice at last.

We don't stop. As soon as we're outside, I take a large gulp of fresh air.

"You alright?" Nichole asks me, still holding my hand.

Bruce awkwardly lets go of my hand and stares at the ground.

"Thank you," I whisper to both of them. "I feel wonderful. Now, who wants coffee?"

"I have to get going, but it was lovely seeing you ladies again," Bruce says.

"Oh, okay," I say, standing on one foot and then the other.

"Text me." He waves to us and walks over to his car to get in. We watch him drive off.

"I think he likes you," Nichole teases.

"Maybe. Can I take off this costume now?"

"I guess."

"You still mad at me?"

"Nope. All better," she says.

"Good."

CHAPTER FOURTEEN - NEW JOB

I've invited Nichole to my new job at Menchie's downtown. She squealed in excitement when I told her about the job. It's only my third shift, but I can't wait to see Nichole. She, of all people, knows how much I need the money. I've only attempted the food challenge once, and I'll need to save up for future attempts.

Nichole throws open the front door and steps inside. She's wearing her usual miniskirt and strappy sandals. The three customers who are still in the shop turn to look at her.

"Holla if you like froyo!" Nichole greets the room.

I smile and shake my head.

"Nice rags." She points at my uniform.

I'm wearing a pale pink t-shirt with the shop's logo on it and a pair of baggy slacks I have never gotten rid of.

Nichole peers around at the shop. It's small and narrow, with a short row of overly large white bucket seats that are off-kilter like they belong in a modern art museum. The tables are bulky bright plastic pastel colors with swirls on top that actually move in circles like a lazy Suzan. The back wall holds a bank of self-serve froyo dispensers with a row of ten spouts. A cubby on one side of the spouts has all the accoutrements for samples and the overly large bowls for when a customer has made up their mind and they're ready for a pound of yogurt. This downtown Sarasota shop isn't as big as the one on University, but it could easily fit 20 to 30 people inside.

"God. Doesn't everyone know how these things work by now?" Nichole points to the sign above the froyo counters that explain how the self-serve works.

"Not everyone knows. This one guy came in on my first day and he was very excited when he saw the bowls. He tried a few flavors, I asked if he needed any help. He said no. Then he filled that bowl up like it was an all you can eat buffet where you can only use one plate and go through the line once. So he fills up a bowl over the top. If he didn't start digging in, it would have dripped onto the floor. He comes up to the register where I'm waiting and plops it down on the scale. It was nearly thirty ounces! I told him the total."

"How much?" Nichole interrupts.

"I was getting to that part! It was…" I playfully tap a finger to my chin and look up and to the right, where the signboard proclaims that each ounce costs $0.48.

Nichole pushes on my shoulder "Go on," she says.

"It was $15 even. Like a sign. Oh my God, his face when I told him the cost was priceless. I was worried he'd leave the whole bowl, but after muttering to himself for a moment he paid and even left a tip! He ate the whole thing, too."

Nichole grabs a bowl and fills it halfway with an assortment of flavors and too many toppings, waffle cone pieces, a maraschino cherry, chocolate sauce, raspberry sauce, Skittles, gummy worms, and crushed Heath Bar. She puts it on the scale and I wave her away with a quick glance towards the back room to make sure my manager isn't watching.

"On the house," I whisper conspiratorially. I grin at her.

"So how's it feel to be a regular working Joe?" Nichole pipes up in between mouthfuls of froyo.

"Eh, it's okay. I can't believe how busy it gets here, and it's the middle of winter. Why would anyone want something cold when it's cold outside?"

"Frozen yogurt's always good, besides, this is Florida, and it's never that cold." Nichole says.

The tinkle of the doorbell indicates more customers.

"One moment." I hold up a finger and excuse myself.

Since the store is so small and I've already gone through my two days of training, I'm all by myself unless we get busy. Granted, my manager, the great and powerful college student Heather, is in the back working on employee schedules for the next two weeks. I have to take care of all the customers, a family with three small kids and two giggling pre-teens, by myself. Nichole occupies herself with her phone as I wait for the customers to finish getting their froyo. I tap my fingers on the counter and watch the looped nature video on the store's T.V., checking the customers out of the corner of my eye every now and then. It takes the pre-teens forever to figure out what they want. They both get vanilla and one of them slathers it with chocolate and caramel sauce while the other one puts every single type of fruit on hers. They pay and sit down in the corner, giggling and eating. Eventually, after two dropped sample cups and a mini tantrum from the youngest kid, the family steps up to pay for their frozen yogurt. They sit in the other corner. I take a rag and clean off the messy yogurt drips from the machines and pick up the dropped sample cups. My work, for now, is done.

Nichole scoops large spoonful's of yogurt into her mouth, pieces of candy piled on top. I envy her. She can eat candy and junk food all she wants and nobody will judge her for it because she's thin.

I wait for the family and the teenagers to finish their treats and leave the store before walking around the cash register and up to Nichole.

"Ugh, this is so not as exciting as I thought it would be," I say.

"It's about to get more exciting." Nichole tips her head toward the door as its familiar tinkle brings me back to reality.

"Be right back," I tell Nichole.

I flit over to the entering customers, but stop in my tracks when I recognize Anja and Becky.

"What the hell," I mutter.

Becky eyes my flowery pink t-shirt with disdain and walks past me to say hi to Nichole. Anja stares at the T.V. on the wall as it shows a silent film about deep sea fish. The other customers walk out, tossing their empty bowls into the trash as they pass by.

I watch Becky joke with Nichole. It was one thing to bring Becky and Anja to the movies. To invite her friends to the beach and hang out during lunch at school. I can't believe she'd invite them here without asking me, public place notwithstanding.

I walk up to Nichole and Becky. "Get out," I say coolly to

Becky.

She stops talking to Nichole and turns to me, standing tall and towering over me, her eyes as dark and unyielding as stone.

"Bitch you are not the center of the universe and this is a public place," Becky says, tilting her head and raising her eyebrows.

Anja looks over from where she stands near the front of the store. Nichole puts up her hands in a stop motion between Becky and I.

The doorbell tinkles and we all look over, the tension and apprehension in the room so thick one could choke on it. And I do at the sight of Ben. A large, surprised cough.

He looks from Becky to me and takes a tentative step back toward the door.

"Becky," Nichole says, imploring her friend to do something about her brother.

Nichole's hands falter and I spit a racial slur in Becky's direction, my voice so low it's almost a growl.

Becky flies past Nichole, shoving her away from us and slaps me hard across the face. I didn't even have time to put up fists or protect myself. My head flies up and to the side from the impact. All that jujitsu training and she slaps me. I'm so surprised for a moment that I stare at her smug, self-satisfied face as I rub my cheek. She thinks I won't fight back, but I have other weapons at my disposal.

I grab a handful of Oreo crumbles in my left hand and those squishy popping Boba balls in my right hand and throw them at Becky. She's too surprised to duck and takes a face full of toppings square in the face.

Anja laughs. Ben freezes mid-step. Nichole is looking past me, her mouth open in surprise.

Eighty percent of the time that I'm working, I'm alone up front handling all the customers, but Heather chose this moment to enter the front area and she saw what I just did.

Becky looks back and sees the manager and tosses me a smug glance before walking out of the shop.

Minimum wage managers usually don't give a smack what you do as long as you don't involve them in any minor problems. In the last three shifts that I've been a regular working schmo, this is what I've learned:

1) Don't bother the manager unless it's an emergency that requires the manager key.

2) Don't let anybody see that you're giving away freebies.

3) Don't count on tips.

I'm going to have to add a fourth suggestion.

4) Don't throw food at the customers.

I can't imagine this ending well for me. I smile tentatively at my manager and she shakes her head at me.

"I'll, uh, catch up with you later." Nichole walks out the door. Anja has already disappeared and I'm all alone.

Dark crumbs litter the floor, interspersed with the small liquid filled Bobas that have rolled to all corners of the store. My manager hands me a mop.

"Clean this up and then you're fired."

"But." I don't bother finishing my sentence. I have no excuses. I hang my head and grab the mop, wondering how far three shifts' worth of money will get me.

CHAPTER FIFTEEN - NOW WHAT

Hours after my third and final shift at Menchie's, I jump in the shower, scrubbing off my long shift and anger.

I get out of the shower and towel dry. I stare at the red mark on my cheek and frown. Before I've even put on my clothes, I root around in my makeup drawer and find my three-year-old foundation, hardly used, that Mom gave me on my fourteenth birthday. It covers up the redness on my face and evens out my skin tone.

I hang up the towel to dry and grab my phone from my dresser. I dial Nichole.

"Hello?"

"It's me," I say

"I know."

"I'm sorry. Can we talk?"

Silence.

"Nichole, you there?" My voice squeaks and I swallow.

"That was some stunt you pulled today."

I sigh in relief that she didn't hang up, that she's still there. "I know. Meet at the Tab in ten?"

"Alright, see you there," she answers.

Twenty minutes later, Nichole walks across the Tabernacle church lawn. I wave down at her from where I'm standing on top of the Nativity set.

"Sweet! We haven't been this year." Nichole runs the rest of the way to the set and climbs over the padlocked door and up the rickety wooden stairs to where I'm standing. We're in the angels' and choir section that overlooks the front of the church, almost a story above the ground. I take Nichole's hands and lead her to the middle of the set, front and center to an absent audience. The bleachers down below stare at us blankly, empty.

"This Ben thing has me all messed up," I say.

Nichole looks at me sharply. I shrug.

"I don't know, it's just, hard to see him at all. It would be easier if I could forget he existed, you know? But having to see him all the time just brings back everything and I hate that he exists and I hate that he's here and Dad isn't. But who am I to hate someone that Dad saved?"

"So you have been thinking about it."

"Well, duh. And another thing, why do you always avoid looking at him, it's weird."

Nichole stares off into the distance. A car passes by on the road in front of the Tab.

I wait for her to answer and finally she says, "Worry about your own problems, Ness."

"That's rude. Besides, you're always worrying about me. What's really going on?"

"I'll talk to Becky about making sure Ben doesn't pop up again. I'm tired of him tagging along, too."

We sit in silence for a moment more. Another car passes.

"What about at the restaurant, doesn't he work at the Hero's Bar and Grill?" she ask.

"What, does he work all over town?" I say.

"It's his family's restaurant, but we don't have to go back there," Nichole says.

"Uh, yes we do. The food challenge," I remind her.

"You don't have to do it. You rode the motorcycle. You've been doing more things than you've ever done in your life. You don't have to do the things on the list."

"What?!" I'm shocked that she's pushing aside Dad's bucket list when she was the one who pressured me to do the things on it.

"Come on, it's not that important. You tried."

"Nichole, what are you saying? Of course it's important. Remember how you told me I should do his bucket list items for him? How is that not important?" My voice rises and I stand, staring down at her.

"Okay, okay. Sorry. I'll go with you to the restaurant."

"Thank you," I snap. "It's just that, if I finish all of Dad's bucket list items I get this feeling that I'll finally get closure or something. I can truly forget about Ben."

It takes her a moment to process what I just said. Then she bursts out with, "God, Nessa, you can't let Ben get to you. It wasn't even his fault."

I shouldn't be shocked at her words, but I have a hard time keeping my expression neutral.

"But it was his fault. I can't forgive him for that."

"You've got to let it go," Nichole insists.

"Ugh."

"Don't you dare roll your eyes. And what you did today to Becky was not cool." Nichole says.

I pace back and forth in our little viewing area. "I don't like Becky."

"Big deal, she's my friend. You can either live with it or not hang out with us."

"How about she doesn't hang out with us?" I insist.

"Cool it, Ness. Why are you being such a smack today?"

"Am not, you're the one who can't say no to anyone and you continually get me into trouble. I was fine in my room, reading my books and watching movies with you."

"Is that what you really want?" Nichole's voice carries finality to it and I hesitate with my next words.

"No," I say, defeated.

Before Nichole can respond, bright lights flash in our faces and I throw my arms up to block the lights.

"Shit," Nichole mutters.

Tab security has arrived.

We scramble down the nativity set and take off.

The whine of a golf cart follows us and the headlights beam our shadows onto the grass. Pumping our legs, our feet slam against the wet grass. I don't have time to scratch at my legs where dew and small flecks of dirt paint my shins. We run for the end of the church grounds, not far away. I risk a glance behind us. The old night-time security guard is speeding toward us in a golf cart outfitted with bright searchlights. He careens up the path, cuts onto the grass and races after us going at least 10 mph.

We're in a dead run now, sprinting across the ditch and onto the road. We race across the asphalt and over the other ditch, into someone's back yard.

"Keep going!" I shout at Nichole next to me.

She's not next to me for long. Her longer legs carry her farther with every stride and I'm getting a stitch in my side that rubs against my insides with every breath that wheezes from my mouth. I was never made for running, but the extra thirty pounds that plague my middle and thighs makes it harder for me to move. I lack grace, but I can't stop, even when my lungs begs me to take a deep breath.

We forge ahead through some thin bushes as if one old guy on a golf cart is going to catch up

Our pace slows as we creep through someone's backyard to get to the neighborhood road beyond. I laugh nervously and the stitch in my side explodes. I limp-run, trying not to move the muscles on my left side as we jog through the back streets of the neighborhood adjacent to ours.

"Come on!" Nichole grabs my arm and drags me along.

We find ourselves walking on a path between thickening trees. Water trickles cheerfully in a stream beside us. This is new.

"Have we ever been here?" I ask Nichole.

We have to walk carefully, using our phone flashlights to light our way so we can see where to place our feet. The path is narrow and looks like it ends up ahead.

"How disappointing," Nichole says, searching the brush with her phone light, as if another path will appear.

"Hey, look!" I point to my right.

On the ground small sparkles of crushed grass twinkle in the moonlight. Nichole skips over to my side and we shine our lights into the bushes.

"This is it." Nichole takes a step into the tangled growth and walks into a thin branch.

"Ouch!" she breathes.

"Maybe we should come back when it's daytime," I offer.

"Don't wimp out on me now, Vanessa Smith."

Nichole is halfway in and halfway out of the supposed path's entrance.

"Fine." I sigh and point my flashlight in front of Nichole so she has more light and take a step toward her.

"You go first." She smiles at me sweetly and steps aside so I have room to move past.

"Who's the coward now?" I make a grand gesture of sweeping her aside and step forward into the gloomy dark, my phone light barely penetrating the growing ground fog.

I'm not afraid of the dark. I'm not afraid of the dark.

"You're not still afraid of the dark, are you?"

"No…"

But I've always been afraid of the dark, so I can deal with this fear much easier than any of my newer fears.

A crunch of leaves in front of us makes both of us freeze. A lump rises in my throat and I try to swallow it down. It makes my nose burn and my eyes tear. Stones of fear weight down my stomach, rooting me to the spot. Only my arm moves, the flashlight beam wavering in front of us as I point it this way and that. Its light is so weak and seems to dim before my eyes.

We listen and wait. The noise might startle whatever it is that's most definitely in front of us.

I shine my light ahead, waving it back and forth, its shaky beam illuminating nothing.

"Oh, for heaven's sake!" Nichole steps around me.

She pushes some branches aside and walks out of sight between them, her light getting fainter. I'm still frozen in place. Oh my God. Oh my God. I pull up one foot from the ground and set it down again. I can't decide if I should go backwards or forwards. Fear rises like bile and I taste acid in the back of my mouth. I need to move. I need to leave. But Nichole. I can't leave her. I can't let something bad happen.

I unfreeze and crash through the trees, swiping leaves and sticks out of my way, frantic to see what happened. I trip over something and fall to my knees, catching my palms against the ground, coating them in dirt. I look up with a sob in my throat, the terror rising like a scream and see Nichole. I swallow down the scream. She's smiling and making cooing sounds.

I crawl forward, my hands shaking, too tense to stand up. I wipe a hand across my sweat streaked face, smearing dirt along my forehead.

"You're okay," I say.

"Why are you on the ground?" she asks.

I get up and see a small black cat twining itself around Nichole's legs.

"What?"

In the dim light shadows move around. I hold up my own flashlight and hear hisses and meows.

"It's some sort of cat shrine," Nichole says.

Cats. A more curious tabby walks up to me, twitching tail in the air. I let it rub against my leg, easing my tension. I sigh out in relief and swing my flashlight around to see what else is here besides cats.

"Wow," I say.

"Yeah, there's gotta be more than ten cats and they all have food bowls and water and there are even pet beds over there." Nichole points and I shine the flashlight to look. I walk up to a bench swing that hangs crooked a foot off the ground. Next to it are several cages lined up with cat beds inside like a pet store. At night. In the dark. Several cats saunter over to me and rub against my legs. One of them mews at me and I melt, all fear of the dark and thoughts of heroics forgotten. I reach down beside Nichole and we scratch and rub the cats' backs, swatting at their tails as they pass us by, and baby talk to them.

This is a pleasant surprise indeed. Who knew this was here, in our neighborhood?

My hands still shake as I pet the first tabby and he growls when I stroke him too hard.

"Come on. Let's go back to my house. I have something to show you," Nichole says.

I follow her around the neighborhood and to her house. It's not far from the cat haven to her street and in no time Nichole is opening her front door.

"I thought I told you to be home before dark?" Sharon says as she emerges from her room. "Dinner was ready an hour ago."

"Sorry," Nichole says.

"What happened to your face?" Sharon says, staring at me.

"Huh? Oh, my hands were dirty," I say sheepishly.

I squeeze around two love seats stacked on top of each other in the kitchen hallway. The living room has no room left for furniture. I enter the kitchen to wash my hands in the sink. Dishes are piled up on both sides of the faucet.

Nichole yanks open the fridge and pulls out a plate of cookies. She takes a bite out of one and sets the plate on top of the oven as she pulls the milk out of the fridge. I grab two cups from the cupboard and Nichole pours us each a full glass of milk. I close my eyes and enjoy the thick creamy fullness of it. Mom hasn't stocked milk since Dad died and I started gaining too much weight.

"Next time I tell you to be home at a certain time I expect you to be here," Sharon says flatly.

"I said I was sorry," Nichole's voice takes on a sullen tone and she shoves the milk back into the fridge and slams the door.

"I heard that you got a job, Vanessa." Sharon stares at Nichole while she says this and I'm hesitant to respond.

"Um, yeah. The froyo place downtown." I cringe as I say this, but neither Nichole nor her mom notice as they're too busy with their staring contest.

"I think all teenagers should get a job. Maybe think about college. Put a few plans in place."

Nichole glares at her mom. I shuffle from foot to foot and tug on Nichole's arm.

"Uh, sure, Ms. Adams. I've been looking at some schools." I lead Nichole to her room before Sharon can say anything else.

"Have you thought about college?" I ask.

"Yeah, I've thought about it. Are you ready for finals?" Nichole asks me.

Nichole fishes around in one of her plastic temporary bins and pulls up a package of cookies.

"Here, have a cookie."

I grab the bag and pull out half a cookie, cupping my hand under my mouth to catch the crumbs as I take a bite.

"Finals?" Nichole asks again.

"I've been so preoccupied," I start to say.

What with the new job, preparing for the Hero's Challenge, and spending all of my free time with Nichole, my studying has dropped off. I'm not ready at all for finals.

"Yeah, I know. You've finally been spending time outside! But yeah, don't fail."

She smirks at me.

"So, anyways, what happens if you can't finish the food challenge?" Nichole asks.

I frown. "I can do it. I will do it. Maybe not last time or next time, but I have to."

"I'm just saying, you can't do everything and maybe you should-"

"No! This is what I want and I'll do it. I thought you supported me?" I interrupt her with a squeak.

"I do support you. I just wanted to make sure you understood what you were getting into."

I huff and stand up.

"What were you going to show me?"

"It's not about your dad's bucket list, but I think it's just as important."

"And?"

"Don't be mad at me," she prefaces.

I sit down and she grabs something and holds it out to me. It's a lighter.

"Nichole!" I fall off the chair in my haste to get away. The acrid smell of smoke chars the insides of my nostrils and I start to hyperventilate, trying to get clean, memory-free air in my lungs.

Nichole clamps a hand over the lighter.

"Overcome your fears. I think this could be good for you. It's empty. See?"

She flicks her thumb on the switch and the click grates through my ears with dread, but nothing happens. No flame.

How did I end up on the floor? I'm crouching into myself and holding my knees, rocking back and forth.

I let out the breath I was holding. Nichole's flowery scent invades my nostrils. She holds up the cookie bag and I get to my feet and inhale the sweetness, calming down my nerves.

"Just think about it." Nichole holds the lighter out again and I back up a step, nearly tripping over a chair leg.

She frowns, then opens up the cookie bag and drops in the lighter.

"Hey!"

"What? Sweets calm you down. Here, can you hold the bag?"

She dangles the bag from two fingers and I grab it at the very top so tightly my hands turn splotchy red and pale.

"You can do this. I think it's more important than the food challenge."

"Okay, I'll try."

"In with the new, out with the old," Nichole says.

"I don't think that expression refers to phobias."

"You don't have any phobias."

"Yes, yes I do." My voice rises, "I have phobias."

"No, you have PTSD."

"Right."

"You can do it; I know you can."

"Wow, your motivational speeches are just as bad as Mom's," I say with a frown.

"Don't push this aside, Ness."

Nichole grabs the cookie bag and shoves it at my chest. I squeak out and push it away from me. Nichole opens the top wide and holds it under my nose. My wild breathing brings in the thin scent of stale cookies, sugared air from the crumbs.

"See, not so bad. You love cookies."

"I prefer donuts," I mutter.

Nichole laughs and I chuckle.

"Promise me to try, okay?"

I nod. Not only will I take the damn cookie bag full of crumbs and the lighter, but I'm going to take another look at Dad's bucket list. I'm going to surprise Nichole. Yeah, I can do this.

CHAPTER SIXTEEN - READY FOR ANYTHING

The day after Nichole forced her lighter on me, I lie in bed for at least ten minutes more than usual. I don't want to open my eyes. I'm so tired from sleeping poorly last night. I couldn't stop thinking about Dad's list and that stupid lighter. It's dark outside still and my sheets are tangled around my legs, as if my bed doesn't want to let me go.

This is one of the last days before Christmas break. Senior year and I should be excited. I wiggle farther under the comforter when I hear a honk outside. I wipe the crust from my eyes and drag my blankets down as a rush of goosebumps erupt over my skin from the cold. I jump out of bed and rush over to my dresser to get some socks.

I get dressed in tall boots that will hide my fuzzy socks and my thicker ankles. Nichole need never know what's on underneath the boots. I quickly clasp my bra and pull on my favorite loose shirt from the floor. I hear another honk from outside.

I forego a belt and, grabbing my backpack, rush out of my room and into the bathroom to brush my teeth and pee. The scale is back in the middle of the bathroom floor and I shove it all the way behind the toilet, turning it sideways to fit.

I grab a Pop Tart from my secret stash and let out a thin, high pitched squeak when my hand touches the metal of the lighter and I see what is. I hold the Pop Tart box and shove at the lighter with it like I'm removing a bug with a cup. I shove the drawer closed and take a deep breath before leaving my room.

I lock the front door behind me and peer around the driveway. Where's Nichole?

Wait, where's my car? I walk to the middle of the driveway. What happened to my car?

Tires burn on pavement and I see my car. My car! It's going way too fast down the street. Is it really going to? Yes, it careens into the corner and turns into my drive. I leap to the side as it stalls and dies in front of me. Nichole hops out of the driver's side.

"What the hell were you doing driving my car like that? Where the effing smack did you get my keys?" I demand.

"Calm down. Geez. You left them on the kitchen counter and when you didn't bother coming out here in a timely manner I decided to teach you a lesson."

"Give me the damn keys."

"Fine. Here."

Nichole holds out the keys and I yank them from her hand so fast they scrape down her palm and she pulls her hand back to her side.

"Ow, Vanessa."

"Don't you dare drive my car. You don't know how to drive a stick."

"Uh, I did just fine. Lose the attitude, Nessa. We should get going if we want to make the tardy bell."

On the entire way to school I'm brake happy and take pleasure in the way she jerks forward and back every time I accelerate, pop the clutch, and then hit the brake. The seat belt tightens around my stomach, pushing fat over and under it, but I don't care.

"I get it, okay. I won't take your car, but you'll have to speed it up if we're going to make it," she reminds me.

"Shut up," I say under my breath, going faster and faster.

"Whoa, Grandma, slow down."

I grip the steering wheel harder.

"Go faster, go slower, make up your mind," I say through gritted teeth.

Nichole taps on her thighs and the sound makes me look over.

"Watch out!" Nichole screeches.

My head swivels fast back to the road and I swerve to avoid a squirrel dashing across the lane. My foot jingles nervously on the clutch pedal and I grind back into third. Nichole looks over at me, but doesn't say anything. I grip the steering wheel hard and keep driving, pretending I'm not as shaken up as I feel.

We're only several minutes late, but still have to go through the whole process of checking in at the front desk and being judged by the tardy lady. This is why I don't like breaking rules.

"I'll see you at lunch. Bye." Nichole waves to me.

"Later."

I wave goodbye and head off to AP calculus. Everyone stares when I open the door and I scuttle toward Mr. Brown's front desk to drop my tardy note on it and then slink to my assigned seat with my head down.

The lesson for the day is on parabolas. I flip to the appropriate section in my book and set my elbows on my desk. I disappear into thoughts, every now and then nodding toward the front and glancing at the new equations and numbers Mr. Brown draws on the whiteboard.

The skydiving place I found last night on the internet requires parental consent if you're under 18. Thank God their maximum weight requirement is 220. I'm still far below that, but I haven't weighed myself lately. I already printed out the forms and forged Mom's signature.

I researched gun ranges as well. I chose the range that was closest to my house, plus it has a cool name. Take Aim Gun Range is an indoor, fully air-conditioned facility.

Dad's bucket list only contains five items – skydive, shoot a gun, win a food challenge, ride a motorcycle, and the pay it forward crap. I don't remember why I didn't want to do his list before. The food challenge is hard, but riding the motorcycle was easy. Skydiving is spendy but doable and Sarasota has so many gun ranges I could close my eyes and point to a map and find one.

My other classes are absurdly boring and I barely pay attention. I'm so tired from researching late last night and constantly thinking about that stupid lighter stuffed in the cookie bag that when my eyelids start to close I don't fight it. I prop my head on my elbows and arrange my hair over my face and-

"Vanessa!"

I hop in my seat and my elbows bump into the desk hard. The

Spanish teacher, Sra. Ciancarelli, stands in front of my desk. The classroom is empty.

"Vanessa, I know the last year has been tough and that you must have a lot going on, but you have so much potential. I'd hate to see you waste it."

"English?" I scoff at her.

"This is important," she says in her enunciated English.

"Yeah, like I haven't heard that before." I get up and she steps back out of the way as I brush by her. I walk out the door. Classes are the least of my worries. This weekend I'm going to conquer the food challenge. Hero's is going down.

The bell rings. Crap. I've only got a few minutes before the tardy bell. If I'm late for two classes in a day, the office will send Mom an automatic voice message. Unacceptable.

I hightail it down the hall, keeping my head down so nobody will talk to me. I make it just in time for the next class and the day goes by in an agonizingly slow blur. It's difficult for me to pay attention to anything any of the teachers or my classmates say. I'm concentrating on the challenge, thinking about fries and burger patties and trying to stay awake.

I spot Nichole in the lunch line and jog to her side. I didn't even bother taking my mom's brown bagged-lunch off the counter this morning.

"No lunch?" she says, noting my empty hands.

"I'm tired of that healthy crap."

Nichole and I both get the scuzzy looking macaroni and over-boiled broccoli. I add a petite pint of milk to my tray and Nichole grabs a chocolate milk.

"You really shouldn't be drinking extra calories," Nichole says.

I frown and automatically reach to set the milk back into the cooler, but pull it back at the last second and set it down on my tray again.

"Sorry, I didn't mean that," Nichole says.

"Doesn't matter. I really shouldn't be drinking milk, but…" my voice trails off. I don't even have an explanation.

"Sometimes you just need a pick me up."

"Exactly," I say. "At least I went for the real milk."

"Chocolate milk is real milk," she protests.

"Says the girl who thinks Yoo-Hoo is chocolate milk," I say.

"Why is that even a question?"

"Says the girl who thinks Spam is real food," I say.

"Oh, stop it. I've seen some of the things you eat. Kale. Rice pasta. Broccoli chips. I mean, what the hell? How do you even make broccoli chips? That's disgusting."

"That's why I like eating at your house."

Nichole laughs and pays for her meal. I scrounge around in my pockets for the proper amount of change. I'm already running out of my final and only paycheck money. I've only set aside enough for one Hero's Challenge attempt and after that… I don't know what I'll do to pay for it.

The macaroni looks like globular slop, but it's creamy and cheesy even though the cheese sauce tastes watery and bland. It's still better than my mom's gluten free pasta with organic vegan cheese. I moan in satisfaction and Nichole rolls her eyes at me.

"You know what it's like at my house," I say.

"You don't have to remind me. Broccoli chips," she emphasizes.

"Yeah, I don't like those either."

I smile at my pile of regular broccoli and chow down. Neither Becky nor Anja interrupt our lunch.

"Where's your fan base?"

"You mean my two friends you hate and threw food at?" Nichole says.

"I only threw food at Becky."

"Whatevs. They skipped today."

"Oh," I say. "Thanks for sticking around."

"You're welcome."

The bell rings.

"Time for class," Nichole sighs.

"Yay, homeroom," I say without enthusiasm.

I get up and we throw away our trash and follow the thinning crowds toward the classrooms.

Nichole and I plop down into adjacent seats just as the bell rings and class begins.

"Nichole, what's your goal of the week?" Mrs. Mills prompts.

I sigh. Here we go. I'm sure I'll be next. I try to wrack my brain to think of an acceptable answer.

"Pass my economics test, finish my <u>Beloved</u> paper for English and get at least a B on it. Um, that's it this week."

I'm surprised Nichole has more than one goal. Mrs. Mills walks up to my desk and peers down at me.

"Your goals?" Mrs. Mills asks.

I open my notebook.

"In a sense," I stall.

"Explain, Vanessa. We would all like to hear how you're doing on your progress." Mrs. Mills turns to sweep her hands out to all the other kids in class. They look too bored to care.

"Well." More attempts at stalling, but I can tell I've reached my limit. "Um. I've been thinking more long-term goals."

"And?"

"And," I pause. "I want to do something newsworthy, something larger than life, something so big that everyone will remember me by it."

"It's great to have long-term goals, Vanessa, but I want you to work on goals with measurable results. For example, how will you know when you've done something big enough? See how the vagueness affects the goal here?"

She waits for me to nod before turning to her next victim. "Sophie, what are your goals this week?"

I tune it all out and doodle in my notebook until the bell rings.

Nichole follows me to yearbook class.

"My least likely career paths are veterinarian, waitress, and working in IT. Totally wrong, except for the last two. I think working with animals could be fulfilling. Vets make good money."

She continues to ramble and I half listen as we wind our way through the hall and into the administrative building.

"I'm so glad we decided to do yearbook together! It's way easier than that stupid arts class I took sophomore year."

"No kidding. I thought volleyball would be easy, but some of the electives teachers take their classes way too seriously," I reply.

"Look, it's Jenny Lyons," Nichole whispers. Jenny's carrying a book bag with a handle and walking with purpose. "I'd get so bored if I took yearbook six semesters in a row like her."

"She wants to be a journalist," I say.

"Whatever, yearbook is for slackers, not teacher's pets. Do you think she brought her laptop today?"

"Probably." I giggle. Jenny Lyons brings her own laptop to every class even though we have desktop computers at our disposal.

Jenny slides into class ahead of us and takes a seat in the front, the center row like she usually does and slides her laptop out of her book bag.

We slip into our seats.

"Ready?" I turn to Nichole.

"Go!" she says.

We both press the on buttons for our ancient computers and wait for them to power up.

"I win," I say as I open up our latest assignment folder, with the senior yearbook pages we've been formatting.

Nichole leans over and scowls at my computer screen. Hers is still booting up the desktop icons. They appear one by one.

I open up Nichole's and my senior yearbook page and check out our recent formatting changes to see if I still like everything we did during last class.

Everyone's assignment for the last month has been to find seniors who want to fund the yearbook by purchasing their own Senior Page. A whole page is $200, half is $100, and so on. Nichole and I have decided to go halfsies on a full page and we've been working together on it.

Nichole's half is full of baby pictures. Most of my pictures are of us and a good majority of those are from this year. Nichole doesn't mention the difference between our two halves.

"Did you come up with anything for our caption?" Nichole asks me as she too opens up our assignment file on her computer.

"Naw. One hundred characters is nothing. All the words I want to use are too long. How about you? Anything?"

She shakes her head.

I chew on the end of a pen as I try to think up something quippy to include on the page and pull out my notebook to jot down a few ideas.

"Hey, can you approve my photos real fast?" Nichole ask.

"Sure." I hop out of her seat and we switch places.

I stare at the foot in her picture.

"Is that my foot?" I point at the screen.

"No. That's the guy I dated for all of two weeks. What a puppy dog. He followed me everywhere."

"Wait a minute! You don't mean Darrell? That guy was creepers extreme. He drew you that awful picture and truly thought it was good. I seem to recall it was a picture of you."

"Ew. Don't remind me." Nichole turns away.

"Didn't he punch the wall when you broke up with him?"

I look closer at the picture.

"Hey! I remember this picture. You were in the courtyard drawing on the graffiti wall when I took it."

"Good times," Nichole says "Too bad they took down the graffiti wall."

I nod my head. "Yup, but it was full within two weeks and then everyone started tagging trees and spraying the sidewalks, what were they going to do?"

"The principal could have just painted over the wall every week, but no, the administration had to take it down," Nichole says

"Whatever. I think your pictures are fine. I like the border on the one of us at the park. I might have to use it on one of mine so we can have another matching thing on our page," I say. "And the background. Polka dots? I don't like that. Can we please do the tie-dye?"

"It'll clash with all the colors in our photos. Honestly, Nessa, you have no eye for fashion." She looks over my choice of clothes.

"What? This was the only clean shirt I had left."

"You sure it's yours?"

My favorite loose shirt is two sizes too big and when I sit down and lean over the scooped neck falls down my shoulder like I'm in an 80's dance movie.

I glower at Nichole, but a cough interrupts us. We turn and Jenny hands us a camera.

"You have an assignment. The freshman fine arts class is doing something special out in the courtyard today, art on shirts or something. You're going to capture it for the yearbook."

"Uh, thanks," I say and grab the camera from her.

Nichole and I look at each other and laugh. We still have half the period left so we leave our stuff behind and head out to the courtyard at a slow walk.

"Are we doing anything later?" I ask.

"Well," she starts.

"Cancel your plans. It's time to skydive. I looked up all the information and booked a reservation."

"Oh my God, are you serious! I'm so down."

I want to keep talking about all the time and effort and planning I put into the skydiving plans last night, but we've arrived at the courtyard.

"Wow," Nichole says, swiveling to take it all in.

We step forward and are surrounded by shirts pinned up on clotheslines between the trees in the courtyard. Students walk amongst the shirts with clipboards, writing things down every now and then. I peek at one of their sheets. It's an evaluation of the art.

"How can you evaluate art?" I ask.

"Exactly," Nichole says.

"Oh no."

"What?" Nichole turns and sees what I just did. Ben. Can't he just stay out of my life already?

"Are you here from the yearbook?" a thin kid with glasses and hair gelled into a Mohawk asks.

"Yup. We're going to take pictures of your installation and ask for quotes," Nichole recites.

"This is mine," the boy says and points to a shirt covered in red splotches and dirt. "Zombie invasion."

Okay then. "Great, anything else you want to add?" I ask.

"Nope."

We walk to the next shirt and take a look. It's covered in flowers and the girl next to it beams up at us. I take a picture.

"So, tell me, what do the flowers symbolize?" Nichole asks.

I walk down to the next shirt and snap a few pictures. I don't wait for Nichole to catch up and continue taking photographs of the artwork.

"Nice job, Ben," the art teacher, someone I don't know, tells Ben loudly. Several students snicker and mouth things at him. Ben's shirt hangs on the end of one of the clotheslines. It's a chaos of lines and I can't tell if they mean anything from this far away. I don't hear what he says back to the teacher and continue taking photographs.

Eventually, I make my way around to Ben's shirt. I hold the camera by my side. I'm not taking a picture of his piece of artwork but if I knew anything about art, I'd say it wasn't bad. The shirt is covered in words, some large and bold-font while others are small or in cursive. I casually step closer to read the words.

Frown. Survive. Victory. Monster. War. Power. Struggle. Dark. Fight. The words push back at me as I read them and I look away.

I walk back over to Nichole and we head back to yearbook class in silence.

CHAPTER SEVENTEEN - VANESSA UNLEASHED

As soon as the final bell rings, Nichole and I hightail it out to the parking lot. Instead of going home, we head to the skydiving rendezvous area off 41. The sky is cloudless and the sun shines down on us. I breathe deep the clear air and tell myself to focus.

We're about to do something completely insane. My heart flutters at the back of my throat and I can hear it pattering. *Do it. Do it. Jump. Jump. Dad. Dad. Dad.* It beats faster and faster as we go through our short training session and get harnessed up. It's all straps and buckles, bunching up my shirt and pushing out all my extra skin in all the wrong places.

The instructor tells me what to do, but the words fly past my ears in a rush.

"And head tilted back," the instructor says.

I try to hold onto the words, but they have no meaning. He crosses his arms in an X shape across his chest and I mimic his movements.

Nichole waddles over and we hi-five. My palm is so sweaty that it slides off of hers.

"Sorry." I rub my palms on my legs, between the straps.

"Let's do this!" Nichole says, her eyes wide and intense.

"Yeah!" My voice cracks and Nichole slaps me on the back.

"This is going to be awesome and you're going to love it. Much better than riding a motorcycle. I think."

As soon as we're airborne, en-route to our destination drop, my stomach trades places with my heart and I want to vomit.

"You got this," Nichole tells me.

A shiver runs up my spine as the plane turns and I feel the dip through my fingers, gripping the edge of my seat.

"For Dad," I say to her, my voice muffled and pitiful.

"For challenges and doing crazy shit," Nichole answers.

I want to howl to the sky, but the instructors give us a two-minute warning and my cheeriness whisks away with the wind. A shiver turns into a full body vibration. Nichole grabs my hands.

"For you and me," she says.

"For us," I repeat.

And then it's time.

"I'll go first," I say before Nichole can ask. I'm ready to get this over with and if I wait any longer, I might never leave this plane.

I take my place at the door, with my tandem instructor holding me back, giving last minute instructions - a pep talk that's stolen by the wind whistling all around us.

I'm in the eye of a hurricane. A tornado. I cross my arms in an X over my chest and then I tilt forward. My instructor points down and then pushes us out of the plane.

Dad! My stomach pushes into my brain. I can't breathe. Is there no air up here? The panic clouds around me. I fight to stay sane. Air pushes against my face with relentless fingers. Hair escapes from my ponytail and whips into my eyes.

I take a breath.

I can breathe.

But then I look down and scream and scream. The ground, flat, and unappealing doesn't look real. Houses are squares. Cars are ants. People are dots. Everything's so far. Still far. Flat. Then it becomes reality and everything is normal-sized and we careen toward it. Two minutes is an eternity until we're on the ground. I wonder where all those airborne seconds went.

"You did well." The instructor pats me on the back and helps me out of my harnesses because I'm shaking so hard.

"Sorry," I apologize and try to stand still.

"No problem. Adrenaline," he says.

"T-thanks."

Nichole whoops when she spots me. "Oh my God, I feel so alive!" she screams. "I'm starved," she adds as an afterthought.

"I don't even know where I left my stomach."

Nichole laughs and grabs my arm, tugging me along. "You'll find it. You always do. Let's go!"

"Parkway Plaza?" I ask.

"Hell yeah. I've got mad cravings for a Wendy's burger."

"To Wendy's it is."

She gets three burgers and I order a Frosty with fries, my favorite combo.

I pull back out onto the main road and shoot across to the Walmart parking lot and pull into the far side, away from peering eyes. My guilt at eating junk is quickly forgotten as I chow down on the fries and stuff my face with one of Nichole's burgers.

"Oh my God, the mayonnaise," I moan.

"What's that stuff you have at your house called?"

"Vegenaise," I tell her.

"Ugh, even the name sounds gross."

"Don't even get me started. I could go on for days about the weird vegan cheese she gets."

"Yeah, I know. You made me try it once, remember?"

I smile at her, sauce oozing out of the corner of my mouth.

Scrunching up all my wrappers, I stuff them into one of the bags and put it aside. Nichole is still munching on her last burger. I hop out of the car. It's started to drizzle and wind whips strands of my hair into my face. I shut my eyes and turn so I'm facing into the wind.

Nichole joins me outside the car a minute later and I can hear her audible intake of breath at the chilly air. We walk as fast as we can into the Walmart and stuff our trash into the nearest garbage can. I breathe a sigh of relief that it's warm inside. I pull Nichole into the nearest aisle and we sprint down its length, giggling. This is our home element. This is our local Walmart. We know every aisle, every nook and cranny, and…

I stop fast, pulling Nichole up short with me.

"Look!" I whisper.

Nichole peers at the shelves on either side.

"No, there."

She looks down at the ground where I'm pointing. It's like a squat, square skateboard. Four wheels and a base about as big as a small poster.

I crouch down and sit on the thing. Nichole gets behind me and pushes. I giggle.

"Faster!" I tell her.

She pushes her hands into my shoulder blades and we zoom down the aisle. We're in the toy area and at the end of the aisle a small boy, only about three feet tall steps into our path. I put a hand down to steer us away just as Nichole shoves hard on my left side. I fly up and out of my seat into the ball net. I grab at the thin netting with my hands to keep my head from hitting the ground and I pull the structure with me as I fall backwards.

Balls fall out of the top. The boy gasps and watches as balls tilt out of the opening and fall down around him, bouncing higher than his head and out into the rest of Walmart. He laughs and sticks a thumb into his mouth.

I let go of the netting and it snaps back, shoving balls out of the opening toward the other direction.

"Oops," I say as I get to my feet.

I step out of the aisle and see two blue-shirted employees jogging over to us.

"Uh oh," I hear Nichole say from behind me.

"Let's get out of here." I take three steps back and turn and run down the aisle in the opposite direction. Nichole runs beside me. We race around the outer aisles of the Walmart until we're back at the doors we came in at and walk out as fast as we dare.

"The night is not over," I say to Nichole as we brace ourselves against the chilly wind outside.

"Brr!" Nichole hugs her arms around her sides and pulls her head into her shoulders, shaking in the cold.

"I have just the thing to warm us up. I've been scouting this place for a few days and I think it will suit our purposes perfectly."

Nichole follows me mutely to my car. We get in and I flip the heat up to high. The first blast is sharp, cold air and we both suck in air as we wait for it to get warm. I turn the car on and rev the engine to get the heater working and we set off down the road doing the speed limit exactly.

I can see my breath as it rises in the cold humid air and too soon we've fogged up the windows and I have to switch from blasting heat to defogging the windshield. The car grows noticeably cold.

"Almost there," I reassure Nichole.

Her lips are pressed tight.

"This is going to warm you right up," I continue.

I pull off onto a darkened side street and meander through a neighborhood, pulling into an apartment complex off to the side. It's only nine or so in the evening, but it's shadowy and cold and devoid of people. The perfect night for what I have planned.

"Are you going to stop?" Nichole chatters through her teeth.

"Stop what?" I ask.

"You haven't been this spunky since I first met you."

I laugh. "It's senior year. I'm living life."

"Yeah, about that, I've been meaning to talk to you——"

"We're here." I cut her off, not wanting to have this conversation.

I shut off the engine and headlights, immersing us in the fog of the night and steam rising from the front of the car. Dang, it's cold. I get out and open the trunk, digging around for the two towels I stashed there earlier.

"What are we going to do with those?"

"They've got a coffee maker here and I brought this. Ta da!" I pull out several packets of instant hot chocolate.

Nichole eyes me warily.

"I don't have a swimsuit," she says.

"You don't need one."

I march toward the main building, where the pool and lounge area are deserted.

"I'm not so sure about this. It's still pretty early." Nichole's eyes flit back and forth.

"Who's scared now?" I tease and continue marching forward.

Nichole runs to catch up to me and we stride into the apartment's communal area. The door to the office is unlocked, just as I found it when I was here scouting. I flick on the lights and go straight for the coffee maker. Nichole stands at the door, keeping watch outside as I prepare our hot chocolate.

"Then what are the towels for? There's no way we're going swimming in this weather."

"Not the pool. Hell no. But the hot tub is open for business." I grin as I pour the hot chocolate packets into two mugs I've pulled from the cabinets.

Nichole grins at me and walks out of the communal area back toward the pool. I follow her and watch as she peers around. The hot tub is covered, but steam rises through the air where the tarp corners don't meet the hot tub's corners.

She helps me pull off the tarp and we set it down on top of a row of tight-packed bushes. It's dark out but the pool area, including the hot tub, is lit up with outdoor bright lights and mosquitos fly around.

Nichole strips to her panties and bra. I can't help but laugh at her matching lingerie set. It's frilly, with pink lace edging the bra and ruffling along the hem of the panties.

She steps into the hot tub. Her hands drop into the water and she leans back against the side of the hot tub, her legs out in front of her. She takes a breath with eyes closed and sinks further under the water so that small waves lap against the bottom of her chin.

The hot chocolate cups are so toasty, I think I might burn my fingers as I carry them over near the hot tub and set them down.

I strip down to my underwear. I've taken care to wear darker colored panties and bra. The waistband of the panties is tight against my belly. Red lines crease under my belly button where the waistband pushes into my skin.

I put a toe into the water and sigh, dunking my leg and following with my lower body. We both sink up to our ears, sighing in pleasure.

"This is the life," I say and grab my mug to slurp down a

boiling sip of cocoa. I set it carefully on the ground.

Nichole smiles at me. She lies back in the water, wetting the hair at the nape of her neck and closing her eyes.

"Hey there, good looking,"

I splash out of my reverie, but immediately sink back down in the water to cover up my exposed body. My hands splash drops as they whip around to enclose my front half.

The pool area is closed off from the rest of the apartment complex buildings because of the tall bushes, but it's lit up and the gate doesn't lock. The stranger is not security. He's hardly even an adult. He's young and his face is smooth without wrinkles or age spots. The skin on his arms is tight and he's not wearing a shirt.

Nichole has her back to him and she turns slowly to acknowledge him. I lock eyes with Nichole, before she's completely turned to face him. She wrinkles her nose at me and then finishes her slow pirouette in the sluggish water.

"Hey there," she says.

He grins and raises his eyebrows at us.

"I haven't had the pleasure of seeing either of you around here before. You gals new?"

Busted. Before I can reply, Nichole oozes her cool charm at him.

"No. We're visiting her aunt and she told us about the Jacuzzi. Care to join us?"

He steps forward, sets his towel down and deftly puts one leg into the water, his stomach tightening across his six pack.

"You girls look a bit young to be unaccompanied." Super jock boy points to the sign at the edge of a storage building, where a large, bold-font sign hangs. I scan the rules and note that no one under the age of 14 is allowed unaccompanied in the hot tub. Fourteen, really?

"We're seventeen," I say haughtily.

He raises his eyebrows at me and turns to Nichole.

"You too?"

"Yeah, but we'll be eighteen in January," she says suggestively.

He turns from Nichole back to me.

"You don't look like twins," he says.

"We're not," I say coyly.

"I'm Chase." He points at himself.

Muscles on his chest flex. I try not to stare. Nichole doesn't bother with that sort of etiquette. Her eyes are devouring him. She swishes closer to him in the water, now less than a foot away.

"I'm Stacy and this is Jessica," she says smoothly.

Fake names. I should have thought of that.

"Nice to meet you. Stacy. Jessica." The names fall off his tongue like mints, cool and spicy. "I hope you don't mind my friend Dan joining us in a bit."

Nichole and I exchange looks. No. I wanted Chase. Ugh. She tilts her eyes up and toward the guy. Fine. I blink hard. I'm stuck with Dan.

"You sure you're not twins? That was some unspoken communication going on there."

His smile is flawless, white, straight teeth and a slight dimple. What if he wanted me? Truth is, compared to Nichole, they never want me. Nichole always out-flirts me, isn't afraid to be seen eating cheeseburgers, and doesn't have a muffin top. Besides which, she's wearing Barbie doll underwear and I'm basically wearing granny panties. Ugh.

"We're best friends," Nichole says, her smile larger than ever.

"Well, Best Friends. I'm glad you're visiting your aunt."

Dan shows up after another ten minutes of Nichole's overt flirting and Chase's cool responses. Interestingly enough, the first words out of his mouth are, "Dude, I got lost finding this place. How do you know when to turn off?"

Then he turns the corner and sees the full Jacuzzi. He stops and stares before shaking his head from side to side with a knowing smile. Dan is shorter and broader shouldered with floppy brown hair, unlike Chase's pristine crew cut.

I glance at Nichole, making sure she won't change her mind. She's whispering something into Chase's ear. Already within inches. She doesn't waste time when it comes to someone cute.

Dan kicks off his sandals and takes his shirt off with one hand. My eyes go to his chest and my cheeks burn. I look off into the surrounding bushes nonchalantly and I peek at him through my peripheral vision. Unlike Chase's Hollister-smooth chest, Dan sports curly dark chest hair.

"Dan, meet Stacy and Jessica," Chase says.

I squint and frown when he says those fake names. Stacy is the hot blonde name and I'm stuck with the girl next door name.

Dan steps over to the hot tub and sticks a toe in before he places his whole leg into the water and holds his hand out to Nichole.

"Nice to meet you, Stacy."

Nichole's obliged to grab his hand, droplets falling from her hand into the hot tub. She smiles at him but he's already turning toward me. She stiffens and frowns at him and I stifle a laugh at her annoyance.

Waves from Dan's movement break against my chest, reminding me how naked I am in my granny panties.

Dan towers over me and holds out his hand. "Pleasure to meet you, Jessica."

Was he emphasizing my fake name or did I just imagine it? Not once does he glance down at my chest. I'm impressed.

"Is this something you girls do often?" Dan asks.

"No, they're just visiting," Chase speaks for us.

"Her aunt," Nichole pipes up. "But we only live fifteen minutes away, so we visit her all the time," she adds.

I catch on to what she's trying to do.

"But she just moved here, so this is the first time we've visited her," I say.

Nichole nods and we beam at the guys.

"You're both excellent liars. If that had been true you wouldn't be here past dusk in your-" Chase peers down his nose at Nichole, "underthings."

Nichole and I exchange looks.

Dan laughs beside me and I give him a quizzical glance, trying to raise just one of my eyebrows at him.

"She didn't tell us there was a Jacuzzi until we got here and it was too late to go and come back," Nichole explains.

Dan and Chase don't say anything. Have they bought it? Does it matter? Nichole is in see through underwear and I'm sure I'm almost bursting out of mine. Even if they don't believe it, they must appreciate our presence. However, I still haven't caught Dan glancing down.

I peek over at Nichole. She's continuing her pursuit of Chase, her hand rubbing the back of his neck. I try to catch her eye, but she won't look over at me.

"So you and Chase come here often?" I ask.

"Uh, not exactly. We just come here for the hot tub. This one's the best in town." He smiles at me, daring me to accuse him of what we're doing: trespassing.

"You don't live here?"

"Nope. Chase used to, that's how we know about it. I just come when he tells me there are hot girls." He winks at me.

He still hasn't looked down. I want to make sure my chest is still there.

"Oh," I lower my voice, "we don't live here either and I don't have any aunts. My mom's an only child."

"I guessed it was something like that. How'd you find this place, then? It's in the middle of nowhere out here."

"It's only half a mile from the main road. One day we were rollerblading-"

Dan holds up a hand, "Stop, you were rollerblading? Who does that?"

"It's still a thing. Anyways, we were rollerblading around the neighborhood and came across the complex. I came back to see if they had a decent pool and found the hot tub too. So now we come here all the time for hot tubbing." I attempt to raise one eyebrow at him again.

"No need to scowl. Hot tubbing, eh?" Dan says.

Nichole moans and we both look over. Chase's giving Nichole a back massage. Typical. Men will do anything for her. I blush, thinking of Dan giving me a back massage.

"Props to her. She knows how to get what she wants," Dan says.

"Don't I know it," I mutter.

"Do I detect a hint of jealousy?"

I roll my eyes.

"I know how to fix that, may I? He holds out his hands and leans toward me. I struggle, trying to decide what I want. To hell with everything. To hell with holding myself back. I nod.

He makes a twirling motion with his finger and I turn to face the storage shed. He brushes up against me from behind and I tighten from my shoulders to my toes. His hands tickle my neck as he moves my hair from my shoulders, bunching it up into one wet roll and setting it on one side of my shoulder, so that it hangs down my collarbone. That was singlehandedly the sexiest thing anyone has ever done for me and I melt under his fingers, slipping lower into the water as my knees wobble.

"Is this okay?" his voice is barely above a whisper.

I smile and then realize he can't see my face. My mind whirls, still thinking about the way he scooped my hair up like he owned it. "Mmm hmm."

I hear him crack his knuckles and then his fingers roll over my back. I let out a moan and hurriedly clap a hand over my mouth in embarrassment.

I hear clapping. I whip my head around, torqueing my neck so that my back is still in place for Dan's massage. Both Nichole and Chase are staring at me and clapping. I redden.

"We were wondering how long it would take," Chase says with a smile.

I can feel Dan behind me stiffen, his whole body rigid in the water, no little waves lapping from his front to my back. Is he upset by the sudden attention?

"Is that what you were whispering about when he came up?" I

ask Nichole.

She nods her head. Dan's hands are resting on my shoulders. I'm not sure if I want to shrug them off or have him continue. Chase points to Dan.

"He's studying massage therapy, so I'm sure Jess is getting the better work over."

I frown, even though it's a fake name, him shortening it to a familiar nickname irks me. This is starting to feel like a setup, but I brought Nichole here. She didn't know where we were going. This is just a coincidence. It was her initiative that took Chase and left me with Dan.

"He likes to practice whenever he can."

Chase winks at me and I wrinkle my nose at the innuendo as I lurch forward out from under Dan's hands. They flop into the water with a plinking sound. I twirl around to face him, stubbing my toe on one of the stairs. I scowl at the fleeting pain and peer up into Dan's face. He looks stricken and my mood melts. Chase is just making fun of him. Now what? Thinking on my feet, I make a turnaround motion with my hands and he raises his eyebrows at me, but does what I've indicated. My hands hesitate before settling on his back. He shudders. I knead his back, trying to remember pressure points.

How can this end? It's beginning to get late and I don't want to be here all night in my underwear. No way am I going to hang off of Dan like Nichole's hanging off Chase, licking his ear and telling him all her secrets. I may have found my wild side, but I'm not that wild. I try to catch Nichole's eye, but she's preoccupied.

The smacking noises reach my ears before the visual of them kissing does. Seriously? I roll my eyes, even though no one's watching me. Typical Nichole.

Dan shifts in the water in front of me, turning to see what's going down on the other side of the hot tub. Nichole and Chase grow louder and larger waves beat against my sides. I shift awkwardly in the water. It's too hot and my face is cold-sweating in the chilled air, a line of moisture tickles my upper lip and cold hot tub water drips from my hair onto my shoulder. I shiver.

"Um," I stammer, turning to face Dan.

"Want to ditch them?" He jerks his head at the smooching couple that used to be our friends.

"Yeah."

I nod emphatically and stand up. The hot water that clings to my body turns frigid and I wrap my arms around myself. Dan climbs out, avoiding the stairs where Nichole and Chase lounge. I peek at them. Nichole is on top of Chase now, her arm draped lazily across his back.

I splash out of the hot tub in a hurry and scamper over to our towels. Dan stands in front of our stuff, holding out my towel like a gift.

"Thanks," I murmur and grab it from him, wrapping it around my exposed parts.

"I brought an extra one, you can use it for your hair if you'd like."

He holds out what appears to be a hand towel.

"Thanks."

I reach out to grab it and brush against his fingers. My cheeks are on fire.

"No problem."

Now what? What to say? "Uh, are you from here?" I ask, leaning over to towel my face and hide my blush.

"No, actually. I'm from Minnesota. And I know what you're going to say."

"Oh, yeah, what's that?"

I can do this. I can flirt too.

"You know. Did you move here for the weather?"

His towel slips and he lurches down to catch it.

"No actually. Never heard that one," I say. I'm trying too hard not to stare where curlicues of dark hair accentuate his sexy 'v' shaped lines.

"Do you think they'll go on all night?" Dan interrupts

"God, I hope not," I reply.

"Well, I've got an English test in the morning," Dan says.

"Kind of late to get started."

"Yeah, well." Dan runs a hand through his hair.

"Right. Okay." I blink and try to clear my head.

"I'll walk you to your car," I blurt out.

"Sure."

We walk out of the pool area and around the side of the communal area for the apartment complex. Our cars are parked in the visitor parking and he points to his, a sleek Charger like Jason's.

"That's my ride."

"This is mine," I say stupidly, pointing to the Honda.

"Well, it was nice meeting you, Jessica."

"Nice to meet you too, Dan."

I go to my car and open the trunk and pretend to move things around. I'm disappointed that he didn't try to kiss me or anything.

Fuck it.

I grab my notebook and a pen out of my backpack. I shut the trunk and walk up to Dan's car.

"Wait." I scribble my number on a blank sheet of notebook paper, tear it out, and hand it over. "Here's my number."

He smiles at me as he pockets it with a flourish. I jog back over to my Honda and hop in, blasting on the heat, shivering and shaking uncontrollably. I grip the steering wheel and laugh nervously.

Nichole walks out of the pool area ten minutes later, the towel tied around her waist and her entire upper half visible. Chase walks beside her. They say something to each other before Nichole waves to him and walks over to the passenger side and gets in with a long, exaggerated sigh.

"So, that good, huh?" I ask.

"Better."

She rolls down her window to wave at Chase again before I take off for home.

"What a great day," Nichole tells me on the way home.

"I'll say. Even after the Walmart disaster, it turned out alright. See you tomorrow?"

"Yup. Bye Jessica."

"Buh bye Stacy," I say.

I wait until she's opened her front door before I head for my house. I park and shut my door as quietly as possible before sneaking in the door. It's past midnight as I brush my teeth and go to my room. I'm too keyed up to go to bed just yet so I snag a book off my shelf and scuttle into bed.

I hug the blankets up to my chin and settle into the soft mattress to read the night away and daydream about Dan.

CHAPTER EIGHTEEN – DONUTS IN AN EMPTY FIELD

Geocaching isn't very hard, and it's not as exciting as the opportunity to shoot a gun. But it's an opportunity to cross an item off Dad's bucket list.

We're outside an abandoned mini golf course on a Friday afternoon.

"Can't we just go to the range first?" I ask. "It's not even that far from here."

I jingle my car keys and look longingly at my car, which I've parked in this abandoned and creepy lot near the old, forsaken golf course.

Nichole raises her eyebrows at me. "Sure, if you want to disregard my plans entirely. It was really difficult putting this together."

Nichole hands me what looks like a phone, but it's bulky and the screen is small. I open my mouth to ask her what it is, but she holds up a finger.

"Ah, ah, ah. No questions. This is a GPS. I've programmed the coordinates for you. Normally, you can do it with your phone, but you don't have the app, plus it's a pain in the butt to try to load and I have a crap plan. Alright, quick tutorial on the GPS and geocaching. Then we're off."

"We're already here," I point out.

"Yes, but we need to get to ground zero. Duh."

"Where is it, exactly?" I ask.

"I said no questions!" she barks. "Tutorial time."

Nichole explains how to use the GPS. She, on the other hand, gets to use her phone.

"Why can't I use your phone?" I whine.

"The GPS is more accurate."

"And that's why you're using your phone?"

"Hey, those things aren't cheap! I was planning on giving it to you for your birthday, but I couldn't wait."

"You could have given it to me for Christmas, you know," I point out.

"No I couldn't, I just got it and your birthday isn't for another two weeks."

"Ten days," I correct her.

"I know that. January 19, same as mine, stupid."

"Don't be a smack," I say automatically.

She grins at me.

"Okay," I say. "So explain to me again what this geocaching thing is? I remember you mentioning it last summer, but you never really explained it when we were at the tree beach."

"Essentially it's just using a GPS to find the cache or container that someone hid in a certain location."

"And?" I ask.

"And you find it using the GPS, but there's more to it because sometimes it's disguised."

I stare up at the sky.

"Hey, earth to Nessy! Pay attention. There's going to be a quiz on this later."

I groan and tune back in.

"And then you can go see what everyone has written in the comments about the hide. It's a good source of clues if you're having trouble finding the cache."

"Tell me again, you didn't hide them? Someone else did?"

"Exactly. See, you're catching on… slowly."

She gives me a sidelong glance and I soften. I've been taking us places, telling her what we're doing for weeks and she just wants some control. I can understand that.

She continues to drag out her explanations until I'm sure I could teach someone else the basics without actually having done much geocaching myself.

Nichole points to the GPS in my hand. I glance down at the screen and press the on button.

"So this listing has been found 23 times, see." Nichole holds out her phone so I can see the comments section of this particular geocache.

She has a data plan and can access the internet as we go. The GPS only has the coordinates and as I bring them up and start walking in the right direction, Nichole follows, her eyes glued to her phone.

"It has a hint. When we've searched a bit and get stumped, I'll open it up," Nichole says.

"Just tell me what it is."

"That ruins the fun. You've got to use your wits to find it."

"Ugh, fine."

I continue walking and following the GPS until we're near the back of the property, abutting a tall wooden fence. A large sign hangs at an angle up against the fence, a billboard with half the letters missing. The white background is gray with dirt. Nobody in their right minds would go back here unless they were taking down the sign.

"I think it's here," I say to Nichole.

She's distracted with her phone, but looks up at my words. She scampers over to my side. We both peer up at the sign. Why would a sign this large be in the back? It's large enough that the edge of the sign starts around head height and the sign part is at least eight feet taller than that.

"It might be in the back," she says.

We step around to the back of the sign and squeeze between the fence and the billboard, shielding our faces against cobwebs with our hands. We scrutinize the back of the sign. It's blank, littered with cobwebs and leaves thick enough to obscure the edge on both corners.

"It could be hidden in the corners, under the leaves," Nichole muses.

"I'm not touching that," I tell her.

"Yeah, me neither, maybe there's something on the front?"

We both go back to the front and stand perplexed for a few

moments.

"Maybe the letters on the billboard are a hint?" I ask.

"And you're sure this is ground zero?" she asks.

"Yup, the coordinates on the GPS match up right here in this corner, near the billboard," I say. "But this isn't where the geocache is?"

"Nope, it's a puzzle-cache. You figure out the clue at ground zero to find out where the real cache site is located."

"That seems unnecessarily difficult," I comment.

"That's what makes it fun. Aren't you good at puzzles?"

"Yeah." My voice catches on the word. "Dad was into puzzles."

"Oh," she says quietly.

We used to race to complete the 100-piece puzzles and he would ask me all sorts of riddles.

"You okay?" she asks, putting a hand on my shoulder.

I sniff and say, "Yeah."

"You think you can solve this?"

"Maybe." I glance back up at the letters on the billboard. "You think it's an anagram?" I ask.

"A what?"

"An anagram. Scrambled letters that form a word or words when arranged properly," I explain.

"I don't know. You're the wordsmith,"

"Thanks," I say flatly. "I thought you said the hint is in the listing?"

"Yeah, but there can be clues at ground zero," she says.

"Can I see the hint?" I ask.

"Don't you want to figure this out first?" she asks, pointing up at the sign. A leaf falls from the top and flutters to our feet.

"An anagram my ass. I think you're stretching it. This isn't a Dan Brown novel."

"Fine."

Nichole whips out her phone and holds it up so we can both

peer at the screen. She navigates to another part of the app to open the hint.

Scrambled eggs aren't hard to find. The sign is the key and the words do the work.

"See?" Nichole says. She might as well have said "I told you so."

I sigh heavily and take another look at the words on the sign. They're mostly letters close enough to have once been words.

"You got a pen and paper?" I ask Nichole.

She claps her hands together in glee. "I knew I could convert you!" She ruffles around inside her purse before pulling out a small notepad and a gel pen that is dark pink.

"Wow," I say.

"No comments! It was a present."

"Gel pens are so '90s," I say anyway.

She shakes her head, "Don't be a smack. Just crack the code, please."

I put all the letters down and move them around, crossing and shifting them until I've gotten them close to a sentence. I show Nichole.

"Nice work!"

"But it doesn't mean anything,"

"Sure it does. Down the bayou. Come on!"

"That was a tough one. Bayou isn't a common word you know," I say with hands on my hips.

"Yeah, yeah, you're a genius. Come on!"

Nichole grabs the pen and paper from my hands and jams them into her purse.

I trail behind Nichole as she comes to a stop at a gray, crusty-looking fake alligator. She bends down and reaches into its mouth. I suck in a breath and she pulls her hand back out.

"Relax. It's just the geocache," she tells me.

She holds out her hand to show me a black container.

"Film canister. Classic hiding container for small items," she says. "Even though it's not that watertight."

"What about the container at the beach?"

"Don't worry. There's no matches in here," she tells me.

"How do you know?"

"Uh, see?"

She pops open the canister and shows me the inside.

Paper.

It's just rolled up paper.

Nichole pulls out the tightly rolled piece of paper and holds it under my nose in triumph. I snatch it out of her hand and hold it away from her.

"Careful," she says.

She doesn't try to take it away from me though so I unwrap it, cautious not to rip it. The paper is thin and faded, as if it's been unrolled and rerolled too many times. The writing has bled through both sides. At the top is an official "you found it" note and then below is a listing of names and dates. I scan down the list. Macbeth40. Tonio4square. Trollgamer. Bikegardener. Babaoso13.

"Weird names," I comment.

"They aren't real names. They're like gamer tags. You choose your profile name," Nichole says. "Then we sign it and stick it back and voila."

Nichole hands me back the gel pen and notepad. I set the roll of paper on the notepad and hold it open. It tries to curl back in on itself. I write lightly in the next available space.

01/09/08 Nikki and Nessy.

"Cute," Nichole leans over to see what I wrote. "I approve," she adds.

"Good, because you don't get to make all the decisions,"

Nichole scoffs at me and goes back to searching the alligator's mouth. She pulls out another film canister with a matching gray lid. As an afterthought I add to our names "For Dad" before putting the paper back in the canister.

Nichole shakes the new find, teasing me. This other film

canister has grit around the edges of the cap and it makes me suck in my breath.

"Just open it already," I say.

She doesn't pop open the lid but hands it over to me.

"It's your turn, do me proud," she says.

"How very kind of you."

I don't wait for all of the thoughts of nasty possibilities to rain down on me. I pop the top off. Pieces of paper and dirt flutter out and I leap around to catch them. They fall to the ground and Nichole helps me pick them up. We go over to a rotting picnic table and she sets her bits down on it and I dump the rest of the treasures from the canister out next to hers. Miniature animal plastic figurines smaller than my little finger fall out, a marble, several pennies, and a few stones. We stare at the odd bundle of items.

"Well, I wouldn't want to trade any of the stuff you brought for this junk," I tell her, breathing out a sigh of relief. "I'm glad there was nothing creepy here," I add.

"Totally," she agrees.

Nichole stuffs the Ziploc baggie full of tradeables back into her purse.

"So that's it, then?" I ask.

"Yup. You sign the log. Trade treasures if you want and then put it all back exactly how you found it."

"Okay then, now I want to show you something."

"Um, what?" Nichole asks.

"You'll see. You're not the only one with surprises."

Nichole stuffs the trash and papers back into the canisters and shoves them as far into the alligator's mouth as she can reach. After brushing her hands on her jeans, we turn to go.

"That was boring, but wait until you see what I bought," I say as we get back into the Honda.

Nichole frowns at me and crosses her arms. I pull out my little surprise and Nichole's frown deepens.

"What, it's just an air horn," I explain.

"Vanessa. An air horn? Really?"

"Oh, come on. You love pranks. Here, you get to do the first blast."

I hand her the air horn and start driving. We're still surrounded by the dying mini golf course, but Nichole doesn't move to use the air horn. I push the button for the windows to roll down.

"Give me that, wuss." I grab for the air horn, jerking the wheel to the left and overcorrecting a little. Nichole gasps just as I push the accelerator and the air horn, letting out a long and satisfyingly loud blast of sound.

"Jesus, Ness! That is not cool."

"Oh yeah?" I blast it again as we pass by a neighborhood.

Nichole grabs the air horn and throws it into the backseat.

"Hey, now who's being the smack? I did your geocaching, now you get to do my fun thing."

"This isn't fun, Vanessa. You're just being crazy."

"Just like you were being crazy when you ditched me for that boy in the hot tub?" I accused.

"Uh, newsflash, you left me."

"Whatever."

I yank the wheel and drive up the curb onto some random stranger's front lawn and speed up and yank the wheel again, the car tires shooting grass as I drive in a half circle.

"Vanessa!"

I careen off their lawn and speed up as I leave that neighborhood behind. I laugh out my open window, ignoring Nichole.

"Isn't this what you wanted?"

"Stop being such a shit." Nichole glares at me.

"Okay, fine. Like you're a model princess. You do stupid things all the time and do I complain? No. You get to do whatever you want and I never get to do anything that I want."

"I was going to the gun range with you, stupid. Besides, you're the one that holds yourself back. And this," Nichole indicates the air between us, "is not doing what you want. This is what stupid kids do. You want attention? Fine, you got it."

Nichole leans toward me, her seatbelt straining to pull her back in her seat. I turn to look at her and she slaps me. Hard. I stop fast and the car stalls and dies. I was only going about 25 in another empty neighborhood area, but we both jerk forward and back into our seats.

I blink a few times and put a hand to my face, feeling where she slapped me, the skin hot under my fingers.

"Get out," I say.

Nichole unbuckles herself and opens the car door. I don't turn to look at her.

"This is over," I say, louder.

She slams the door and the entire car wobbles. I turn the key in the ignition and press down so fast on the accelerator that the car jerks forward.

At the end of the neighborhood I drive the car over the curb and onto the pristine grass of a small field. I drive in fast, tight circles but the fun is gone. I'm just mad and alone. I'd much rather a donut right now than these sad, lonely donuts in an empty field.

CHAPTER NINETEEN – JUST BECAUSE

"Vanessa, come out here." Mom's voice is full of reprimand; the words sharp as tacks. I didn't go to my scheduled therapy session earlier today. Instead, I took a nap and I'm still in bed.

"Vanessa!" Mom yells outside my door.

I pull a pillow over my head to drown out the sound. Mom knocks on the door, her fist pounding the wood.

"Go away," I shout through my pillow.

"Vanessa, I need to talk to you. I'm coming in."

The doorknob rattles. It won't open because I've locked it.

"Vanessa, your mother would like to speak with you." Walter's deep voice seeps under the door and I sit up with a scowl, the pillow falling back onto the bed.

"Why are you even here?!" I shout back.

"Please come out, Vanessa," Mom begs.

I groan in disgust and roll out of bed, the clothes I slept in wrinkled and twisted around me. I straighten them out and redo my ponytail. Unlocking the door, I put on my best scowl, and push it open.

"What do you want?"

"Can we come in?" Mom asks.

My glare is pure poison but Mom doesn't notice. She walks in and starts straightening my bed. Walter doesn't move from the hallway.

"Perhaps I'll let you two talk alone," he suggests.

Mom stops tucking in my blanket and her shoulders sag as she looks from me to Walter.

"Fine." She pats the bed and I walk over, shoving the door closed behind me. "That was uncalled for."

I just shrug. I'm tired and have a headache. Nichole probably won't even talk to me. I didn't even get to shoot a gun.

"Nichole told me what you two did, with the car."

And now I want nothing to do with Nichole. What a smack!

"Sit down," Mom says.

I cross my arms and stare down at the bed in front of me.

"I wanted to tell you that I want Walter to move in, but in light of recent events I'm not sure that's a good idea. I also don't think it's a good idea for you to continue using the car. You've abused that privilege."

"What!" I shout. "You can't take the car away."

"You can ride the bus to school. If you need a ride to your job, I can get Walter to drive you while I'm at work."

My heart sinks.

"I don't need a ride to my job," I spit.

"Okay. Well, when you've shown that you're ready to accept the responsibilities that come with driving your own car, you'll get that privilege back. In the meantime, I've rescheduled another session with Dr. Bryan next week for you."

I bite back a reply. Therapy has done nothing for me. I'm still afraid of fire. I'm still angry. And I'm still not over Dad's death. So what's the point?

"Also, I think you should talk to Nichole."

"Don't tell me what to do!" I shout. Anger tightens my stomach, clutching at it like there's a demon clawing its way out. "She's the one who won't get a job. The one who isn't going to college."

I breathe a few times and Mom opens her mouth to say something, but I continue speaking as if I didn't stop. "She sleeps around. She skips classes. She eats junk food. Did I do that before I met her? NO!"

Mom sighs and looks at her hands in her lap.

Since I'm on a roll, I might as well tell Mom what I really think about her new boyfriend.

"And Walter? Really?" I'm not shouting, but every word is a punch.

That's not even what I wanted to say but my breathing is loud in my head and I can't concentrate.

"Vanessa."

"No, I'm not done. This isn't just about me. You. You haven't helped. You wonder why I'm doing this? It's not for attention. This is who I am, so deal."

A tear rolls down Mom's cheek. "What did I do to deserve this?" she says to the ceiling.

I scoff and walk out of my room.

"Vanessa-" Walter starts to say, but I'm already out the front door.

I walk toward the Honda, but I don't have the keys. Mom can't just start grounding me now, taking away things.

I walk.

The Parkway Plaza isn't too far and, after about 30 minutes, I'm there. I walk up to the fast food counter and dig in my pocket for my wallet. My fingers grasp at pocket lint. I don't have my wallet. As if I even had money in it.

Swiveling on my heels, I ignore the confused stares of the fast food workers.

"Shut up!" I say to nobody and continue planting my feet hard into the pavement as I retrace my steps all the way back to my house. Curse words escape between shallow breaths and I pound my feet with every step, grinding them into the sidewalk through my sneakers.

The Honda is gone and the lights are out. Good. I go inside and root through Mom's drawers until I find her stash of $20s. I pocket two, heading back outside into the dusk of a brilliant sunset.

I don't go back to the fast food joint. I have a new destination: The Hero's Bar and Grill. I have enough money for the Hero's Challenge.

Hottie waiter isn't working. My waitress is a plump, middle-aged woman, like my mom should have been, all "dearie" this and "honey" that. She seats me in a booth set for four people. I scoot all the way to the inner seat and drum my fingers on the table.

"Thanks," I tell her when she sets down a large glass of water.

"Hero's Challenge," I tell her when she flips open a small notepad to take my order.

"Aw, Honey, you sure?" she asks.

"Yes." My voice is hard, sharp around the edges and she backs up and walks off with a frown, slipping her notepad into her apron's front pocket.

I fidget in the booth, the cushion new and hard under my butt. I think I hear my phone and pick it up, but only Mom has texted and called. I set the flip phone back down with a sigh. I thought Nichole would call me. I open my text messenger and choose Nichole. I type out a message. *I can't believe you did that.* I erase it. *Why? I thought you were my friend?* I erase that as well. *Are you still going to the college party tomorrow?*

I set the phone down. I don't send the last message, but I don't erase it either. A sob works its way up my throat and comes out like a pathetic small mewl. I pick my phone up and slap it back down on the table with a satisfying smack. If I can't have Nichole, I won't miss her. I won't. I rub my eyes so hard I see spots when I open them again, but they are dry. I won't cry.

"Challenger!" The waitress sets down the large tray and places each plate on the table in front of me. It's been several months since the challenge first began and the new items include the hot pepper, a full glass of milk, an extra pound of fries, and they've added hot pepper sauce to the burger patties. Well, at least the burgers won't be dry and tasteless.

"All this in 20 minutes?" I ask the waitress as she sets down the timer.

"No, sweetie, 15." She winds the clock up and looks to me. I nod and she lets the timer go.

"Hero's Challenge!" she proclaims cheerily and walks away.

I push the hot pepper aside and start in on the fries. Five minutes later and all I've done is eat fries and burger patties, sipping on the milk in between. Nobody in the restaurant notices me and my pace slows and slows.

This is impossible.

I'm not hungry.

The empty pit in my stomach just grows wider and emptier.

I give up after ten minutes. My heart just isn't in it. The waitress waits until the timer goes off to come up to me and give me the bill. I hand her the two twenties and walk out, not bothering to take anything with me.

The walk home takes forever. My stomach hurts and my head pounds and my feet are tired from walking so much.

I drag myself through the front door and ignore Mom when she starts talking to me. I go straight for my room, humming in my head to drown out all other noises.

"Hey! Vanessa, I'm talking to you," Mom shouts.

I shut the door. Mom yanks it open. She doesn't come into the room, but glares at me from the doorway as I slump onto my bed, fully clothed, still wearing my sneakers.

"Vanessa," she says softly.

I don't even look at her.

"You're grounded."

I hear the door shut. I get out of bed and open my dresser. Ants crawl all over my socks. I shove socks and underwear aside until I find the bag of cookie crumbs. I shake it to dislodge the stream of ants on the outside of the bag and hold it open. With shaking fingers I carefully pull out the lighter. I shake the ants off of it, but my fingers are too buttery, too sweaty, too hesitant and the lighter falls to the floor. I shove the bag of crumbs deep into my trash can, automatically covering it with some paper and tissue.

The lighter.

I reach down and pick it up, heart thumping in my chest. My hands shake and I flick the spark wheel, but it doesn't click. I take a deep breath and flick the spark wheel again and this time it clicks so audibly I think the sound comes from inside of me. Like my heart is ticking.

Nothing happens. I do it again. And again. I do it so many times that, finally, I don't react to the motion at all.

CHAPTER TWENTY - BACK TO BEN

I forgot I couldn't drive the car today. I searched all over the top of my dresser for the keys before I remembered Mom took them away.

Nichole doesn't know I'm grounded and without a vehicle, but she didn't call or show up this morning.

I walk to the bus pickup area by myself. I stand to one side of the street, away from the other high school kids, mostly underclassmen. I hide my face in my phone, pretending to text someone, while sneaking glances at the other students to see if they're looking at me.

They aren't.

"Vanessa?"

I whip around and spot Jason through the window of his Charger. I walk up to the window and lean my elbows down to poke my head inside.

"Yeah?"

"Where's your Honda?" he asks.

"In the shop," I lie.

"Tough break. Where's your other half?"

"Yeah, we're not talking right now."

"Ah," he says. "Well, I'm headed to school. Want a lift?"

I perk up and hit my head on the top of the window. Jason winces at the sound, but I don't feel it at all. I don't feel a thing.

"You don't have to ask me twice."

I hop in and shut the door, placing my pack on the floor between my legs. Jason looks over at me as I buckle myself in.

"What?"

"Are you okay, Vanessa?" he asks as he accelerates the car smoothly down the road.

"Just fine."

He peers at me critically for half a second before looking back at the road. The bus stops behind us, the freshman file on. Suddenly, I wish I was on the bus and not in this car. Jason glances at me again and his mouth twitches like he wants to say something.

"What?" I demand.

"Nothing. It's just. I never see you without Nichole."

"Oh, so it's all about her?"

"That's not what I said," Jason says, frowning.

"Yeah, but you would rather it was Nichole here right now, not stupid, fat Vanessa."

Jason grips the steering wheel and grits his teeth.

What am I saying?

I turn to apologize, but Jason clears his throat and lets me have it. "You're the one who says those things. I've never said that. You know, I used to have a crush on you. When we did that scavenger hunt thing, I was impressed by your no shit attitude. I always thought you were shy, but you blew me away riding behind me on my bike."

"You liked me?"

I turn my head away so he can't see my blush.

"I did."

"Did?"

"Never mind," he says.

"No, not never mind." I turn to stare at him, but his eyes don't leave the road.

"Nichole went out of her way to set up that scavenger hunt. She convinced me to do it. For you."

"We lost the scavenger hunt," I interject.

"So? Nichole set that up for you."

"What the hell? Have you been talking to Nichole behind my back?"

"What's wrong with you? Everything isn't always about you."

"I know that."

"No, you don't. You think everyone is out to make you feel

bad or make fun of you or talk about your dad or something."

"Stop the car."

Jason glances over at me and gulps. My hand is already on the door handle, trying to push it open. I realize the door is locked at the same moment Jason yanks the car to the side and slows to a jerking stop.

"Vanessa."

"You can go to hell."

I hop out and shove the door closed. He leans his head out the window, but I ignore him and start walking. After a minute his car revs past me and I continue walking with my head held high.

My feet hurt by the time I get to school. Why the fuck did I put on my flimsy sandals? Grit and pebbles are sandpaper between my toes and I'm sweating underneath my boobs and armpits. I'm smelly, gross, and stuck at school now.

I walk the halls alone, keeping my head down and my arms pulled into the sides of my shirt. I walk through the open chemistry classroom door. I pause for a moment as I spot Kenny already unloading his backpack in the desk in front of mine. I have to walk past him to get to my desk and do so quickly, plunking my backpack down on my seat.

Kenny turns to ask me something, but I glare so fiercely at him he turns back around without saying a word. I pull out my chem book and my notebook and shove my backpack under my desk before I sit down. The chair creaks.

I drum a fingernail on my desk and scratch into one of the deeper graffiti pencil drawings. It's been traced again and again into the wood, like a river of graphite running through it.

As soon as the bell rings Mr. Poole takes a whiteboard marker and writes out several chemical questions for us to balance. I copy down what he wrote and work out the answers. Iron and sulfuric acid is equal to how much sulfuric acid and hydrogen? ($Fe + H_2SO_4 \rightarrow Fe_2SO_4 + H_2$).

I yawn as I figure out the five equations and doodle in the bottom corner of the notebook paper. I draw Bluster as a stick figure. Just as I'm drawing in a thought bubble over his head, someone behind me clears his throat.

I look up and over my shoulder at Mr. Poole and smile guiltily. I start copying down the last five problems he wrote on the board. Mr. Poole sighs and then walks back down to the front of class.

"Who would like to write down the answer to the first problem?"

Classes drag all day until lunch and then time speeds up with my heart. Should I go over to Nichole's table or avoid it altogether? Anxiety makes me hungrier than usual, but I can't stomach the thought of food. For once.

I'm halfway to our usual lunch spot when I stop to compose myself. Students walk around me, like I'm a rock in a stream. I can't stand them.

"He totally likes you."

"Do you think that will be on the test tomorrow?"

"Did you get my text?"

It's all so meaningless. I step off the sidewalk and try to block out everyone. I'm left with my thoughts. How dare Nichole tell Mom about the air horn and driving donuts on strangers' lawns. Anger rises up my throat, growing into words I can't keep to myself. Words for Nichole. Words for Jason. Words I've been holding inside since Dad died.

I march with clenched fists across the courtyard, my eyes trained lasers onto Nichole's always perfect blonde highlighted hair. I'm three steps from the table when someone bumps into me and I go sprawling.

"Watch it," I snarl, whirling my head to the side to see who bumped me. "You again."

I can't take Ben's crap today.

"What are you always doing here? Can't you just leave me alone?"

Ben takes two steps backward and glances to the side, toward Becky. I roll my eyes.

"What, you're going to let your sister protect you, you little shit? You're always messing everything up for me!"

And that's when I lose it. Again.

I step forward and punch him in the jaw. I've never been in a fight. The force of the blow surprises me, pushes me back. Pain radiates from my knuckles. He staggers back as well, eyes larger than ever. He holds up his arms and backs up another step. I glare at him. I mutter a few curse words under my breath until he takes two more steps back, his hand shaking by his side, the three fingers blurring into a whole hand for second. I slump against a tree, spent. All that raw negative energy leaves me out of breath.

"Hey!" Nichole barks.

But Becky is already in front of me, pulling me up by the shoulders and yelling in my face. I push back and Nichole grabs my arm to yank me sideways. Becky glares at Nichole.

"Don't act like you're all innocent," I say to Nichole. "You're so self-righteous. You never say no to friends," I mock her. "Well, you know." I turn to Ben, "She can't even look at your face because it's so ugly. Me, I can't look at you because I despise you as a person. I couldn't care less how you look."

Nichole's jaw drops.

"Seriously? Vanessa, can't you leave my brother alone already?" Becky says.

"And you. You and Anja don't want him around either. He's a pathetic little hang-on that you only tolerate because he's your brother. You people make me sick!" I shout.

"You people?" Becky echoes.

Becky grabs hold of Ben and tries to push him away. The crowd around us has grown thick and Ben hesitates in front of them.

"I can't believe you can't just let it go. Why are you even in therapy?" Nichole says loud enough for the crowd to hear.

An "ooh" comes from behind me.

"How dare you." I narrow my eyes at Nichole. "Your mom was right; you should get your head out of your ass. Get a job and grow up!" I shout at her.

The crowd is noisy behind us, like chattering, hooting

monkeys. Nichole's eyelids flutter rapidly and she stalks off. Becky follows her, Ben trailing behind.

"Screw you," I say to the crowd. Someone laughs and gives me the finger. I give it right back. Teachers and the rent-a-cop security run up and I fade into the crowd like I'm used to being such a troublemaker.

I make it through the rest of the school day and get on the bus to go home. Nobody pulled me out of class. Nobody stopped me. By tomorrow someone will have told and I'll be in a world of trouble.

Mom isn't back from work yet, so I grab my party clothes from when Nichole and I went shopping, lament on the fact that I have no friends anymore and grab another $20 from Mom's stash. I stuff everything into a used plastic grocery bag before pulling my bike out of the very back of the shed behind the house. Amazingly, it still has air in the tires and appears to be in good, working condition. I can't believe I have to ride my bike, but I have no other choice. I'm not even supposed to leave the house, but nobody's going to stop me so I hop on the bike and slowly pedal my way to New College and the big Friday night party.

I make a pit stop at Safeway and raid their donut section. I grab a pint of milk and a half dozen assortment of Dad's favorite donuts: jelly-filled, powdered, glazed, maple, and chocolate. I practically inhale the powdered donut before I've even unlocked my bike and devour another two donuts as I walk the bike out of the parking lot.

By the time I get to New College I'm sweating hard, perspiration trickling down my back and neck, slicking up the back of my neck. My fingers are sticky. I contemplate a sink shower somewhere on campus before putting on my costume. I have hours to kill, nothing to do, and I don't know anybody. Bathrooms have to be near the classrooms or in the cafeteria.

I rest my bike against a tree in the middle of a green field between a dorm looking building without a name and a squat building labeled 'Hamilton Cafeteria' to finish the rest of my donuts and dispose of the donut bag and my receipt. I wheel my bike around until I discover an odd hammock in a tree and climb up and take a nap. I'm tired, I'm still hungry, my limbs are heavy, and my gums ache from all of the sugar.

By the time I wake up from my nap, the sun is setting and I have no clue what time it is. I pull my phone out of my pocket to check. It's after seven. I slide down the tree, ripping the sleeve of my shirt. Stupid loose shirts that always get caught on everything!

Students stream away from campus, some in costumes like Indiana Jones. I hide my bike behind the tree and walk into Hamilton Cafeteria. The door is open, but most of the dozens of round tables are empty. I walk all the way to the middle of the fake tiled flooring before I spot the restroom sign.

I march into an empty stall and change into my party clothes, adding extra rips to my wife beater shirt and the fake blood leftover from last Halloween on all the clothes. In an effort not to make the entire bathroom into a crime scene, I carefully smear the blood into the clothes with my fingers and set paper towels down around myself to catch any splatters from my work.

The result is marvelous.

A girl with her head down barges into the bathroom looks up and sees me.

"Oh, my!" Her hands fly to her face.

I smile at her and she goes into the furthest stall, shaking her head.

I inspect my hair in the mirror. It's both oily and frizzy, the worst combination, but for a costume it works. I fluff it up even more, grimacing at the greasy texture.

I shove my sweat stained clothes into the grocery bag and head out of the bathroom after washing my hands. I'm not really sure what I'm doing or where I'm going, so I sit down on some random couches in the middle of the cafeteria to people watch and get my bearings.

"Dude, look what's on the free table," one college student exclaims, pointing at a six-foot table loaded with shirts and pants and surprisingly, boxers. The table is shoved against the wall near my couch.

The other guy laughs and picks up the underwear with two fingers and holds it up against his waist.

"Not my size. Too bad. I love SpongeBob," he says and tosses the pair of boxes back onto the table. They laugh and walk away.

I wonder if this is the clothing swap place Nichole talked about before. I walk up and take a look through the clothes. None of them are in my size. I dump my own dirty, sweaty clothes onto the table, dropping the grocery bag near them for good measure. I don't want them anymore and walk out of the cafeteria, ready for some fresh air and adventure.

"Wow, you look neat, what are you, some safari gone wrong type character?" Asks woman as she gathers up books and papers at one of the round tables near the door. I can't help staring at her hair. She has thick fiery orange curls that cascade all the way down her back.

"Uh yeah, something like that," I say, finally looking at her face instead of at her hair. She has amazingly bright green eyes with a set of lengthy false eyelashes and neon green eyeliner.

"Cool," she says.

"Thanks, hey any pre-parties going on?" I ask.

She chuckles. "Yeah, want to join?"

"Yes. I'm Vanessa," I say.

"Emma," she says with a smile.

She points to a part of campus I haven't been to. "We're in Goldstein."

I follow her around a building and through a walkway between two more buildings with balconies. Students peer out windows and a banner is strung across one sliding glass door that reads 'zombies is people too.' We walk past a large outdoor chess board and she leads me into the back of a three-story building.

"Come on in, we've got snacks and beer," Emma says as she walks through an open door on the first floor.

"Hey!" several guys shout as one utters a high pitched squeak.

The one who made the mouse sound comes forward and points at my chest for a closer look. "Wicked!"

One of the guys leaves through the door behind me. I'm standing in a small living space that adjoins a petite kitchen and a tiny living area. Five guys are squeezed shoulder to shoulder on the couch. Several more dudes line the floor, their backs against the wall as they watch T.V. I can smell fake cheese wafting over from the kitchen and it makes me swallow in anticipation.

"You guys hungry? We're about to make a run to the Third Court Café, wanna join us?" one of the couch guys asks me.

"Sure. Is it a restaurant?" I ask. I swallow again.

"Townie?" he asks.

"Uh?"

"She's cool," Emma says. "The Third Court Café is what we call the communal kitchen in the first year dorms when they make late night food and sell it."

"Oh, great," I say. I don't ask for clarification on 'Townie' since it probably just means outsider and I don't want to seem even more like I don't belong.

Guys peel themselves off the floor and we all flow out of the door in a hodge-podge. I notice one gal and the macaroni chef stay behind.

We move along like a school of fish, in a large, tight group. It turns out the Third Court Café is a fast food type setup in one of the shared kitchens where three students of questionable sobriety are cooking up a storm. Each of the four burners behind the galley style kitchen houses a large pot. A table holds even more pots and a portable grill plugged into one of the outlets above a rickety table. A handwritten sign above the table proclaims the food I could purchase, if I had any money left over from my donut raid that is.

Several words are crossed out on the menu. The choices, as I read them, are rice and beans, tortilla soup, fried plantains, and spaghetti.

I'm amazed these students have it together enough to pull out their crumpled $1s and $5s to pay for the food. Emma buys me a plate of rice and beans.

"I'll pay you back," I tell her.

"It's no problem."

We wander back to Goldstein where we spend the next hour watching YouTube videos and munching on our snacks. Surprisingly, the grub is good. The beans and rice are seasoned and flavorful.

"Want a beer?" Emma asks me.

"Sure."

I sip the Natty Ice slowly, hiding my grimace behind the can, but I finish mine before Emma finishes hers and she hands me another. By the time Emma gets up, crushing her can and tossing it into an overflowing blue recycle bin, my head is woozy. We walk over to where the party is thumping just past Third Court. Lights flash into our eyes and a large dinosaur hovers over a dance area. I giggle. Jurassic Park. Dinosaurs. Ha.

I slip away from the group and the open courtyard area for some fresh air. I go back to the tree I took a nap in. My bike is still behind it. I retrace my steps further to the field I walked across to get to the cafeteria. Two bouncy castles sit in the middle of the small field. As soon as I recognize them I break into a run wearing the biggest shit-eating grin.

The walls of the bouncy castle are shimmying and shaking from all the people. I slip inside, falling and trying to get up and falling again and again. The air tastes stale like body odor and cheap beer. I try to bounce up and down but end up bumping side to side against the wall of people. I giggle and push against everyone as we jump and jump. We're sardines in a can. We're grasshoppers. We're smelly and fun and this is amazing.

The sound of the air continuously being pumped into the castle overrides the distant music coming from the main court I walked by to get here. I giggle harder, which makes me fall and I take my closest neighbors down with me.

We end up in a dogpile of laughing, sweating, smelly bodies. I try to disentangle myself from the bodies around, above, and below me and catch against someone's necklace.

"Ow, ow, ow my hair!" I moan.

"Sorry," someone says.

I twist and turn as I try to free my hair from her clasping necklace. I can't stop giggling. Someone grabs for me and pulls me out of the bounce house entrance, yanking me and my hair too.

"What are you doing here?" Nichole asks.

I look up and down, scrutinizing her version of my outfit.

"I could say the same to you." I cross my arms and stare her down.

"Haven't you had enough of the arguing?"

"Haven't you had enough being a bitch?" I say back.

Nichole rolls her eyes.

"Fine, I'll be the bigger person. This isn't you, Vanessa. This is some wacked out girl trying to get attention and some BS type closure for something that happened years ago."

"I thought you were going to be the bigger person? All you're doing is being a big bitch."

"Have you been drinking?" Nichole yells after me.

I walk toward the other bounce house, looking at Nichole over my shoulder. I stick my tongue out at her and giggle as I walk right into someone and fall on my butt.

"Again? Seriously?" I must have built up some really bad karma to keep bumping into Ben. My head is still fuzzy and my tongue feels thick. I only had two beers, right?

Ben sways above me and Nichole finally moves from where I left her to stand over me. She helps me to my feet and I scrunch up my face in displeasure, pushing her with soft, noodly fingers. I turn to Ben.

"What are you doing here?" I accuse him.

"What are *you* doing here?" he echoes, his stance going more rigid. I see two of him and blink him back to one person.

"We were invited," I say pointedly. Why is he talking back?

"Everybody's invited," he slurs the words and opens his arms wide, his body relaxing into a stagger.

I almost put a hand out to keep him from falling over, but catch myself and so does he. He plants a foot in the grass like he's a telephone pole and pivots until he faces us again.

"You," he points a wavering finger at us and we both take a step back as if he might touch us. He's obnoxiously close. I sober down into reality.

Several more students wander out of the bounce house and stop next to us, as if sensing something's going to happen.

"Look at his face."

"Is he a high schooler?"

Whispers crowd around us.

Ben puts a hand out, probably to steady himself, but he overreaches and his hand pushes on my shoulder. I fall over again.

"Hey man, be cool," one of the gathered onlookers says to Ben.

"I'm cool," Ben says to the crowd that's growing by the second. Ben's voice gets louder, "I'm so cool. I'm the e-pit-o-me of cool."

I cringe. He takes a step toward us. I'm still on the ground and try to scramble backwards, but my belt loop gets caught on something and I'm stuck. He plants a foot next to my head.

He opens his mouth wide to say something else, but his swaying overcomes his ability to talk and he just staggers back and forth like he's in a windstorm. I'm afraid he'll topple over onto me or kick me in the face.

"I think you should leave," I say coldly from the ground.

He holds out his hands. "I'm invited. We're all invited." The belligerence is back in Ben's voice.

"Actually man, this is a closed campus, you have to have an invite to come here," the guy from before says, staring at the visible scars on Ben's neck.

"You from Booker?" someone asks from the back of the crowd.

"Look at me!" Ben shouts.

He sways again and punches one of the students from the crowd, his fist glancing off the guy's cheek. Ben staggers sideways and stumbles over to the bounce house. Nobody moves.

"I'm calling the campus police," says a gal and runs over to a glowing blue phone in the distance. It's a police box. The wooziness I felt earlier from the alcohol is dissipating at an alarming rate and my head is almost clear enough to do quadratic equations.

I disappear into the crowd and watch as campus police arrive and chase Ben around the field.

"What an asshole."

"Where do you think he got those scars?"

"Are they burn scars?"

I open my mouth to answer, but close it again and just watch. Students scatter in Ben's wake until the police officer finally catches up to him and grabs hold of his arm.

I slip away to the courtyard where the music is really blaring. Nichole is gone. Ben is gone. I can finally be myself, have fun, and forget everything. But I'm too aware of my thighs jiggling as I move and my arms are awkwardly waving every time I try to mimic some other student's dance moves. The party goes on around me and I stand still in the middle of it, like an invisible observer.

Ben was drunk and alone. What was he doing drunk at a college party and where's Becky? Guilt burrows its way into my mind. Did I push him to this when I hit him earlier at school?

I shoulder my way out of the crowded courtyard, back toward the hammock tree. I spot Nichole immediately. She's near my bike, standing by it like she's guarding it. I also see Mom and Walter near the parking lot, heading our way.

"I'm sorry, Vanessa. You've been drinking. I had to do it. I don't want you to get hurt, honest," Nichole says.

She steps to the side like the traitor that she is and lets Mom have me.

"I'm through talking to you," I tell Nichole.

"Vanessa!" Mom's shout is like a whip and she stares at me. I hang my head and walk up to her.

"Did-" Walter starts to say but stops.

I follow them to the Honda mutely. I don't know what else to do. Nichole wheels my bike behind us. Her mom's Jeep is parked next to the Honda.

"Do you mind taking Vanessa's bike back?" Mom asks Sharon.

"Not at all," Sharon says, but I can hear the disapproval in her voice.

Walter helps Sharon put my bike in the Jeep. We get in the car and drive home. Walter and Mom talk in hushed voices in her room. If I wanted to eavesdrop through the thin walls I could, but I don't want to hear them talking about me. I go to my room to change out of my ridiculous safari outfit. This was such a stupid idea. I throw the clothes on the floor and pull on my pajamas and get into bed, pulling the blankets over my head. I breathe in the familiar smell, perfumed with sleep and familiarity.

I never want to see Nichole again. I punch my bed, bringing my fists straight down at my sides and scrunch up my nose to keep from crying. I don't want to think about Nichole or Ben or something that will make me cry.

"Vanessa?" Mom knocks softly on the door.

She walks in and takes a seat on the edge of my bed. I sit up and fold my hands in my lap, the blanket falling off my face. Bluster pads in after her and curls up on the floor in his corner.

"I know things have been hard for you and I'm sorry to have brought Walter into your life so suddenly. I'm partially to blame for you acting out like you have."

I scoff out loud at her pity, but inside I feel terrible.

"I love you, Vanessa. I miss Dad, too. It hurts. I deal with it in my own way. Walter is a part of that, but I can see that you're not ready to let him be a part of your life right now so he won't be moving in anytime soon."

"Good."

"But your behavior has been unacceptable. You're still grounded."

"And the car?" I can't keep the hope out of my voice.

"The car is off limits until you can prove that you're ready for that type of responsibility again."

I slam myself back onto my bed with a groan. "I just wanted to be connected to Dad." The whisper falls out from between my lips.

"Pumpkin."

"No." I sit back up so fast that I see black spots. "He couldn't do them because he didn't have the time. I can't do them because I'm not good enough."

"Vanessa, that bucket list isn't real."

"Of course it's real, how could you say that?"

Mom holds up her hands and breathes in deep, closing her eyes.

"It's real. I'm real. Dad's dead, Mom. If he won't do them, I will. You told me to, you can't change your mind now."

Mom sighs out and rubs her hands down her cheeks. I lean back onto my pillow and close my eyes. The bed creaks as Mom gets up and quietly shuts the door.

Why would Mom say the bucket list isn't real? It's the most real thing I have left. Without it I'm just stupid and angry and friendless. I get out of bed and heft Bluster onto the bed. He whines and stares up at me. I push the covers around him and get in beside him, snuggling up against his fur. Bluster is real, just like the bucket list, and my motivation to complete it, with or without Nichole's help. I don't need her.

CHAPTER TWENTY-ONE - OVERCOME YOUR FEARS

Mom tries to wake me Monday morning when I don't get up. She won't let me stay home. I stumble out of bed and into the bathroom. The bathroom scale is back on the floor near the tub. I inch onto it for the first time in months and gasp at what I see. Ten more pounds. I promise to get rid of my candy stash, to stop eating Ritz at every opportunity, to stop – but I can't. The food challenge. Donuts. I can't sacrifice them. Brushing my teeth as fast as I can, I dump that resolve. I pause with my toothbrush sticking out of my mouth and pick up the scale and hide it behind our extra toilet paper rolls in the sink cabinet.

"Ugh," I groan as I catch sight of myself in the mirror. My hair is atrocious! It sticks out funky in the back and sides, like I wore a hat to bed. I spit and rinse as Bluster wags his way into the bathroom and I pat his head.

I race back to my room, now almost all the way awake and throw open my closet. It's a mess. Hangers dangle askew on the racks and clothes hang this way and that on them. Dirty and clean shirts and pants intermingle on the floor. I pick through the skirts on the side rack and find my favorite, a pleated dark blue that isn't too tight in the waist. It's actually Nichole's favorite, but it's also mine because she gave it to me. I hesitate before putting it on. Nichole isn't my friend anymore. I put it on anyway. I put on one of my loose white shirts and then push and pull myself into a denim vest that accentuates my cleavage and makes my shirt sleeves all billowy.

I grab the lighter and shove it in the skirt's shallow pocket hiding in the pleats.

I hustle out of the house, crooning goodbye to Bluster. Maybe if I miss the bus, Mom will let me use the car today. I get to the bus stop just in time and hop on behind the other students. All the empty seats are taken and I stare down at the ground as I scrunch into a seat next to a girl I don't know.

I get off the bus and head for the courtyard where Nichole and I used to hang out together before school.

The courtyard is chaotic. Students run every which way like crazed chickens. I spot Anja stumbling towards me and grab her wrist to slow her down.

"What's going on?" I ask her.

She shakes my hand off and points back toward the arts building. Before she can say anything, an alarm goes off, tearing through my head and filling it with a flashback.

It was the loudest sound I'd ever heard in my twelve years. Long and piercing, straight through my hands covering my ears. Tears came to my eyes from the sound and the acrid smoke filtering into the room. I coughed and turned to Mom. She mouthed something, the sound drowned out by the shrilling.

I cover my ears in the present with trembling hands as I shut my eyes tight. I push the memory down. My heart beats loud in my throat, but I'm not panicking. I'm breathing faster and thoughts are slamming around in my head, but I'm not in a fetal position on the ground. Yet. The alarm isn't as loud as the one in my memories and I open my eyes. The student swarm has slowed to a trickle. Anja is gone. I see Becky flitting across the courtyard. She runs up to me and shakes my shoulders.

"Have you seen Ben?" she shouts above the noise.

I uncover my ears. The alarm is far away, inside the building. I shake my head no. Why would I know where Ben is?

"What's going on?" I ask her.

"Lockdown."

Lockdown for what? "Shouldn't we be inside?" I ask.

"Lockdown," she repeats.

The alarm pounds in my skull and the panic claims me, clouding my head until I can't push it away like my memories. Where's Nichole? I hear two successive bangs above the sound of the alarm. My brain clears.

We never got around to the shooting range, but I know that sound. My worst nightmare is a fire. Smoke and flames and suffocation through carbon monoxide. Being burnt from the outside in. But that sound, it makes my heart beat hard like runners in the last few feet of a head-to-head race. That sound is real. A gunshot.

One time, in the Honda, Nichole and I were driving down the highway and we opened the windows and screamed our heads off. Just because. That is the scream I hear now, but louder. Nichole. From the direction of the gunshot. From the direction of the fire alarm. From the direction of the art building.

The alarm continues to ring. It is white noise in my ears. A sizzling panic grips me and I breathe raggedly, the air coming in gasps. Panic. The sound of the fire alarm. Its ring vibrates in the back of my head. The echoes of gunshots rip me apart. Why did Dad run into a burning building? The same reason I'm pounding up the stairs and yanking open the art door, the metal lighter slapping against my leg with every step.

What I see makes me want to vomit. No smoke blurs my vision. No flames light up the space. No smoke chars the inside of my nose.

This is no fire.

It's Ben.

He has a gun.

I'm completely unprepared for this.

Ben.

It's a small gun, if that matters. He points it at a group of students. They stand up against the whiteboard at the front of the classroom. Ben holds the gun with both hands. The door slams shut behind me. His eyes meet mine and they narrow.

The gun. It moves and the students flinch. The gun points at me. I gulp. I will not panic. Where's Nichole? The gun shakes. The alarm rings. The students edge toward the door. My right hand jiggles uncontrollably. My eyes twitch. I close them. No gun in my memories. The fear tightens around me. I was afraid then. I'm terrified now. The flashback pulls me in.

Eyes tight with fear, I stared unblinking at the front door to Estefano's, sirens in the background. My hands shook. Two firemen appeared, a limp man between them. Dad. Unconscious. But in his arms he cradled the young boy, face pressed tight to Dad's shirt. Dad and the boy were covered in soot. Dad's hair was a mess, his face blackened. His shirt and pants torn up, white dust coating his clothes. I looked away and cried into Mom's shoulder. All I could hear were the whispers, even the sirens faded into white noise. "He saved the boy."

I want the comfort of Bluster's fur, of a sugary donut, of anything but the sight of Ben and his scars and the reminder that my dad is dead.

The door behind bangs open. I jump, nerves on fire. I want to turn and look, but I can't look away from the gun. It wavers up and down as if it's waving at me. The door creaks shut with the smallest of clicks.

"Ben," I say, holding up my hands.

"No, don't even. Vanessa."

"But —"

"Vanessa!" Nichole shouts behind me, but I'm too mesmerized by the boy with the gun. I can't take my eyes off him.

"Shut it!" he shouts, squeezing his eyes closed. A shock of hair falls over his forehead and he brushes it away with one hand. Three fingers. Another reminder. The barrel vibrates up and down in his other hand.

I hold my hands up higher, mind racing. What do I do? What do I do? Nichole bumps into my side. I can't look at her. Words die in my throat.

You know how they say your life flashes before your eyes in the face of death? All the moments I was mean to Ben flash through my mind. The countless times I'd pushed him, yelled at him, called him names. Accused him of playing with matches. Laughed at him.

He stares me down and I wince. Fear turns into guilt and I want to disappear. Away from those accusing eyes of his.

"At least you looked at me. You saw me for what I really am," Ben growls.

Is he talking to me or Nichole? Even if it was his fault Dad died, I shouldn't have been so awful to Ben, taken everything out on him.

"Ben," the word is a whisper, too small and too late. An apology would mean nothing. Actions speak louder than words and my shout is a whisper. I mouth the word sorry. It's not good enough. I'm not good enough. I've done everything wrong. I'm screaming in my head. *Sorry. So sorry. Sorry. I see you, Ben. I see you.*

Adrenaline throbs in my veins. My hands tremble from the need to run, to move, to stop Ben. The gun keeps me rooted to this spot. *Move. Move. Run.*

Ben's wrist makes a sharp, slight snap to the left. The gun now points to just past my left shoulder. Where Nichole stands beside me. Time freezes and pushes me off the floor. I twist and jump to the side. Ben's fingers twitch on the gun. Adrenaline pushes me off the ground. I'm in front of Nichole and falling.

The sound is deafening. An explosion of noise too big for one bullet. I didn't feel anything when he pulled the trigger, his arms popping up from the recoil. It's a funny thing, really. All of this and he misses. I stare into his eyes. I've seen them before. Young Ben's eyes when he was in Dad's arms. Eyes full of guilt. For shooting at Nichole? For missing?

I can't find my train of thought. Wasn't this a big, life-changing thought? I'm glad Nichole wasn't hurt. I'm glad Ben didn't actually shoot anyone. I think I understand now. I think…

I'm on the floor. I'm still looking at Ben. He towers above and beyond me. Out of reach. It occurs to me finally.

"I forgive you," I say, but it's too late.

He holds the gun to his head.

"This was never about you. I started the fire. It was always an accident, but now I'm in control," he says.

When you are at fault for the death of another, how does that feel?

He pulls the trigger and the sound echoes over and over in my mind before a cloud passes through my vision and I'm reaching and reaching for that epiphany. This was it, this was my moment and I've blown it. My concentration taken from me at the last minute and all I can think is this is such a crazy stupid thing I did and for what?

    My last thought before I close heavy eyelids is Nichole....

CHAPTER TWENTY-TWO – HERO'S CHALLENGE

"You didn't even hardly get shot," Nichole says to me, pulling her chair up to my bed with a scraping sound.

I'm already tired of talking about Ben, but it's the latest topic in everyone's minds. It's only been a few days since it happened. .

"Yes, I know," I reply.

"And yet you passed out and now aren't even going to school? You don't look that bad. You hardly hit your head when you fell," she offers.

I've got a lighter shaped bruise on my thigh where the bullet bounced off and grazed my skin, leaving a comet like trail along my leg.

"Can I see it?" Nichole asks.

"No."

It's near one of my stretch marks, like white nails scratched my inner thigh. And now I have a matching red streak on the other side of my thigh from the bullet. In the middle is the blotchy, blue bruise with a square outlined in red where the corners of the lighter cut into my skin.

Nichole's sitting on the edge of her chair beside my hospital bed her hands clasped, eyes looking everywhere but at me. It's good to talk to her again, to have a friend again. We didn't even have to make up. Me jumping in front of the bullet was enough of an apology.

I know without having to ask. In the end, even though I know I did the right thing, it wasn't enough to stop Ben. But, I realize, not everything is possible. Sometimes it's not our fault when we can't do the impossible. Ben was an impossible. The Hero's Challenge is an impossible. The bucket list is an impossible.

"There are so many crazy rumors. They say you saved three witless freshman art students. They all know you saved someone at least," Nichole says.

"I don't really want to talk about it," I say, staring at the wall behind her head. I frown and sniffle back tears.

Ben, more so in death than in life, is tearing me apart. The guilt has replaced the bucket list in my mind. It's all I can think about.

"Fine, but you know you're going to have to. Everyone thinks you're a hero and that screams for media attention. I've already had two reporters question me."

I sit up suddenly, "They don't think we're involved?"

"No, stupid," she crimps up her lips. "They want to know the scoop on why you rushed in when everyone was running the other way." Nichole pauses. "Thanks for that, by the way."

She stands up and goes to the window, staring out at the dull view of the parking lot below us.

"Speaking of, here's your lighter."

Nichole hands me the lighter and I burst into a grin. Stupid thing saved my life.

Mom bursts in and Nichole steps aside.

"I'm so glad you're okay. I will never ever make you go to school when you don't feel up for it and I'm sorry about Walter and bullying you into eating his food and not listening when you were trying to tell me something was wrong," she babbles.

I roll my eyes. "You were parenting. I get it. We've had this conversation already."

"But you're still grounded," Mom adds.

"Way to parent, Mrs. S," Nichole says.

Mom sits down and worries at her bottom lip. "I never knew the trouble you were having with that boy."

"It wasn't him, Mom. It was me."

"Of course it wasn't you. I'm just sorry for his parent's loss. First their business and now their only son."

She stares off out the window. She doesn't have to say what our loss was.

"When can I get out of here?" I ask.

"They've already started the discharge process. I talked with your doctor while you were napping."

"Oh, great," I say. "So that's it?"

"That's it. Let's get you home. I'll go check with the nurses about this." Mom points to my monitors. I smile at her and she walks out of the room with slow measured steps.

Nichole steps up to my bed. "Now that you're awake and feeling better, I think I should tell you something." Her eyes flit to the open door.

I sit up. "What? What is it?" My voice rises.

"Nothing bad. Really. Do you remember your dad's bucket list?"

"Duh. Why?"

Nichole drops her head. She's making me uncomfortable and I squirm.

"I wrote the bucket list."

I laugh.

"Seriously, I planted it behind the picture. I wanted you to get out of yourself, to leave the house and try new things."

"Shut the smack up."

"I'm sorry. I didn't know that it would lead to all of this. That you would go crazy and get all wrapped up in Ben and everything."

"I can't believe you would do something like that."

"You needed a push," Nichole explains.

"No, I don't believe you." I push the blankets aside, my feet hitting the floor, pain shooting across my thigh. I sway and grab for the bed and miss. Nichole reaches out to steady me and I push her away, falling back onto the bed. "You wouldn't do that. You wouldn't do that!" I yell at her.

Mom rushes back into the room, followed by two nurses in matching teal scrubs. I close my lips tight and breathe heavily through my nose. I open my mouth to gasp at the air.

I wait for the smoke to invade my nostrils, for flames to creep up behind my eyelids, for memories to distract me from real time.

Nothing happens.

I open my eyes.

"Vanessa? Pumpkin?" Mom asks.

I hunch over, becoming smaller on the bed, head whirling. But the smoke and everything. Gone. Forever?

"Why would you do that?" My voice is barely above a whisper.

Nichole looks at Mom with pleading in her eyes.

"Vanessa, I told you not to get too wrapped up in that list," Mom says.

"You knew?" My voice comes out barely above a whisper.

I wait for the anger to hit me, to push me off the bed and out the door. I wait. Nothing.

Dr. Bryan's voice commands me in my head, "count to ten. Breathe. Think about what you want to say. Don't let your emotions have control. You control your actions and your words."

I see Dad in my memories. Not at the restaurant. I see him smiling and laughing and waving at strangers. "Do you know that guy?" he asks. I shake my head and laugh and he waves. I wave too, giggling. Ten years old and I didn't know any better. All I knew was that I loved my Dad and he was my whole world.

I turn to Mom first. "I don't like Walter, but not because of him, because you're always spending time with him. And I hate vegan organic gluten-free food. Just because you're on a diet doesn't mean I want to be on one. I'm fine the way I am." I'm not completely fine with the way I look, but that's not really important right now. "And I promise to pay you back for the credit card charges and the money I borrowed from your dresser.

Mom stares aghast at me.

"I'm ready to go now," I tell one of the nurses.

He moves toward me and starts unhooking the wires and pulling out my IV. When he's done he walks out.

"So you're okay?" Nichole breaks the silence.

"I can't believe you lied to me," I say. "Both of you."

Mom and Nichole look at me with guilty frowns. I hold up a hand before they can say anything.

"But I forgive you. I don't understand it all, I might never get it, but for now all I can do is forgive you and maybe someday, I'll let it go."

Tears trace twin paths down Mom's cheeks and she leans in to hug me. Nichole waits back, a relieved and proud smile on her face. The nurse brings in a wheelchair and helps me into it.

"We're going to talk later," Mom assures me.

"I know." I sigh. "Now, please, take me home?"

Mom smiles at me. Her phone rings. She looks at it for a moment.

"Hello?" she says into the phone.

I watch as she nods and frowns.

"I'll ask her," she says. She holds the phone away from her face. "It's ABC 7, they want to do an interview."

Nichole shakes her head no. Mom's expression is blank. I wet my lips. Do I want to talk about it? It couldn't hurt, right? "Okay."

Mom puts the phone back to her ear. "You can come to the house this afternoon." Pause. "Three." Pause. "Yes, thank you." She hangs up and turns back to me.

"Are you sure?"

"No, but it can't be as hard as some of the other crazy things I've done lately."

Mom reaches over to pat my hand. "I'll go get the car. See you in a minute."

She walks out. The nurse wheels me down the hall, through the maze of the hospital and out into the sunshine. Nichole follows us.

"Thanks," I tell the nurse as Mom pulls up in the Honda.

Nichole helps me into the passenger seat and she gets into the back. I've never wanted to go home so much in my life.

I fall asleep on the ride home and wake up when Nichole shuts the back door.

"I'm so tired," I yawn.

"That's okay. Here, let me help you." Mom helps me out of the car and I lean on her and hop-step to the front door. "Do you want to do the interview in your room or out in the living room?"

"My room. I think I'm going to take another nap. You can go home now, Nichole."

"I'll stay here with you. I'll read one of your books."

I shrug and hop-step into my room and onto my bed with a sigh.

My eyes are starting to close when Nichole speaks again. "Are you sure you're okay?"

"You mean with how you totally lied about Dad having a bucket list and everything I've done this year having been a total lie?"

Nichole hangs her head with a heavy sigh.

"I still can't really believe it. Everything was so real."

"It still is real. You did those things. I've never ridden a motorcycle."

"Hold up. You've never ridden a motorcycle? I've done something crazy that you haven't!"

Nichole smiles.

"I guess I'm not really mad, just disappointed. Not at you, really. At the world or something."

"Yeah. I feel like such a total bitch."

"When aren't you a bitch?" I giggle.

"Friends?"

"Best friends. Now eff off so I can take my nap."

Nichole slinks out of the room and shuts the door.

I wake up to knocking.

"Can I come in?" Mom asks.

"Yeah," I say groggily as I wake up. My eyes are unfocussed and I blink several times before I can read the clock on my phone.

Mom walks in, closes the door and sits down on the bed.

"Why didn't you wake me, it's almost time for the interview!"

"I didn't want to interrupt your sleep."

"Ugh, Mom. You need to do things sometimes. You're the parent. Be the parent."

Mom purses her lips. "The lady from ABC 7 is here. Her name

is Sofia Rodriguez," she says.

"Oh. How's my hair?" I sit up in bed.

Mom runs her fingers through my long hair.

"Do you want it in your ponytail?" she asks.

"You noticed?"

"Of course. You like to snack on Ritz crackers and watermelon Jolly Ranchers are your favorite flavor. You keep pushing the scale out of sight and your favorite donut is glazed."

"Wow."

I haven't eaten a donut in front of Mom for years.

"How do you remember?"

"Oh, Pumpkin. You're my daughter. I love you." She reaches over and hugs me gently. "But you're still grounded and I have a list of chores for you to do when you're ready so you can pay me back."

I groan and lie back in bed, but I can't help the grin spreading across my face.

"Thanks Mom. I think I'll do the interview with my hair down."

"Ready then?"

"Ready as I'll ever be."

Mom springs off the bed and with a last smile to me she opens the door.

"We're ready for you, Sofia," she calls into the hallway.

Heels click on the wood floor, reminding me of Nichole. Sofia is nothing like Nichole. She's got hair that would rival Emma's from New College. It's styled like a halo around her head, curls cascading to her shoulders. She wears a tight fitting dress that ends above her knees and bright red high heels that match her fire engine red lipstick.

A camera crew follows behind her.

After a brief setup, Sofia turns to me.

"Alright. Ready?" she asks.

Mom tucks a loose hair behind my ear and smiles down at me.

The cameraman says something quietly to Sofia and she nods curtly at him.

They start out their segment with the camera fixed on Sofia, without me in the shot.

"Last Monday there was an attack at Booker High School that ended in one death, that of the assailant. In an attempt to get information about this attack, I am here today to speak with one of the witnesses, Vanessa Smith."

Sofia walks over to my bed and I sit up straighter.

"Now, Vanessa, "When everyone else was running away from the situation, what made you go toward the source of the chaos?" she asks.

"Um," I stall.

Why did I go in?

"It's kind of personal, I guess."

I should really say something more. But who runs toward a gun or a fire?

"Everyone wants to do well in their life and I just took this moment as my turn," I say lamely.

Do something for someone else without expecting something in return. From Dad's bucket list, well, Nichole's list.

"That was very brave of you. Did you know at the time who the gunman was?"

"No. I thought Nichole was in trouble."

"So you went in toward danger not knowing what you would find?"

"That's about the gist of it."

I resettle myself on my pillows.

"How well did you know the attacker?" she asks.

"Everyone knew him."

Ben was hard to miss. Everyone stared at him when he walked by. Everyone knew him by face if not by name. But I can't say that.

"Did anyone think he was unstable?"

"All teenagers are unstable." She waits so I add, "It's a tough time of life. You're just figuring out who you are, where you come from, and who you want to be, what you want to do in life. Sometimes the answers aren't so easy, ya know?"

"What do you want to do in life?" her question cuts through me. What do I want? I look straight at the camera.

"I want to beat the Hero's Challenge. I want to leave my mark on the world for me and my dad." I pause. "And my best friend, Nichole."

Sofia turns to the camera, "The Hero's Challenge is a local food challenge that has remained undefeated for the last nine months at the Hero's Bar and Grill. The winner of this challenge gets a spotlight on the news and a $550 certificate for the restaurant. However as of two days ago, the restaurant is closed until further notice."

She pauses and then looks at me. "Why is it so important for you, this particular challenge? Now that you've saved someone's life, wouldn't you say that you've left your mark on the world?"

"Yes and no. The Hero's Challenge is unfinished business and will probably remain that way. It's too hard. My dad would be proud if I were to win something like that." Even if it wasn't ever on his bucket list.

"Isn't your dad proud of what you did at the school, saving your best friend?"

"But Dad didn't even know those other people in the restaurant!" I sputter. Again, I'm thinking about Dad's actions. "It's not just about Dad. He cared about strangers, but he also cared about his family. He wanted me to be a good person and he was a good role model. I want to be a role model, too."

Dad was always proud of me. I swipe at my eyes, hiding the gesture in a scratch to my temple as if I'm thinking, then I smile at the camera.

"The Hero's Challenge was for my dad. I ran into that building for me. Even though I couldn't defeat the Challenge or save Ben, I know that my dad would be proud. I don't blame Ben anymore for my dad's death. I just wish I could have told him that before -

before everything."

"Thank you, Vanessa, for telling your story and inspiring us to overcome our own challenges. This is Sofia Rodriguez with ABC 7."

The news people pack up and leave and Sofia bends down so she's not towering over me and my bed.

"Thank you for telling your story. This segment will run during the evening news hour, though we may have to cut out the part with Ben's name until the investigation closes. Thank you so much for allowing this interview. It's important to tell the truth."

I tell Mom I'm tired and she leaves me too after another large, crushing hug. Then I'm alone. I eventually fall asleep, but am roughly woken. Groggily, I open my eyes and see Nichole standing over the bed.

"You're still here?" I ask.

"Of course. I can't believe you were still sleeping," she says.

"What time is it?"

"Five something."

"Did you see the news segment?"

"Yeah, that's why I'm here..."

"Do you think it'll be on the news again?"

"I don't really think-"

Mom walks in with her laptop and sets it on the bed.

"You didn't wake me!" I accuse.

"It's online now. See?" she swivels the laptop toward me and I pull it forward. I press play.

My segment runs. I look pretty darn pathetic in my bed, but at least my hair looked good. Maybe I should wear my hair down more often. I slide the laptop away from me as it nears the end, but it's not over. The segment auto plays to another, where Sofia welcomes viewers again, this time from outside Booker High School.

My mouth drops open. The shot is of the high school. People crowd around the outside of the cafeteria in a hodgepodge of a line.

Sofia Rodriguez approaches the camera.

"This is the scene outside Booker High School. The response to Vanessa Smith's indirect plea has been overwhelming and all these people have shown up to support her. She may not be able to complete the Hero's Challenge, but all these supporters have pledged to win for the student who died and Vanessa's father. The school and local fire department, Station 17, are sponsoring the food challenge.

"Did you-?" I start to say.

Nichole shakes her head.

"This is amazing. They're there right now?" I sit up in bed. "We have to go!" I forget where I am in my excitement.

Mom walks in and rubs her eyes, yawning. "Sweetie?" she says.

"I need your help," I say to both Nichole and my mom.

"Pumpkin, maybe you should lie back down," Mom says to me.

"I'm 18, Mom. I can take care of myself, plus I just slept for like fifteen hours. I think I've had enough sleep."

"Okay. I'm listening."

"I want to go to Booker."

"Are you sure?"

"Yes. I'm sure."

"Okay, I'll get the car."

"Now let's get us some Hero's Challenge!" I say.

We drive in anxious silence to the school. The parking lot is packed and Mom drives up to the building and parks in a no parking zone.

"Mom!" I say.

"What? You can't walk all that way," she explains.

Nichole giggles and gets out. I get out, leaning on the cane the hospital gave me. A line of people, students and parents and people I've never seen before trails from the inside of the building all the way to the corner of the parking lot.

Someone spots me and points. I almost don't notice, but it causes a cascade of pointing and the noise level outside rises.

I make up my mind and walk resolutely to the doors, limping with the help of the cane.

Becky walks out the door. Her eyes are red-rimmed and her shirt is inside out.

"Becky?"

She looks up at me and stops, her whole body straightening until she's taller than me and much more formidable than I've ever seen her.

Nichole puts a hand on my upper arm. I stare straight at Becky. She has no power over me.

"It's okay to be mad," I tell her.

She sniffs and doesn't look me in the eye. Nichole lets go of my arm to give Becky a hug. Becky glances at me over Nichole's shoulder and nods once. I smile at her and nod back.

"This is your party," Becky says as Nichole backs up and takes my arm.

"I'm just here for the food." I grin at her and she walks off, shaking her head.

The door opens again and a guy walks out. A big grin lights up his face when he sees me. He holds the door open for our party and watches us go in, grinning like an idiot. I hear him behind me talking to the person at the front of the line.

"Was that Vanessa?"

His voice fades as the door shuts closed and we enter into chaos. It's late in the day, the school should be empty, but it's packed like a Cheesecake Factory on a Sunday after church. I gawk. Every chair is occupied.

We stand in the doorway, next to the line of people still waiting for a table or seat to open up. The cafeteria staff run around in their hairnets and aprons. Nichole and Mom don't move, waiting for me to indicate what I want to do now that we're here. Shouts and yells and timers are going off all over the place. The sound is deafening, but the smell is even more overpowering. The frantic looks of the cafeteria staff are comical. They can't keep up.

It's complete bedlam and it takes my breath away.

"Hero's!" I hear chanted from all sides and corners of the cafeteria.

I continue to stand in the doorway until a couple trying to leave have to maneuver around us. The commotion is overwhelming. The place barely looks like the school's cafeteria.

I march up to a random table with a lopsided step.

"Vanessa!" A girl from our school says excitedly. "I'm Annie. I'm a sophomore and I was totally inspired by your speech!"

"Want to watch me decimate this challenge?" A guy from the table asks me.

I don't know who he is, but he looks our age. I smile at him.

"Can you guys tell me what's going on?" I ask.

"Don't you know?" Annie asks, looking at me incredulously.

Annie indicates the cafeteria with a sweep of her hand that ends with her almost smacking the guy in the nose, "This all for you."

"And your dad and Ben," the guy adds.

"School was let out early today, but we stayed to support you," Annie adds.

I sweep my eyes once more across the cafeteria. Now I can see what is really going on. Platters crowd the tables. Glasses of milk litter tables in place of soda. Almost everyone here is attempting the Challenge. Every table has a timer. Everyone is eating the same thing, or attempting to, and tables are littered with half-eaten Hero's burgers.

I turn slowly like I'm in a movie, taking in all that I'm seeing and smelling and hearing. A roar whooshes in my ears and I blink stars. The roar steadily rises until I can't hear myself think. It's the thunder of a hundred people clapping. Vision clearing, I see that almost every single person is standing by their chair. They are clapping and cheering, some even punching hands in the air. And they're all looking at me.

My face radiates heat and I want to hide my blush from the crowd, but Nichole claps me on the back and reaches out to grab my hand. She holds it up in the air and gives a hoot herself. The crowd roars louder, people stamping their feet, cheering, and clapping. The noise pushes at me and my fingers twitch.

Nichole seems to sense my discomfort and pulls me over to an unoccupied chair, but instead of helping me sit, she tries to get me to step up onto the seat. I baulk at it and Nichole leans down to whisper in my ear.

"They're here because of you and what you said on the news. Give them what they want."

It's not Nichole's words that finally prompt me to take a halting step onto the swaying chair with my good leg. I have to say something. Nichole stays close. The clapping dies away as slowly as it grew. Several timers go off. I scan the crowd. Some kids rock side to side restlessly, already bored.

"Thanks, I really appreciate all of you showing up, or rather, staying in school," I start.

"Louder," someone yells from the back corner.

I clear my throat nervously and tilt my chin up as if that will project my voice farther. I try to speak louder.

"Thank you all for coming. The Hero's Challenge is something that is really important to me, especially as I failed at it. Again and again. My dad was always into these weird Guinness World Record type challenges. I wanted to beat the Challenge for him in honor of his memory. It may look like I can eat, but I just couldn't finish the Hero's Challenge."

Puzzlement stands out on people's faces. A few people titter. I clear my throat.

"Uh, my dad was a hero in his own way all his life because he was a dad, my dad. He was no more and no less a hero on the day he died. Uh."

I glance down at Nichole. She lifts her chin at me and smiles. I wet my lips.

"Thanks for coming." My voice squeaks and I clear my throat. What am I supposed to say?

I scan the crowd and almost fall over when I see Ben's parents and Becky sitting in a corner.

"I stood up. I let go. Now it's your turn to stand up for something or someone important in your life. Something that's challenging you right now. This challenge, the Hero's Challenge, I haven't given up, but I want you to beat this Challenge. For me. For my dad. For Ben. Whoever can beat this thing, well, I can only say my dad and I will be very proud of you!"

I breathe. Clapping resumes. I step down from the chair.

"I always wanted you to let that go. I wanted you to have fun and to think that some stupid food challenge could change your life," Nichole says.

"I know. Thanks."

But I'm really saying that I forgive her for lying to me about Dad's bucket list and making me face my fears at the restaurant and with the lighter. She's my best friend.

Nichole grabs my hand. "Are you up for another surprise?" she asks. "Ben's parents are here."

I look around and spot Stefan. I nod to Nichole and we walk, hand in hand, up to Stefan and Maria.

"I'm so very sorry," I say.

Tears threaten the corners of my eyes and I try to keep them from falling. Ben's mother, Maria Russo, reaches over to hug me and I let out sobs. I let out all the anger I felt at Ben and at my losses. I let out all the tears that needed to get out.

We cry together for a few moments before breaking apart from our embrace.

"Because of this," I say as I sweep my arm out to indicate the full and lively cafeteria. "Ben will never be forgotten. Because of you, my dad will never be forgotten. Thank you." The words feel right for once. I'm not some stupid, fat, ignored person.

Maria and Stefan clasp hands and walk away. I look out over the cafeteria, admiring the chaos.

This isn't exactly what I wanted out of the Hero's Challenge, but it's exactly what I needed. I've beaten death, guilt, and anger. I've forgiven but not forgotten. This one's for you, Dad.

VANESSA AND NICHOLE'S BONUS BUCKET LIST

- Try laughter yoga
- Visit a castle
- Go out in public in your pajamas
- Do the top 5 tourist things in your city or state
- Have breakfast in bed
- Learn how to crack an egg with one hand
- Master a yoga pose
- Spend a day without saying a word
- Make ice cream
- Climb all the stairs in the tallest building in your city
- Try the hottest sauce your town has to offer
- Buy an original painting
- Be a character in a haunted house
- Write a positive note and leave it in a library book
- Make up your own lyrics to a popular song
- Participate in a zombie walk
- Learn a magic trick
- Ride a Segway
- Fast for a day
- Eat a bug

Read on for a sneak peek of Book 2 - Seize the Donut

CHAPTER ONE – NICHOLE

Where are you? Nichole texted her best friend, Vanessa, her fingers stabbing at the keys. Nichole was terrified that Sharon, her mom, might discover Johnny's wallet. The wallet he couldn't find after their extravagant meal. The meal Nichole paid for as every second pushed her further and further into panic.

"Vanessa!" Nichole said in complete exasperation. Nichole kicked a toe into the pavement and stared daggers at some dude who looked away from her chest as he went into the 7-11. She noted with dismay that she'd smeared grit into the toe of her wedges.

"I'm like ten minutes away. I'll be right there, chill," Vanessa replied. "Just hurry up, okay?" Nichole pleaded. "Going as fast as I can," Vanessa said. Nichole punched "end." She shouldn't be taking her frustration out on Vanessa, but it was hard to keep her growing panic to herself. A woman exiting the 7-11 wrinkled her nose at Nichole and steered wide around her. Nichole stood, leaning against the side of the building for another ten minutes, anxiously peering around for Vanessa's Honda Civic. She slid to the ground in dismay, not caring if she got her short shorts and halter top dirty. After another ten minutes, Vanessa pulled up and flashed her lights.

Nichole rocketed up, accidentally slamming the car door as she got in.

"Sorry, Mom made me clean up after Bluster," Vanessa said. "He puked all over the rug."

Nichole crossed her arms after strapping on her seat belt. "Why couldn't Johnny drop you off?" Vanessa asked, pulling onto the road.

"I already told you. Mom doesn't like Johnny." "So?" Vanessa said. "Well," Nichole said, looking away from her bestie. "I, uh, never told you but Johnny's a bit older than me."

Vanessa glanced briefly at Nichole. "I didn't want you to worry," Nichole added. "Nichole, how long have we been friends?" Vanessa asked. "Four years. Ever since the beginning of high school." "Exactly. I thought you were done keeping me out of the loop." The unspoken words, "since last year" echoed in Nichole's mind, making her wince. Yes, she'd fudged the truth to Vanessa when they were seniors in high school, but she'd eventually come clean. Besides, it was for Vanessa's own good.

Nichole glanced briefly toward Vanessa's upper leg where she'd been grazed by a bullet just months ago when that little lie had caused major consequences.

"You're right. I shouldn't have. Can you go any faster?" "Why are you in such a hurry?" Vanessa asked. Nichole chewed on her fingernail and shifted in her seat. "Johnny left his wallet at my house."

"So. No big deal." Nichole's right foot pressed down as if she could make the car accelerate.

"You can tell me," Vanessa insisted. "He's 29." "Shut up!" Vanessa exclaimed. "Yeah." "No wonder your mom doesn't like him."

"She doesn't know!" Nichole said vehemently. "You sure about that? Where's his wallet?" Nichole sighed. "I don't know. It, uh, might be in her bed." "No!" Vanessa said. "Yes." "You should have told me. I would have come sooner." Nichole shook her head. "You had to take care of Bluster. I understand."

"I came as soon as I was done." "I can tell. What are you wearing, anyway? That shirt is past your knees," Nichole said.

"It's my corgi shirt and he looks just like Bluster," Vanessa insisted Vanessa always wore baggy clothes, but this one was like an ill-fitting dress.

"I only wear it around the house. And I know it's way too baggy and I know you're always telling me I don't have to wear baggy clothes."

"Well, fashion aside, I'm glad you came as soon as you did. I know how long it can take you to make dressing decisions."

Vanessa smiled as they turned into their neighborhood. "You ready? What if your mom found it?"

"She would have sent Lewis to come get me." "Your mom's harsh, but not that bad," Vanessa protested as she pulled into

Nichole's driveway.

"It's been getting worse all summer. She's been on my case to do something and work harder and clean my room. She can't even clean the house and she expects me to clean my room!"

Vanessa glanced over and narrowed her eyes. "Don't chew on your fingernails," she said.

Nichole pulled her finger from her lips and looked out the window. "Whatever happens, you can stay at my house tonight, deal?" Vanessa said.

Nichole nodded her head, her eyes focused on the closed front door of her house. She got out slowly. Before she could take two steps from the Civic, Sharon burst through the door and threw something small at Nichole. It hit her square in the chest and bounced to the ground. A familiar red Rolling Stones sticker stared back at her.

"You lied to us!" Sharon barked. Nichole bent down to pick up Johnny's wallet. "Don't ignore me, Nichole. And you!" Sharon pointed a threatening finger at Vanessa who shrunk into herself as if her shirt was a security blanket. "You are a bad influence."

Vanessa glanced back at Nichole and took a step back toward the car. "This is my house. I don't care that you're 18. When you live in my house, you live by my rules. I will not have my daughter dating someone more than 10 years older than her! What they hell were you thinking?"

"Mom," Nichole pleaded. "Don't 'Mom' me!" Sharon said, holding up a hand. "You've gone behind my back enough. I don't know how you got involved with that boy at Booker, but now you've lied straight to my face about Jerry!"

"Johnny," Nichole corrected, her eyes narrowing. Sharon threw up her hands. "How do you know he's not married? Hm? He could have any number of STDs! It didn't escape my notice that I found his wallet under my bed."

"Calm down, Mom!" Nichole shouted. She stepped closer to Sharon, jutting her chin out in defiance. She was still an inch shorter than her mother, so she placed her hands on her hips and glared."

"Why can't you go to college like Vanessa and meet a nice college boy?" Sharon said. "Someone closer to your age?"

Vanessa gasped behind Nichole. "I don't have to take this. Like you said, I'm over 18. I'm an adult," Nichole shouted.

"Not in my house!" Sharon shouted back. "Fine, then I won't stay in your house. I'll move in with Johnny. And he's only 29!" Nichole yelled.

"What!" Sharon spluttered. "You want me out? Then I'm out and I won't be coming back." Nichole stared over at Vanessa. "Come on Ness, let's get out of here." Vanessa opened and closed her mouth several times before following mutely to the car and getting in. "But," Vanessa said.

"Just drive," Nichole said, crossing her arms over her chest like a second seat belt. "I'm not coming back until she's gone," she added. Vanessa backed out of the drive and idled in the street for a moment.

"Just go!" Nichole cried. Vanessa gunned it and the car screeched off down the road. The 2008 charm hooked onto her graduation tassel clinked against her rearview mirror.

"I don't like this," Vanessa said after they'd left their neighborhood behind.

Nichole sighed, her thoughts jumbling into one cohesive thought. Johnny. He was older, he would know what to do. "I can stay with Johnny," Nichole said. "I'm sorry you had to be there. You're okay, right?"

"Yeah, I can't believe Sharon yelled at you like that." "It's been a long time coming. We've been arguing for months. Whatever."

"Are you sure Johnny's the best choice?" Vanessa asked. "Not you too!" Nichole blurted, sitting up straight in her seat. "Don't take this the wrong way, but you barely talk about him and you just told me how old he is. You've only been dating for a month. Are you sure he's the right one?"

"I didn't want you to worry. After Ben and graduating and you going off to college, I didn't want to create problems that weren't problems. And we've been dating for almost six weeks."

"And yet here you are. You don't even have a toothbrush,"

Vanessa pointed out.

Nichole slumped in the seat in defeat. "I'm taking my car. It was my present after all. I'll have Johnny drive me back tonight when Mom's out at her shift. Lewis is almost never home."

"Okay, it's your life. I don't like it, but I'm here for you." "Thanks, Ness. I owe you." "I'm still paying you back for saving my life, even though you lied about my Dad's bucket list. I'd call it even."

"Don't even start on the bucket list thing again! I only lied about it because it was for your own good," Nichole said vehemently.

"Have to keep you on your toes. And FYI, it's only been a couple of months," Vanessa said. "And besides," Vanessa emphasized the word dramatically. "You A wrote a fake bucket list, B stashed it where I'd find it and think it was my Dad's, and C only told me the truth after months had gone by and Ben nearly shot us."

"I get it. I get it." Nichole held up her hands in surrender and Vanessa smiled.

"So, where are we going exactly?" Vanessa asked. "He's South by the Westfield." "Nichole! That's like Osprey!" "Please?" With a sigh, Vanessa nodded her head and made a U-turn, heading down to I-75. Nichole's hands shook the closer they got to South Sarasota. What if Johnny didn't want her to stay?

Seize the Donut (For the Love of Donuts Book 2)
Friendships should never be taken for granted.

The ups and downs of high school forged an unbreakable bond between Vanessa and Nichole. Summer's over and Vanessa is preparing for life at the local liberal arts college. Without her best friend by her side, Vanessa starts to chart her own path. Navigating new friendships and relationships proves easier said than done.

Nichole got kicked out of her mother's house, lives with strangers in a sketchy neighborhood and commutes across town for her job in retail. She doesn't always make the right choices and she can only blame herself when things go wrong.

Something's gotta give. Who will make the first move - or will fate intervene to remind each of them of the importance of their bond.

ACKNOWLEDGEMENTS

Donuts everywhere, especially Daddy's Donuts for making me believe in donuts again.
Suzy Vitello for her inspiration.
Squawk Valley Writers for their helpful critiques and motivation.
FreeValley Publishing for their continual support.
NaNoWriMo for the time and motivation to write the first draft.
D'ariel for her wonderfully helpful critique and handy editing additions in the early stages.
My beta readers who never told me not to tell the story, but told me which parts wouldn't and didn't work. Thanks Jami, Danielle, Katherine, Katharine and Amy.
To the first print readers and reviewers, especially Karen E. for her eye for details.
To Annie my editor for telling me to show and showing me where to tell among other necessary edits.
Starla Huchton for her amazing cover.
My dad for being awesome.
And to all the donut lovers and challenge attempters – keep on being awesome.

ABOUT THE AUTHOR

Many people have influenced who I am today. Having a wild child best friend in high school really helped me grow into an inquisitive person. Because of her, I am stubborn and creative and let myself be who I am without too much care about what others think. My dad also had a great influence on my life. Some of his dad puns and funny quirks rubbed off on me over time.

"Who brought donuts?"
I brought the donuts.

OTHER BOOKS BY THE AUTHOR

Vanessa's Book of Awesome Things
A fun accompaniment/companion book to the for the Love of Donuts Series. This little book of fun contains bucket style lists of challenges, fun things to do with doughnuts, scavenger hunt items, facts about Corgis, top ten donuts you have to try, a doughnuts recipe, and more.

Nichole's Book of Practical Things
A fun accompaniment/companion book to the for the Love of Donuts Series. This little book of fun contains bucket style lists of challenges, fun things to do with doughnuts, scavenger hunt items, facts about Corgis, top ten donuts you have to try, a doughnuts recipe, and more.

For the Love of Donuts Coloring Book
A coloring book for donut lovers of all ages.

Ataxia and the Ravine of Lost Dreams
In Ataxia and the Ravine of Lost Dreams A young girl takes on the mighty powers of the government but is sidetracked by challenges of the academy she attends, the new boy, and keeping her secrets safe.

A Young Adult, Dystopian, Not-So-Distant-Future Adventure Novel with a hint of sci-fi and a bit of romance.

At One's Beast
From once upon a time to happily ever after, At One's Beast highlights the struggles of two young adolescents who have fallen prey to chance evil circumstances. When it took the entire village to create the monster, what will it take to break the spell?

Available in print, e-book, and as an audio book, At One's Beast is a new take on "Beauty and the Beast," with a love triangle, revenge, a spell, evil, fate, forgiveness, compassion, bitterness, capture, betrayal and love.

Made in the USA
Monee, IL
28 April 2026